T0268703

SMALL TOWN SINS

SMALL TOWN SINS

A Novel

KEN JAWOROWSKI

Henry Holt and Company

New York

Henry Holt and Company
Publishers since 1866
120 Broadway
New York, New York 10271
www.henryholt.com

Henry Holt® and Ⓗ® are registered trademarks of Macmillan
Publishing Group, LLC.

Distributed in Canada by Raincoast Book Distribution Limited

Library of Congress Cataloging-in-Publication Data

Names: Jaworowski, Ken, author.
Title: Small town sins : a novel / Ken Jaworowski.
Description: First edition. | New York : Henry Holt and
   Company, 2023.
Identifiers: LCCN 2022052809 (print) | LCCN
   2022052810 (ebook) | ISBN 9781250881670 (hardcover) |
   ISBN 9781250881687 (ebook)
Subjects: LCGFT: Thrillers (Fiction) | Novels.
Classification: LCC PS3610.A944 S63 2023 (print) | LCC
   PS3610.A944 (ebook) | DDC 813/.6—dc23/
   eng/20230112
LC record available at https://lccn.loc.gov/2022052809
LC ebook record available at https://lccn.loc.gov/
   2022052810

Our books may be purchased in bulk for promotional, educational, or business
use. Please contact your local bookseller or the Macmillan Corporate and
Premium Sales Department at (800) 221-7945, extension 5442, or by e-mail at
MacmillanSpecialMarkets@macmillan.com.

First Edition 2023

Designed by Gabriel Guma

Printed in the United States of America

1   3   5   7   9   10   8   6   4   2

To Michele, Hope, and Troy. All my love.

SMALL TOWN SINS

NATHAN

I can trace so much of my life back to a summer night when I was seventeen. Everything starts from then and links the years that follow, like one of those connect-the-dots pages you played with as a kid: Begin right here, draw a line to there, then another, then again. Sooner or later, an image emerges.

I'd recently finished my junior year of high school and was kicking around a few ideas on how to get out of Locksburg, a Central Pennsylvania backwater I'd wanted to flee ever since I was old enough to misspell its name. College was a possibility. The marines, a cheaper one. Either would work, as long as it got me away.

I had a nodding acquaintance with my classmates but no real friends among them. That's not because of bad behavior on my part. The opposite was true: I was the only child of a sweet-spoken, disabled mother and a deacon father who together looked after a struggling church that was too poor to support a full-time priest. When I wasn't doing schoolwork or house chores, I was at Saint Stanislaus, chipping melted wax from the candleholders or cementing the cracks that the bitter winters brought to the stone walls outside.

One Saturday night I was walking home from the church, head down, hands in pockets, when I turned a corner. LeeLee Roland was bounding down the steps of her house, ten yards away. She was a soon-to-be sophomore who stood out from the other girls at school. Even at fifteen, she was brazenly flirty to most every guy but me. I'd watch her with a side-eye, fascinated but wary, as she bounced along the high school halls.

"Hey, Nate!" she called, employing a nickname I didn't use. I raised my chin and hid my surprise. We'd never spoken before, and I was a little amazed that she knew who I was.

"You going to the party too?" she asked.

"Nah," I said, as if I knew which party that was.

"Yes, you are. I'm kidnapping you."

She hooked a hand around my arm, and the breath left my lungs. To feel a girl touch me, even with just a friendly move, nearly froze me. That touch, combined with the warm June breeze, was instantly intoxicating, as if I'd swallowed an entire bottle of altar wine.

"Where is it?" I said, tamping down my voice in the hope of sounding somewhat cool.

"Tracy's house," LeeLee said. "Willow Street."

I nodded a few times too many while piecing it together: Tracy Carson lived there, another girl I'd never spoken to. LeeLee and I walked two blocks then turned onto Willow.

"I'm . . . I'm not really sure I'm invited," I said, entirely sure I wasn't.

"She don't care. Anyway, too late," LeeLee said, and turned to walk up the steps of a house. She let go of my arm. I felt both real relief and deep disappointment.

LeeLee courtesy-knocked then pushed the door open. Inside, about fifteen people were circled around the dining room table, playing some kind of drinking game. All were familiar faces. In a town of about five thousand, you saw everyone at one time or another.

"Look who I found," LeeLee told the group. They seemed indifferent. For that, I was grateful. Anything short of disdain was enough to make me half happy. Like any seventeen-year-old, I was perpetually confused and occasionally anxious, all while acting as confident as I could.

Forty-five minutes later, the number of people had nearly tripled, and the radio, blaring classic rock, had gotten turned up twice as loud. I'd taken a place against a wall, nursing a can of lukewarm Keystone Light and watching the games that no one asked me to join. After finishing my beer, I acted as if the can were full, bringing it to my lips time and again. LeeLee had gone to the kitchen and brought me the beer when we'd arrived. She'd since disappeared upstairs with a pack of other girls.

I debated leaving. No one would notice.

I eyed the door.

Any time up until then had been pivotal, of course. What if I had stayed at church a few extra minutes and never saw LeeLee? Or what if I had taken another route home? But when I look back, that moment seems the most decisive, the last real instant when something could have changed. Had I walked out that door then, how many lives would have been different?

Instead, I decided to hang around the party for a little longer. I wandered into the kitchen and took another can from the fridge, hoping no one would notice or yell at me or say I had to pay.

When I went back to my spot at the wall, LeeLee had returned.

"Hey!" she said. "I was wondering where you were."

I showed her the beer.

"Finish it," she said.

"Why?"

"This place is lame," she said, not caring who heard. "Let's get out of here."

We passed the can back and forth until we emptied it, then left. I imagined that everyone was watching us go. Maybe someone might gossip about me later—a delicious notion for a guy whom surely no one at school ever thought about.

LeeLee took my hand when we reached the sidewalk. I didn't know what to make of it and didn't question her when she led me into a nearby patch of woods, where we sat on a fallen tree trunk.

"Gettin' chilly," she said, and leaned against me. I put an arm around her.

"You don't say much," she said.

I had no response other than a shrug.

"See!" she said, and nudged me.

She smiled.

With no other prelude, we were kissing.

I didn't try to stop her when she unzipped my pants and reached inside. I didn't have the words. I didn't know if I wanted her to stop anyway. Within a minute her shorts were down, and she was on top of me. To hold out, I soon moved her below, then slowed. That extended my efforts for at least two minutes until we finished. Then we lay there on the ground.

"That was good," she whispered after a while.

"Yeah," I said, because I had to say something.

• • •

I pined over LeeLee each day that summer, and scanned the streets whenever I was out in Locksburg. When my parents and I went on a three-week church retreat, I called our home number often to check the machine, in case LeeLee had left a message. I debated endlessly about whether to call her, some days convincing myself that she wouldn't want to talk to me, other days swearing that she was probably waiting for me to make a move. Then in August she knocked on my front door. I couldn't help smiling when I saw her.

"Hey."

"Hey. You alone?"

"Yeah. My mom and dad are at the church."

"Anybody else here?"

"No."

"Can I come in?"

I opened the door. She came inside, then stopped in the middle of the living room and turned to face me.

"I'm pregnant."

Dry words caught in my throat, while terror and anguish and fear swirled in my gut. I can feel the echoes of those emotions still. They sometimes creep into my dreams and wake me with remnants of the panic I felt at that moment.

When I could finally speak, I asked LeeLee every question twice: if she had had sex with anyone else ("No! I'm not some slut—I was drunk! It's your fault too!") and if she was sure ("I had my cousin buy two pregnancy tests for me. Both came back positive.").

"So what do we do?"

"My cousin said I could use her ID. She can take me to Philly for an abortion."

"Good. Yeah. Good. OK," I said, clutching hold of her answer like it was a life raft. We could salvage this without my parents knowing.

"It's expensive," LeeLee said.

"How much?"

"My cousin would have to take two days off work. Then there's the drive to Philly. We were thinking, she could tell my mom that we were going to a concert there, so we'd need to stay in a hotel. Then, you know, the doctor's bill. She thinks almost a thousand. For everything."

"Do you have it?"

"I got like sixty bucks. That's why I'm here. I would have gone already if I had the money. How much do you have?"

The balance of my bank account had only recently topped a hundred dollars.

"When are you going to Philly?"

"Next weekend, if I can get the money. If not, I dunno."

"I'll get it," I promised her. "Make the appointment."

. . .

Over the next few days, I lived in torment, staying up late into the nights to devise ways to get a thousand dollars. None of my plans had a chance of coming together. By Wednesday I was desperate. Theft, which I'd dismissed from the start, became the only option. Anything from the church wouldn't be easy to sell. That brought my thoughts to my mother's wedding ring.

She kept it in a small wooden box on her dresser.

I took the ring, promising myself I'd get it back to her soon, though I had no concrete plan for doing so. Then I borrowed my dad's car and drove forty miles to Harrisburg, where a pawnbroker offered me three hundred dollars. I took the ring and turned to leave.

"Wait," he called. "How much you need?"

"A thousand."

He huffed.

I reached for the door.

"I can do seven fifty," he said.

I shook my head.

"OK, come back here," he said when my hand was on the door handle.

. . .

A week later LeeLee had gone and returned from Philadelphia. When I called her, she said, "Yeah, it's done."

Three sentences later, she said, "Don't call me again, OK?"

. . .

My father tapped on my bedroom door a few nights later.

"Have you been in our room lately?" he asked.

"No. Why?"

"Cleaning up, maybe?"

"No."

"Your mother's very concerned. She can't find her wedding ring."

"Did she, like, lose it while shopping or something?"

"She doesn't wear it except on special occasions."

"Oh."

"I had it appraised at ten thousand dollars for our homeowner's insurance. But it's not the money. My father gave it to me, to give to her. It was my mother's."

"She probably dropped it somewhere."

"Let's help her look, though."

"Now?"

"No. It's too late. But tomorrow. In the light."

"I will."

I tried to get back to the book I was pretending to read, but he remained in the doorway.

"You feeling OK? I've heard you up at nights sometimes."

"I'm good."

"You can tell me anything, you know. I would never judge you."

"Yeah. I know that."

He turned to leave, then stopped and turned around.

"Nathan. You didn't see the ring at all?"

I knew what it took for him to ask me that question. He never spoke when a motion or a sound would serve just as well. In these words were expectations of trust, and truth. Ideals he lived by, and encouraged me to honor too.

"No," I said.

The next day I scoured the house with my mother: dumping out the vacuum bag, reaching between furniture cushions. She'd lost her leg at the knee in a car accident when she was twelve and limped with the prosthetic, so I was the one who climbed up on chairs to peer onto shelves.

I acted like I was seriously searching, even when there were tears in my eyes.

• • •

My mother slipped and fell down the basement steps the next day, shattering both hips and fracturing her skull on the cement floor. She'd been combing the house for her ring and had gone down there to search for it, we surmised.

She died two days after the fall.

• • •

Some people run away from their shame. Others, like me, move closer, try to smother it.

After high school I stayed in town to be there for my father, who was devastated by my mother's death. I lived with him, kept the house, and tried my best to make him happy, all the while remaining silent about what I'd done. I came to quietly loathe myself and the thing that I'd done for money.

I took a job at an assembly plant and sleepwalked through the next few years, never dating, still so thrown by what had happened. Then my father had a stroke, and I spent several more caring for him, before one morning going into his room to find that he had died during the night. I wept, and some of those tears were of relief: I wouldn't have to hold my horrible secret from him anymore.

• • •

A month later, on a late shift at work, I sliced my upper arm on a jagged piece of sheet metal, sending me to Locksburg General, where some young-buck doctor sewed fifteen stitches into my skin.

"You didn't flinch once," the nurse, Paula, said, and grinned after the doctor left the room.

I was enamored of her at first sight: she was tall, only two inches shorter than the six feet I stood, with short brown hair and attentive hazel eyes. All of that could have made her seem stern. Yet from her first words, she exuded warmth in that sterile white hospital room. She made me work only a little to see her smile, a sincere, warm prize that made me immediately respond in kind.

A year and a half later she became my wife.

Paula and I settled into Locksburg and set about renovating a coal executive's old house that hadn't been occupied in years. The six bedrooms would soon be filled with cheery children, we assumed, and we painted the walls in bright colors that would surely match their moods. Though I never escaped this town, I would find joy here with a family, and raise sons and daughters who would go out to see the world, then regale me with stories of their adventures while their own kids ran around my home.

Paula and I finished our work on the house after four years. It was still only the two of us.

But no hurry. We had both only recently turned thirty.

We were still young.

...

Paula turned forty-two last week. For her birthday we drove an hour and a half to Harrisburg to see a traveling production of *Les Misérables*. Paula's a heck of a nurse, professional and no-nonsense on the job. Yet she's got a not-so-secret sentimental streak, and she went through a pack of tissues during the show, before starting on her sleeve. That made me grin. At one point, though, I felt us both stiffen, or at least imagined we did, when the lead character sang a line about not having any children. I didn't move in my seat when those words were sung. I just hoped they'd pass soon, much like I do when the two of us watch television and see some sitcom where the parents complain about their offspring, or when we walk past a children's clothing display in a shop window, or when we drive by a billboard with a cute toddler holding her mother's hand.

When you have no children, everything is eager to remind you of that fact, particularly in a small town. City life may be different, but around here, large families are prized, and couples without kids are considered odd. Even our house, in which our awaited children never arrived, now seems to mock us with its empty rooms. Yet to move out of it would be an admittance of defeat that would be almost as painful as the failure itself.

Only once has Paula asked me how much I was disappointed that we hadn't had children. Only once, I've lied to her. That was when, after asking, she broke down and blamed our troubles on herself. I said, "It's not such a big deal to me. Really."

A year or two ago, an unspoken agreement passed between us. Paula and I started to busy ourselves with added work: her at the hospital, me at the plant. I began to go fishing more. Joined the volunteer fire department. From that I gained twenty pounds from all the beers I'd drunk with the crew after coming back from a call, and I began to take on the general appearance of most every guy my age in town whose stomach, covered by a flannel shirt, was only a few years away from drooping over the brown leather belt that held up his faded blue jeans, and whose well-worn baseball cap covered his soon-to-be-thinning hair. I'd glance in the mirror too often and think: *Well, there you go, Nathan. You're the guy you promised yourself you'd never be.* Soon I began avoiding my reflection.

For nearly fifteen years, Paula and I had been hoping for a child, following every recommendation, reading countless articles, seeing specialist after specialist. Without admitting it aloud to each other, we'd given up on the dream that so many others have achieved so easily.

If we couldn't face that, at least we could find other things to occupy our time.

...

I was returning from Laurel Lake one afternoon when my phone beeped the three-note alert that preceded an incoming fire department announcement. I was surprised at the sound. I was barely out of the state game lands, where cell service was spotty.

"Report of a cabin fire at mile marker 16 on Michaux Road. Pumper truck and ambulance being dispatched. Repeat: mile marker 16 on Michaux Road."

I was already on Michaux, at mile marker 18, so I didn't bother with the dash flash. At least I could feel somewhat useful today. The fishing at Laurel Lake had been fruitless, and I'd found myself sitting in my jon boat staring into the water, wasting time, in no hurry to go home. Someone else launched a boat, a guy about my age, with a boy of twelve or thirteen. The kid let out a joyful laugh when they were free of land. Though I try to avoid thinking of children, I couldn't help it this time. Boys at that age are everything: mischievous, curious, and affectionate, before the world teaches them not to be. I smiled and lifted my hand to wave at the two of them. Caught up in their own delight, they didn't see me. I brought my hand down from the wave, then went back to fishing alone.

I came around a bend on Michaux Road slowly. The boat was in the bed of my pickup with its nose over the gate. Last thing I needed was to have the thing flip out onto the blacktop. After the turn, a plume of smoke came into view.

The house was a single-floor shack, one I'd passed a hundred times, yet I don't think I'd ever noticed it, or, if I had, I'd considered it abandoned. It sat fifty yards off the road, with no driveway other than two ruts in the dirt where cars must have driven to the front. Parked there now was a green Chevy beater.

Most of the houses that remained standing in the region were abandoned or served as hunting cabins. Occasionally the high school kids from town would ride up to party in them, and a couple years back they set one ablaze, either intentionally or not. It burned to the ground, and this one would soon do the same if the pumper truck didn't arrive within the next five minutes. The curtains had caught fire in the room farthest from the front door, and smoke was rising through a hole in the roof.

The thought that some high school kid could be in there both pissed me off and spurred me on. Maybe one of those acne-faced idiots was passed out drunk in a room. Entering a burning building alone is forbidden under fire company rules, yet I decided it was worth the risk, especially with the fire only at the far side of the building. There was time to rush in and scan the place.

At the front door, I felt the handle, then turned it and pushed inward. The room was lit by a table lamp. That was a surprise. The place must have a gas generator. I shut the door behind me to prevent any fire-fueling breeze from coming in.

"Fire! Fire!" I hollered, loud enough to wake any sleepers. "Anyone in here? Anyone need help?"

A window shattered in the back of the house. Underneath the sound I might have heard something. I stepped farther inside. As long as the door was in view, I could throw myself outside if things got too hot too fast.

"This place is gonna come down! Get out now!" Half a foot of smoke was creeping along the ceiling. If the owner of the car was in here unconscious, he'd soon be fried.

"Anyone? Anyone!"

There was a door off the main room, probably to a bedroom. Felt the knob. Cool. Turned it. Inside, there was a mattress on the floor, surrounded by beer bottles and other junk.

A green, industrial-strength trash bag sat on the mattress. Whatever was inside was heavy, judging by the dent it made. I stepped over and opened the top.

When I saw the first bundle of cash, I nearly laughed at the preposterousness. I pushed aside that bundle. Beneath it, dozens and dozens like it: crisp, two-inch-thick stacks of twenties. Fifties. Hundreds. Dug my hand in and felt more and more money.

My crazy first idea—the guys at the fire department were playing a joke on me. Maybe there was a hidden camera in the room somewhere. I shook that out of my head when I coughed on smoke. This place was about to be a death trap.

There was no thought about what to do. I just did it. Lifted the bag. It weighed fifty pounds or so. Then I swung it over my shoulder and hurried from the bedroom.

I crossed the main room of the house and went for the front door.

Someone shrieked, an agonized sound: part words, part wail.

I turned to see a guy running down the hallway, his arms reaching out for me.

He was on fire.

CALLIE

"You're gonna take my blood pressure?"

"No. I'm going to wrap this cuff around your neck and pump it until your face turns purple and your cheeks bulge out like an overfed hamster."

That's what I wanted to say. I didn't, of course. Instead, I forced a pressed-lip smile and nodded.

"Why?" the patient asked through an opening in her face that sat above her two double chins. I had to look twice to see which crevice the sound came from.

"It's standard procedure to check your vital signs."

"But my blood pressure's fine," she said, blissfully ignorant of all evidence to the contrary. "My *ankles* hurt."

"I understand that. But—"

"Can I see the doctor now?" She pointed to the door. The blood-pressure cuff, stretched to the limit and held on by a few hairs of Velcro, popped off, forcing me to start over.

"He'll be in shortly."

"I don't have all day."

"Of course not. You've got Twinkies to eat."

Another thing I didn't say.

Sarcasm, even if only internally, is what gets me through so many of my nursing shifts these days, and pretty much every other minute outside of work. And truth be told, it's barely fun anymore. There's not a lot to smirk at when you're dealing with whining patients like this one, or the woman before her: a twenty-six-year-old who'd been in twice in three weeks, this time for a broken nose and a bruised eye, punched around by her husband in front of their four kids. When I slipped her the number of the domestic abuse hotline, she tore it to pieces and told me to mind my own fuckin' business. Then she looked at my face and said, "How would you know anything about gettin' a man?"

Ms. Sore Ankles grimaced as I reattached the blood-pressure belt then pumped.

"My ankles *hurt*," she said, as if moving the stress to the third word rather than the second was the secret to getting some Nobel Prize–winning research physician to come in and examine her. But the best—and only—doctor we currently had on duty at Locksburg General was Dr. Willis, all seventy-seven years of him. When he sits with a patient, I bring a bedpan with me. Twice I've had to drop it, seemingly as an accident, when he started to nod off midexamination. Ms. Sore Ankles here better watch it or he's apt to misdiagnose her with malaria.

"OK, let me ask you a few questions," I began. Dr. Willis was going to be another twenty minutes at least, so drawing this out as long as possible would keep the woman occupied and, I hoped, distracted enough to quit her bleating.

She sighed, and her extra-large chest heaved.

"On a scale of one to ten, how bad is the pain?"

"Ten!" she bellowed.

"And when did it begin?"

"Yesterday!" Ah, her new strategy: exclaiming every answer.

"Have you visited your family doctor?"

"No! I come here!"

"This is the emergency room. It's made for—"

"I know what it's for! This *is* an emergency. *My* ankles hurt!"

I could handle no more.

"The doctor will be in shortly."

I stepped out and double-knocked on the room across the hall, then entered. Dr. Willis was in there, recounting his years in the navy to a gray-haired widow who'd come in earlier for arthritis pain. I sympathized, I really did, but she's another one who needs to find a family practitioner rather than use the emergency room every time she feels an oncoming ache. And, as usual, Dr. Willis was happy to chatter away as the woman smiled and nodded like she was scoping out husband number three.

"Doctor?" I interrupted. The woman shot me a look as if I were stealing away the last bite of her final meal.

"Yes?" Dr. Willis asked. "Is it an emergency?"

"It's no small problem," I said. Considering Ms. Sore Ankles tipped the scale at over three hundred, that wasn't a lie.

"Ah, I'm sorry, Miriam," Dr. Willis said to his patient. She didn't correct him, though her name was Rita Anne. I had written it on the chart myself. "But keep taking your prescription and you'll be feeling like you're twenty-one again."

I coughed to hide a snort, and shuffled the doctor over to the ankle lady's room. Then I excused myself and headed to the front desk, twenty feet down the hall. Our receptionist had called out sick, so I'd turned the ringer up to its highest volume and kept an ear open. It was a fairly slow Saturday afternoon, though I pitied the night shift. Paula was scheduled as the on-duty nurse, and she'd have her hands full with drunks who'd been skull-cracked by beer bottles and brawlers whose eyes would be swollen shut for days.

The main hospital phone rang. I pulled down my mask and answered.

"Locksburg General."

"There's a fox in my yard."

Silence.

"Didja hear me?"

"This is the hospital," I said. "You can call the police or animal control. Maybe they can help with that . . ."

"No. I need you guys."

"Why?"

"Because, like, I wanna go out there and pet it. But if that fox bites me, I'm gonna have to come into the hospital. You're open, right?"

"Let's not allow it to get that far, OK?"

"I'm just being—what's that word—proactive?"

"Sir, have you been drinking?"

"Well, yeah," he said, his tone implying that I should feel stupid for asking.

"Um . . ."

"Or, wait, is the word *preemptive?*"

"Leave the fox alone and—"

"Dang, he's running off," the guy slurred. "Lookee! Do ya see 'em?"

It took me a moment to realize he was asking me that sincerely.

"Uh," I said, in the hopes of signaling that this call should be coming to an end.

"Catch ya later, buddy! See you next time!" the guy cried out before hanging up.

And that was far from the strangest caller of that month. We'd had people call to ask if the explosive diarrhea they had last Thanksgiving could be a symptom of the kind of liver cancer they heard about on this week's *Today* show, or demand to know which brand of aspirin they should buy and if they could pay with food stamps, before shouting that they're standing in line at the pharmacy and you're not answering fast enough. It's usually easier just to say Excedrin than to explain to them why they shouldn't be dialing a hospital for that kind of advice, or hanging up on them only to have the line ring again when they inevitably call back and spew a stream of insults.

Down the hall, Dr. Willis stepped out of the examining room. I put my mask back up and went to him.

"Callie? Can you fit Ms. . . . What was her name?"

"Mason."

"Hmm?"

"Mason."

"I can't . . ." He motioned to his ear and then to my mask. He's practically deaf even on a good day and can't hear anything when I'm masked up. I pulled it down to my neck.

"Ms. Mason," I said.

"Yes. Ms. Mason. Can you fit her with compression socks for her ankles?"

"Sure," I said. He could hear well enough to gauge my mood.

"I'm sorry, Callie. I'd do it myself, but my arthritis is acting up too."

"I got it, Doctor," I said, and patted his shoulder to let him know I wasn't really peeved. The guy does the best he can.

The patient was sitting there barefooted when I returned. I dug two compression socks from a drawer and rolled a chair in front of her, then patted my knee.

"Can you place your foot up here?"

She made the attempt, but mounds of compressed flesh prevented her from lifting the foot more than six inches from the floor. I slid the chair aside and got down on one knee to slide the sock on. She grunted, uncomfortable, but I'm good at this. The socks were on in record time.

"I'll give you an extra one, you might need it. You should wear them at least—"

"The doctor told me," she said. "And keep my feet elevated."

"Right."

I stood, went back to the drawer, found another sock, then turned to her.

She said, "Were you in an accident?"

She motioned to her upper lip, as if I didn't know what she was talking about. As if I haven't lived with this every single day from the moment of my birth.

Still, I was a little stunned and didn't immediately answer. Then I cursed myself for failing to put my mask back up.

To live with a disfigurement is something you can't forget. It's there every morning when you gaze into the bathroom mirror, in every touch you bring to your face, in every glance of a stranger who wants to look but doesn't want you to see them looking.

Though everyone sees it, very few say anything. People suck, yet I'll give them this—they themselves are loathe to appear rude.

"No," I told her. "It's a craniofacial disorder I was born with. A cleft palate and harelip, with complications. The scar is from one of the operations I had."

"Does it hurt, honey?" she asked.

And goddamn it, what infuriated me most was that she sounded sincere. She really did hope that I wasn't uncomfortable.

"No," I said. "There's no pain."

"That's good, then," she said, and offered a small smile, which I returned. Then I regretted snarking at her inside my head earlier. Really, who am I to comment on someone's appearance?

I handed her the extra sock and told her that she could leave after she put her shoes back on. I might even have helped her with those, but the phone began ringing, and I hurried out of the room and down the hall.

"Locksburg General," I answered.

It was an ambulance driver, telling me to prepare, they were bringing in a burn victim from a house fire out on Michaux Road, and the guy was in grim shape.

"Is it one of the firefighters?" I asked. Paula was on duty next, and god forbid it was Nathan, her husband.

"No," the driver said, "it's a civilian."

I told him we'd be ready, though the best I could do would be to fill Dr. Willis with coffee to keep him standing, call in Dr. Lennard, who was the biggest gun in this small-town hospital, then have the three of us waiting at the front door for the ambulance.

I put the phone down. It rang again five seconds later.

"Locksburg General."

"Callie, that you?"

"Yeah."

"It's Police Chief Kriner."

"Is this about the fire?"

"What fire?"

"There's a fire up on Michaux Road. They're bringing in a burn victim."

"I didn't hear about any of that. My chest radio's busted and I been away from the car, in a house over on Clay Street."

"What's up, Chief? I have to get ready for this patient."

"When that ambulance is done there, I'll need it over on Clay Street."

"You'll have to call them yourself. I may be busy."

"I will. But I called to tell you: when the ambulance comes in again, it'll be bringing you two bodies."

"What kind of care will they need?"

"None," he said. "They're both cold and dead. One's a little kid."

ANDY

Kate quit heroin the day we found out she was pregnant.

I said I'd quit with her, then waited for us to fail. We'd been dosing for years, and shooters like us stopped only when we flatlined. Before that day, we cursed other addicts who tried to give it up. We sneered at their high-minded bullshit, their betrayal of us, their rejection of how we lived.

And then there we were, attempting to do the same.

Two days after our last baggie, Kate and I were screaming ourselves hoarse and sweating straight through our clothes. We trembled violently for hours and dry-heaved into reeking pails. I pissed myself twice, and watched Kate pick at wounds that had no chance of healing.

In the middle of one of those nightmarish times, Kate opened a drawer and took out our old tie-up and spoon. I cackled like some drooling imbecile, ravenous to taste again. Kate stared at those things in her hands. She growled, a sound from high in her throat, sent out between gritted teeth. Then she found a hammer and slammed and banged and smashed that stuff flat. She threw what remained out the window.

That was ten years ago. I'm still amazed. We were both twenty-four, our attitudes foul and our cravings immense. A dealer once told us that we made Sid and Nancy look like Jesus and Mary. He said it with only half a laugh—our sunken eyes made even him uneasy. But after that test stick showed a plus sign, Kate wanted only to be clean. And to have our baby. So we did. The three of us made it through.

Angie was born in a free clinic in Philadelphia. I'd arrived twenty minutes after Kate gave birth. I was out of breath, having snuck away from my job as a janitor at the bus station and run the two miles there. The doctor came in as I was bent over, hands on my knees, puffing.

"Hello," he said. "Are you the father?"

"Yeah, I am," I said. I don't know the last time I'd smiled, but there I was, beaming from ear to ear at that word I'd never been called before.

He turned his attention to Kate.

"Are you familiar with Down syndrome?" he said.

Kate nodded. The doctor looked to me. I stood straight up and said, "Yeah," though I wasn't entirely sure.

He began to explain. Kate stared into his eyes as if to memorize every word about heart defects that were common with Down kids, about special care that would be needed, about services that may be available. With no sympathy in his voice, he said that he was sorry and began to back out into the hall.

"Is this because . . . See, we used to . . ." Kate motioned to the old tracks on the insides of her arms.

"Opiate use . . . I'm not sure. I don't think there's much data," he said. "I can check into it and get back to you."

We never saw him again.

"Whata we do now?" I asked Kate.

She turned her head toward the window, silent.

They fired me when I got back to work, my absence unexcused.

I didn't argue, only walked down an empty hallway to go clean out my locker. There was too much inside my head. I couldn't speak.

We brought Angie home two days later. She mewed rather than cried, and Kate mewed back, holding her, always with a soft smile. Kate would stay in Angie's room until Angie fell asleep, humming to her well past midnight, rocking her when she needed it and telling her long, tender stories. I'd stand outside the room and listen, drinking in the gentleness of this woman who used to shoot needles into the veins of her neck, and who once slashed a thieving junkie with a straight razor that she'd wrestled from his shaking, hairy hand.

We'd push Angie in a stroller along the city sidewalks and glare back at those who looked at her with pity. We were uninterested in being liked, but we demanded respect. We cared for each other, loyal and steadfast, and loathed nearly everyone else with that same passion: the fat middle class and their spoiled shithead kids and the square-faced suits and the fake television families and the overprivileged pricks with their smug sense of entitlement and all the falseness we saw around us, every moment, everywhere.

I worked with the same grit I had back when I was trying to score a dose. Twelve-hour days when they were available, didn't matter the job, anything to bring in a paycheck and let Kate remain at home with Angie. There she'd spend weeks teaching her a new word, to walk without a stumble, to try to hold a crayon.

"Yes!" Kate shouted when Angie finally said her own name, first and last. "Yes yes yes!" she cheered, with a fist pump that Angie copied. I crowed too, then put my daughter on my shoulders and hopped around the room. The three of us walked half a mile to buy an ice cream cone for Angie, laughing aloud, a simple moment that I've never forgotten.

At five, Angie spent two weeks in the free clinic for a heart murmur that had grown worse since birth. Kate stayed there throughout, while I left only for my shifts mopping floors at a retirement home. One night, after Angie was released, I woke to hear Kate in the bathroom, praying to a god she didn't believe in for a miracle she'd never get. On the other side of the door, I prayed too, for both of them.

For Angie's sixth birthday, we drove three hours to a theme park. Minutes after we arrived, I went to use the restroom, and came out to find Kate slamming her fist into some teenager's face. He was a lanky, pimply weasel who, she later told me, pointed at Angie and laughed. Kate snapped his nose with a headbutt, then cracked his teeth with a punch. When she cocked back again, the kid's friend grabbed her arm and yanked. I decked that guy with a roundhouse, then followed with a boot to his nuts. Kate was kicking the other kid's stomach as the security guards surrounded her. I swung at anyone who came near us. Out of the corner of my eye I spied Angie in her wheelchair, munching potato chips, as cool as a tray of ice cubes. She stopped eating and clapped her chubby hands.

We were ejected from the park and drove home with Kate in the back seat reading picture books to Angie, both of them as cheerful as if we'd spent a day at the beach.

I remember glancing in the rearview to see Kate pointing to the letters as she read them, and held back the sob that had started to grow in my throat. I don't think I can explain that moment, the pulsing pain in my face where a security guard had socked me, along with the sadness of our ailing daughter and the beauty of her mother's love. How do you describe that mix of emotions with words? Why even try.

That was how our years passed, filled with pure love or rabid hate and little middle ground. Angie's every triumph was magnified, while every outsider's offense was punished. Angie's scribbles were framed and hung on walls. We wore out a dozen cameras from overuse. We argued with countless hospitals to get her care. When she received it, the treatment merely seemed to slow her heart problems but never to cure them.

Kate's father died and left her a ragged house in Locksburg. We moved there, happy to get away from a city that did nothing but tempt us to start using again.

Our tiny backyard in Locksburg gave Angie a place to skip around rather than a needle-strewn city playground, and for that we were thankful. I got a job at a gas station and spent my off time with Kate and Angie, driving up into the green hills that surrounded the gray town and dipping our toes into ice-cold streams.

"What was the best part of your day today?" Kate would ask Angie after tucking her in. One night Angie went through a list of all the things that brought her joy that day: a hug, a piece of chocolate, petting a neighbor's dog. Then, as Kate was leaving the room, Angie added, "The best part about tomorrow is that there will be more things to love."

Kate adored the phrase and stitched it, off-center and crooked, into a needlepoint pattern, separating the words into a haiku and declaring our daughter brilliant.

At nine years old, Angie began to get weaker and pale. We drove her to Harrisburg, and once down to D.C. The specialist there used words like *inoperable* and *morbidity* before telling us that there was little now that could be done for her heart. Kate petted Angie's head as he spoke, and for the first time since we kicked our habit, I saw a tear slide down her cheek.

A month later Angie lost more strength. She would stumble as she walked, and fell to the ground often. When we'd reach for her, she'd decline our help, struggling to stand up on her own, always the fighter.

"Should I stay home?" I asked Kate the morning after Angie struggled through an especially difficult night, the worst in a string of bad ones.

"Go to work," she said. "Don't lose your job. We need it."

I kissed them both before leaving.

While working at the gas station, I called Kate several times and, when there was no answer, convinced myself that she and Angie were taking a walk or sitting outside in our yard.

When I returned home from my shift, the house was silent.

I called out for Kate and got no answer.

The quiet had a weight it never had.

And I just knew.

I put the coffee pot on and began to weep, and in my head screamed at any god there could ever be, promising anything I had if Kate would just come out of Angie's room and bark at me: "Why are you crying, you idiot?" I stared at the closed door and willed it to open, though I knew it wouldn't. God had always forgotten about us.

I stood in one spot until the water boiled. Then I steeled myself and pushed open the door to Angie's room.

Angie was on Kate's lap, eyes closed, limp. Kate was sitting on the floor, her back propped up against the wall and her own lifeless eyes half open. A needle, just out of Kate's arm, was beside her body. On the bed, a note.

Angie died in her sleep at about noon. I bought a bag of uncut last week, knowing she didn't have much time and knowing I should go with her when it happened. I'm sorry I couldn't wait for you. I didn't want her to be alone for long.

We love you.

NATHAN

I dropped the bag of money and reached for the guy as he ran at me. He was in agony, with flames scorching his shoulders and the back of his head, and even those who are well versed in fire safety can succumb to mindless panic when their skin starts to sear.

I grabbed his arms, stuck out a leg, and flipped him onto the floor.

"Roll!" I yelled. "Roll!"

He shrieked. I held him down—it wasn't tough, he was well under one hundred fifty pounds—then turned him on his back to extinguish the fire there. His hair sizzled, and I sucked up a lungful of that smoke when it went into my face. I ripped his shirt off and tossed it aside, felt my own hands singe.

"Is anyone else here?" I yelled at him. A useless question. He was moaning and probably couldn't hear me. Then I saw that one of his ears was burned down to a nub. "Get up! Hurry!"

I helped him stand, then took both of his arms, bent down, and threw him over my shoulder in a fireman's carry. I opened the door with one hand, then reached back and grabbed the bag of money before carrying both outside.

The rear of the house started to fall in on itself. A section of the roof collapsed as I laid the guy on the ground in front of my truck, then propped him upright. He slumped to his side when I let go. No matter. As long as he wasn't on his back, he'd be OK for the moment. The skin there was charred and would soon be covered in boils.

From a couple miles away, the ambulance siren sounded.

I was surprised, then and after, at how composed I felt. It seemed like only a job to do, and, therefore, one to do right. I picked up the bag, went to the back of my pickup truck, and tucked it under the jon boat. From the utility box, I grabbed a gallon jug filled with distilled water, kept for such an emergency. Then I went to care for the burned man. He mumbled something. I shushed him and began to speak to him—really talking to myself, to make sure I went through all the right steps.

"The three Cs of burns: cool, cover, and call. Help's already on the way, so I'm going to cool you with this, buddy, then cover you up."

He moaned as the water flowed over his back, and that was it: he passed out. Better that than awake and in pain, I figured.

The rest of the roof was caving in on the house. A blast of warm air hit the two of us when the front wall collapsed. I hoped my truck was parked back far enough in case too many sparks came down.

The ambulance arrived and the EMTs got to work, fast. The burned man was in the ambulance and on the road within five minutes, right as the fire truck pulled in.

The crew set about watering down what was left of the place. I began directing the other volunteers who'd arrived, steering them as far away from my truck as I could, leaving me a path to drive out of there as soon as I could without raising suspicion. The fire was fairly under control within minutes, when Jack Naugle, the fire chief, came over to me.

"You went in there?" he asked.

"Yeah, but—"

"No buts. You should know better."

"I was worried that maybe some high school kids were inside."

"Who was it?"

"A guy, he was about thirty or so. Hard to tell. He's burned up pretty bad."

"I hope you stayed close to the door."

"Yeah. I was safe. My hands got singed some. Otherwise fine."

We peered through the windows of the guy's car. Nothing was visible except for some old newspapers and two empty beer cans in the back seat. We both knew better than to open the car door. This was sure to turn into a police matter, and they'd want us away from any evidence.

"What did it look like inside?" Naugle asked.

"There's a gas generator in there for electricity, so . . . maybe drugs?"

"Cookin' meth, most likely," Naugle said. "Out here with no one to bother them."

"Them?"

"Usually takes two or more guys. Maybe the other guy went out. Maybe he's in there under all this shit. If so, he's dead. Did you see anything else?"

I pretended to take a moment to consider his question.

"No. Typical shithole, lots of trash and stuff."

"All those meth chemicals are crazy flammable. Something probably caught a spark, lit the place up. Remember last year, outside of Ranshaw?"

"Right," I said. We both knew it, so there was no need to waste breath. It was the biggest story in the county at the time, thirty acres of woods accidentally set alight by two meth cookers who ended up cremating themselves and saving their families the expense.

"Get your ass to the hospital," Naugle said.

"I don't think I need—"

"That's an order. Have 'em check you out, just in case."

"Yeah. All right," I said. It was a good excuse to get me and the money away from there. "I'll go now."

"Good. And hey, nice work here," Naugle said. "If that guy lives, you saved his life."

. . .

Paula walked in after one a.m. with that half-exhausted, half-exhilarated expression she gets after a busy night at the hospital. It's a look that sometimes makes me jealous, her with a job that can make her feel that way. I've certainly never experienced those same emotions while assembling shelving or bending sheet metal. For the first time, though, I was the more wired one. I'd been that way since returning home with the money. I tried to tamp down the energy as we spoke, though it wouldn't stop pulsing through me.

"There's my brave man!" Paula said, and I couldn't help grinning. So often she greets me with a compliment. I doubt I earn them all, though they always seem genuine.

"Who told you?"

"The ambulance team. They said you ran into the burning building. Weren't you scared?"

"The part of the house I went into was safe. At least for a few minutes."

"And you carried that guy out."

"How is he?"

"Not so good. Callie was on duty when he got in, so she bandaged him up. He's too injured to move, or they would have taken him to Philadelphia."

"Will he survive?"

"It's a coin flip. He may not make it through the night."

I nodded, tried to process this new information.

"Chief Naugle stopped at the hospital. He said he ordered you to get checked out. Why didn't you come in?"

"I felt better," I said.

"Hey, what are you doing up? It's late."

"I couldn't sleep."

"Let me make you a snack. Or I have melatonin. That usually helps."

"No. I want to talk."

"You seem jumpy. Are you OK?"

I thought about it. "I can't be sure how I feel."

She went to sit on the sofa. I pointed to a chair that I wanted her to take instead, across from me, so we could face each other.

"What's the matter?"

Since getting home, I'd been running through everything that had happened to me since finding the money, then wondering how to tell the story to Paula. I'd had hours to think it through and practice. Yet now that the time had arrived, I sputtered my words. I pushed out a few in hopes that the rest would follow.

"In the attic . . . you know that old gun cabinet that's up there?"

"Yeah?"

"There's about two million dollars in it."

"Rob a bank?"

"I doubt there's two million dollars in all the banks in Locksburg combined."

"That's probably true."

"But there's two million upstairs. In cash."

She laughed. "I bet you went out with the fire crew tonight, huh?" she said. "I rode by Maxie's, and they have the sign out for two-for-one drink specials. Knowing you, you probably got eight-for-four! Good for you, hero. You deserve it."

"Paula? Do I seem drunk?"

She used her nurse's eyes, examined me for a moment.

"You don't."

"So listen. When I ran into that burning building? There was a bag in there. It was filled with money."

"Whose money?"

"It was in an empty room. I got there before anyone else. So I hid the bag in my truck. Then drove back here."

"Why do you have it? Shouldn't the police have it?"

"The police don't know about it. No one does. Only you."

"Whose money is it?"

"Mine."

"It's not yours."

"It's mine now. The place was burned to ashes ten minutes after I got out."

"So it's someone else's money."

"It's got to be drug money. And if I gave it to the cops, they'd only skim off the top, then send it someplace, to a politician who'd do the same."

Paula stood up. Took her purse in hand, and her car keys.

"Come on. I'll go to the station with you, right now. You'll say you made a bad judgment. And you'll say that you were—"

"I'm not taking it back."

"It's not yours! It's wrong!"

I couldn't help but snort at that.

"There's no right or wrong here. There's only what is. I've been sitting here for something like six hours, thinking it all through."

"Do I get a say in this?"

"Sure you do. But you need to understand: if I turn it in now, I'll get arrested. Even if I don't, I'll be kicked out of the department."

"You're a volunteer. It doesn't matter."

"And when everyone at the plant hears about it? What are they going to do? They're going to fire me, that's what."

When I saw her consider that, I followed the line of thought.

"Everyone around town will be calling me a thief. I made the choice, now I have to live with it. It's two million dollars that—"

"Did you count it?"

"No. I got scared. Wondered if maybe they put a GPS thing in there, or some kind of remote tracker. That's why I put it in the gun cabinet. It's half-inch-thick steel. No signals can get in or out of there. Before I put it in, I gave a fast count of the stacks."

"And what are you going to do? Go around town spending it?"

"Wait a couple weeks, then leave Locksburg. We're always saying we'd move to Florida."

"That's a joke we say to each other! It's not serious. What would we do there? Our lives are here."

"Our lives." I spat the words, angrier than I'd expected. "I work in a metal shop that's always in danger of closing. What kind of life is that? A shit job, in a shit place, with a shit future . . ."

And that's where I paused. Another step, and we'd be venturing into all the stuff we never talked about and were afraid to admit to each other, almost all of it surrounding our inability to have children. We did such a dance daily, it seemed. When we'd see a father and son having a catch, Paula would ask a random question to distract me, or I'd do the same when we'd be walking through a store and inadvertently find ourselves among the baby furniture. It had become second nature for us.

To change the direction of what I was saying, I went with: "I'm not happy in this place. I've never really been happy in Locksburg."

"I don't make you happy?"

"You do. But . . . think of it, Paula. We could sell this house. Go to Florida or California, buy a nice little place, never have to work again . . ."

"I like to work."

"Then work! We could do good things with the money too. Invest it, then give some away. Charity. Anything."

She was skeptical, but I imagined that she was moving closer to my way of thinking until I blew it by saying, "Come up to the attic. Just see all this money."

Paula shook her head, as if to dislodge any notions that may have started to take root there.

"No. I don't want to see it. It's not ours. And the longer you keep that money, the more trouble you're going to be in."

"Who's gonna know? The cops? The guys at the fire department? No one saw it. Even if they thought there was money inside, the place burned. If the guy had friends, they'd think that too."

"But he saw you. The guy."

"He was in a lot of pain. I don't know what he saw. Or what he remembers. And you said it yourself: he's probably not going to make it through the night."

She disagreed with each rationalization I made, and I worked again and again to convince her, to no avail. We ran around our same arguments for another hour and a half, exasperating Paula and frustrating me to the point where my voice was raising in anger. Finally we called some kind of truce and agreed to go to sleep and continue tomorrow. It was close to four a.m.

In our bed, she tossed for another hour. I know, of course, because I couldn't fall asleep either. Every time I seemed ready to drift off, my thoughts would return to the money in the attic. And those thoughts would alternately excite me and alarm me, again and again and again.

• • •

Paula and I woke in silence the next morning and both went into the kitchen for coffee. And as if we were in the middle of the same conversation we had been in the night before, the first thing Paula said to me was:

"And what happens if he pulls through? What happens if that guy recovers, and he remembers seeing you take the money?"

CALLIE

I called Dr. Lennard in and briefed him that a burn victim was on the way. He's the hospital's chief physician, and better still, he's had some experience with burn patients from when he did his residency in Pittsburgh. Yet even he breathed through his teeth when he arrived to examine the patient: an accelerant or chemical must have splashed onto the victim's back and seared through his skin when ignited. A section of the guy's spine was visible, the flesh burned off and the underlying fat bubbled up. The bone had turned a sickening shade of sizzled red brown. The smell, like some unholy combination of overcooked hamburger and burnt plastic, was appalling.

Dr. Willis came to assist, and the three of us worked to stabilize the patient. For a hick hospital, we provide some decent burn care, at least enough to steady a victim before transferring him to a better-equipped place in Philadelphia, which takes four hours by ambulance or two and a half by helicopter, assuming we can wrangle one.

"He won't survive the ride," Dr. Lennard said, practically reading my mind.

"No."

"If it were closer, half hour maybe, we could chance it. Best to keep him here for a while to stabilize. Then we can see."

"Right."

We cleaned the wounds, hooked the patient to an IV, and set up his oxygen in a non-rebreathing mask. By then Paula had arrived, and she took over with the burn victim, in time for me to meet Joe Kriner, the police chief, who pulled in leading the returning ambulance.

Inside the ambulance were two bodies for the morgue: a thirty-four-year-old woman and her nine-year-old daughter. Since the town had only one ambulance, the two had been placed side by side on the same gurney. The girl had Down syndrome and had apparently died from a congenital heart defect, while the woman had intentionally overdosed on heroin. No matter how many bodies I've seen in my years as a nurse, and no matter how much snark I dish out, at least in my head, I never experience anything other than deep sorrow at the death of a child.

Dr. Willis declared them both dead, a formality, in a whisper. Chief Kriner took off his hat.

I smoothed the little girl's hair before covering her with the sheet.

. . .

All I've ever wanted to be is a nurse. A dime-store psychologist might say that's because I spent so much time in hospitals when I was a kid. Perhaps that's true. The nurses were kind to me. They looked me in the eye when they spoke and never lied. Doctors, on the other hand, would tell me that everything would be fine and that another operation would fix me for life. Then, when my face failed to heal properly, they'd promise that *next* time, things would mend the right way, filling me again with hopes that were ultimately dashed. Nurses made no such promises. They only encouraged me to be strong.

The official name of my condition, bilateral complete orofacial cleft, caused a severe harelip and a badly deformed palate. Today, such a problem in children can usually be fixed with a few surgeries and will result in a small-enough scar if you operate while the child is growing. But nearly thirty years ago, the technology wasn't as sophisticated, and two resulting and nearly deadly infections worsened the problem, until doctors deemed my case too risky to operate again.

"She'll just have to learn to live with it," one surgeon told my mother, addressing her rather than me, though I was sitting in the chair beside her.

So I'm saddled with a thick, two-inch pink scar that runs from my top lip up beside my nose and sometimes pulls my mouth into a bit of a sneer. All of this is made worse, I think, by my bright red hair, which brings more attention to my face. Covid was a disaster for our town, but there was one small, interesting side effect of the pandemic for me. My mask hid the scar so well that I once traveled to Harrisburg, telling myself it was only a shopping trip, but in reality I was curious to see how strangers would treat me if they couldn't see the bottom half of my face. There, in one day, two different men had asked me on dates. I can't say if I was happy or sad about that, or about the fact that I politely declined them both.

I can say that, without a mask, I'd never been asked out once in my twenty-eight years.

...

The next day I returned to Locksburg General and checked the inpatient log to find only one room occupied, that of the burn victim brought in the day before. The night nurse departed when I arrived, leaving me with the receptionist and Dr. Willis, who went to sleep in a vacant room with a request not to be awakened unless there was an emergency.

A ten-bed, one-floor hospital can be a quiet place for hours on end, and I wondered if I should take a snooze myself, when a car pulled up in front. The driver stepped out and came through the automatic doors.

"Do you have a wheelchair?" he asked. His voice held no panic, so there was probably an older patient in the car, I surmised, suffering from a bad back or a twisted ankle.

I wheeled an embarrassingly squeaky chair to the car and found a girl of sixteen, who low-moaned in discomfort. So much for my powers of deduction.

"Hi, hon," I said. "What's wrong?"

"It . . . kinda hurts," she said, trying hard to hold back her anguish. Her eyes, though, couldn't lie.

"I don't want to move you if anything's broken or . . ."

"Nothing's broken," she said. Then, matter-of-factly, "I have cancer."

She attempted to smile and was stopped by a grimace when a new round of pain stabbed into her.

"My name is Callie. What's yours?"

"Gabriella."

"OK, Gabriella. Let me help you from the car."

Her father stood to one side, as if he were ashamed of all of this.

"I forgot her pain medication," he said. "I mean, I forgot to get it refilled."

Hell of a dad, I thought, and nodded only to indicate that I understood his words.

"Who's her doctor?" I asked him.

"Excuse me?"

"Who's her primary physician?"

"Why does that matter? I mean, she just needs something for the pain."

"Dr. Stacy Yellen," the girl said. "We're from Pine Hill."

"Right. Let's get you to a room."

I got her settled in a bed then woke Dr. Willis, who went to her while I called the girl's doctor.

"We have a patient of yours here, Gabriella Stanhope," I told Dr. Yellen.

"How is she?"

"She arrived in severe pain. Dr. Willis wants to know what he should prescribe."

"Give her hydromorphone for the pain," Dr. Yellen said. "Who is with her?"

"Her father."

"Great," the woman mumbled, in a way that meant anything but.

"Why?"

"Do you know the girl at all, or anyone in her family?"

"No. I've never seen her before."

"What's your name again?"

"Callie."

"Callie, can I speak in confidence with you? Between us? I need to know that I—"

"Doctor, I've got a sixteen-year-old girl in another room in great discomfort. Please make this fast."

"Right. Sorry. This is what you do. Give her the hydromorphone via IV, and stay in the room with her. Under no circumstance should she be left alone with her father."

"Why?"

"Go take care of her. Then call me back later. I'll tell you everything. But remember: don't leave the two of them alone. Understood?"

"Got it," I said, and hung up.

Dr. Willis administered the drug to Gabriella while her father leaned forward in a chair, hands folded in some kind of silent prayer. He didn't offer any soothing words to his daughter or ask us any questions. I didn't see what kind of danger this guy could pose: he was five-foot-eight if he was an inch and skinny enough so that his suit jacket hung loosely on him. If I had to grab him, I wouldn't go for the hair, though. His was cut short and slicked back.

To pass some time, I took the needed information and had him sign the usual patient and guardian forms.

"Will you pray?" he asked. I first thought that he was speaking to his daughter, but she had drifted off to sleep. He was asking me.

"I'll pray for her, sure," I said. I've never been religious, but I'd pray to any god for a patient, if it would help or comfort. He blessed himself and I followed suit, feeling a bit like an impostor or even a spy of this faith that I'd never practiced outside of an occasional funeral or a relative's church wedding.

"Let us pray: Our dearest Father in Heaven," he began, and I folded my hands. "We thank you for your mercy, and we welcome our sufferings, in that they shall move us closer to you. We . . ."

I gave up listening after that. A god who would do this to a child was no god who delivered mercy and no god who deserved thanks. After another two minutes of long-winded groveling, the guy ended with an amen, which I echoed, if only out of habit.

He stood.

"Can I take her home now?"

"Um, no," I said, half convinced he was joking. "She'll need another dose of the hydromorphone, and she can't be released with that in her system. She'll need to rest. Overnight, at least."

"Well, OK," he said, as if I were giving him a choice.

"You can go, if you need to."

"I do. I have other children that need attending to. You have my phone number in case you need to reach me. I'll be back tomorrow. Bless you."

After he pulled away in his car, I called Dr. Yellen again.

"Gabriella is sleeping. Her father left a minute ago."

"How is she?"

"Her vitals aren't stellar. But she's better. What can you tell me?"

"Her father is the pastor at Shepard's Staff Tabernacle. Do you know them?"

"I've heard of them. Isn't there a church over there, in Pine Hill?"

"Right. They don't believe in medicine, other than prayer. Gabriella collapsed a couple months ago in a grocery store. Someone brought her in. She has Ewing's sarcoma."

"Her parents didn't know that she was sick?"

"Oh, they knew something was wrong with her. But they wanted to pray it away. Fucking idiots. If you diagnose Ewing's early enough, you've got a good chance of stopping it. Now it's spread all over her body. She's in stage four."

"And there's no stage five."

"Correct," she said. "What a beautiful kid."

"Why shouldn't she be left with her father?"

"I don't trust him. I'm not confident that he gives her her prescriptions. I wanted to make sure he didn't deny her any."

"Why didn't he come to you today, instead of here?"

"I can guess. Last time, I told him I'd have him thrown in jail if he didn't take care of her. He argued over the treatment we provided. Said it was his right to deny it. I said, fine, and it's my right to report you for neglect, and my right to take you to court and see what a judge might say about this. The only thing he hates worse than me, apparently, would be publicity. So now he does the bare minimum for her, so he doesn't have the police on his ass."

"He was in the room, praying about how god was going to save her."

"Yeah, he did that with me. And then I did something really dumb."

"What?"

"Are you religious?"

"No," I said.

"When he went off on one of his rants about how his god can heal, I said, 'Has your god ever healed an amputee? If so, you should show me. I'd love to see that magic trick.' That got him yammering about how he didn't want a heathen treating his child. I'm guessing that's why he came to your hospital."

"What should we do now?"

"What else can we do? Keep her comfortable."

"How long does she have?"

"Based on the last round of tests, she's got a week, maybe."

. . .

The next day I went into Gabriella's room. She'd slept since being admitted the previous afternoon, heavily medicated to help her through the night. Ewing's sarcoma attacks the bones and soft tissue, and her case had caused her legs and hips to swell. Yet her face had regained color, and the sleep seemed to have recharged her. If I hadn't seen her so weak the previous day, I'd have been surprised to learn of her condition. Other than a propensity for plainness—she wore no jewelry, and her corn-colored hair was so long and straight it looked like something out of *Little House on the Prairie*—Gabriella seemed like any other sixteen-year-old you'd see around town, who'd be giggling with her friends and carelessly carrying a bag full of schoolbooks if she wasn't lying in a hospital bed.

"How do you feel?" I asked her.

"Better."

"Better than what?"

"Better than if I were being eaten alive by wolverines."

"That's good for you. Not for the wolverines. I hate it when they go hungry."

"How long will I stay here?"

"At least another night. You've had some strong painkillers, and Dr. Willis took a blood sample that he wants tested. We probably won't get those results back until midday tomorrow at the earliest."

She glanced around the bland hospital room.

I said, "Yeah, it can be boring. Do you have a cell phone or a book or something you might want?"

"No. I sorta fell down when we were out and my dad drove me here. I didn't have time to get anything."

"We have a small library. Mostly stuff that people left behind. I'll bring you some books. What do you like?"

"Anything about the ocean. Seriously, anything—novels or nature books or science stuff. I've been, like, obsessed with it for years and years. And then when I was studying fish and biology, I read everything about the sea."

"I'll check if we have anything like that."

"Can you show me how to use this too?"

She pointed at the television. That was a bit of a surprise: most patients have that thing turned on and are scanning the stations before they warm the bed.

"You don't have one at home?"

"We're only allowed to watch it sometimes, when my dad is there."

"Are you allowed to watch this one?"

"I won't tell if you won't tell," she said, and grabbed the remote.

I turned on the television and went to find her a book. On the way past the front desk, Mona, the morning receptionist, was looking up to the ceiling while attempting, fruitlessly, to get out a few words to someone who apparently wouldn't listen. I tried to speed up and race past her, but Mona thrust out her hand holding the phone.

"He's demanding to talk to someone on medical staff," Mona said.

I crinkled my nose as if she'd handed me a roadkill skunk, and drilled my eyes into hers. She gave me a *What can I do?* shrug.

"Locksburg General!" I said, all cheery.

"You a doctor?" a guy's voice said. I immediately pictured him sitting in a sweat-stained lounge chair and wearing a wife-beater undershirt with more food on it than there was in his moldy refrigerator.

"I'm a nurse."

"Maybe that's good enough . . ."

"Well, we'll take our chances."

"I can't remember shit anymore. What should I take so I can remember?"

"You should take . . . Oh, shoot. I just forgot."

"What kind of nurse are you?"

"The kind who doesn't tie up a hospital phone with lame questions."

"I'll call your supervisor. What's your name?"

"Mona," I said, then hung up.

Mona's mouth dropped open.

"Don't worry. He won't remember." Then I flashed her a smirk that said: *That'll teach you to hand me the phone.*

I found two things for Gabriella to read—one a *National Geographic* magazine that had a cover story on sea turtles, and the other what looked to be a cheesy romance novel set in a fishing village—and brought them to her. I'd been gone barely fifteen minutes, but she'd already shut off the television.

"Gave it up?"

"It's exhausting."

"I know."

"I like real people better," she said.

"I like people too. I just feel better when they're not around."

"That's called cognitive dissonance."

"That's also called life."

"You're a smartie."

"In a good way or a bad way?"

"Sorta bad."

"I'm sorta sorry," I said.

"It's OK. Everyone tries to seem nice all the time, and I kinda do too, but sometimes I don't want to be. Do you think that's wrong?"

"What do you mean?"

"Do you think you should always be a nice person, every single minute of the day, even if you don't want to be? And if you don't want to be nice, but you act nice, is that a kind of lie?"

It wasn't a first, but it was a rarity: a philosophical question from a patient. I'd gotten so used to the crazy callers and the barely ill patients who treat every minor inconvenience as if it were an earth-shaking tragedy that now, when an interesting comment arrived, it caught me off guard.

"I . . . I think you're asking the wrong person," I said. "I'm embarrassed to admit it, but I'm not always so nice. And the opposite sometimes happens: I can easily be nice, but I choose to be . . . well, you said it, a smartie."

"And what happens if you aren't nice in actions, but you're nice in your mind?" Gabriella asked. "Or, wait, what if your actions help others but your thoughts are mean? Like, if you do something kind for someone, but in your heart, you hate doing it?"

"Wow, you won't hear this on TV."

"They're interesting questions, aren't they?"

"They are. Are you a philosopher too?"

"I just think things like that sometimes."

"That's admirable," I said.

"Can I ask you another question?" she said.

"Whatever you want."

"I'm not doing so well, am I?"

I took a while before answering. Checked her water pitcher. Smoothed a section of the bedsheet.

"Not really, no."

She took just as long before saying, "Thank you for the truth."

"I wish I didn't have to tell it."

"Have you ever lied to a patient?"

"I wouldn't do that."

"Seriously? Not even to little kids?"

"A long time ago I promised myself to never lie to a patient. No matter who."

Gabriella stared directly into my eyes, as if she were about to test me. Then she said:

"I'm going to die any day now, aren't I?"

ANDY

I sat with Kate and Angie for an hour, my head in my hands, moaning like some wounded beast in a field. Then I tried to pray, before giving up and telling god: *You know what? Go fuck yourself and take your universe with you.* Finally I rose from the corner of the room where I'd collapsed and called the police. Before they arrived I took the half-filled baggie of heroin that Kate had left and hid it behind the needlepoint in our bedroom that read:

> *The best part about*
> *Tomorrow is that there will*
> *Be more things to love.*

The police chief showed up as I was hiding the extra syringes that Kate had bought in a three-pack from a drugstore. Within an hour I was sitting in front of the chief's desk at the station while an ambulance took away the only two people I'd ever loved.

Chief Kriner checked out that I'd been at work all morning, and asked enough questions at the hospital to ease his mind that I'd had nothing to do with the deaths. In a town as small as Locksburg, he was essentially a beat cop in a cruiser with an extra stripe on his sleeve. As a rule, I didn't trust anyone who wore a badge, though the guy seemed to have at least one measure of compassion more than the Philadelphia police, who were, in many cases, as hard and jaded as the junkies.

"So where's the heroin?"

"I haven't done any of that in more than nine years."

"You're no longer an addict?"

"I'm an addict, all right. I'm always an addict. I crave it every single day of my life. I've just gotten good at holding off the urges."

"Where did your wife get the drugs?"

"I don't know," I said, though I had an idea or three. There were plenty of losers in Locksburg who'd be happy to sell you whatever you wanted. This cop surely had to realize that.

"I didn't see any of those little bags left over."

"Bags?"

"For heroin."

"Oh. I don't know what to tell you. Maybe it's around the room somewhere."

"You're not thinking of doing the same, are you?" he asked.

"No," I lied.

"If this was the city, I'd refer you to a grief counseling center. But the best we got is Father Glynn over at Saint Stanislaus. He's trained in that sort of thing." He took a card from his desk and handed it to me. "This is his phone number. He's a good friend of mine."

"Thanks."

"Go see him."

"I will."

"You won't go, will you?"

"No," I said, figuring a dose of truth wouldn't hurt. I checked the clock on the wall. I'd been at the station for four hours. "Can I leave?"

"I'll drive you home."

"I'd like to walk."

"Sure?"

"Yeah."

He offered his hand, and we shook.

"I'm sorry for your loss," he said.

I nodded and left and started on the fifteen-minute walk home through Locksburg. I never thought much of this town, but Angie liked feeding the ducks at Dykeman Pond and talking to people who seemed to have more time to chat than those who lived in Philadelphia and shied away from strangers. After a year away, I lost much of my strange pride for that city, which fostered such unexamined feelings of arrogance and, to be flat-out honest, deserved none of them. Locksburg was a better place for my wife and my daughter, and that made it good enough for me.

On the walk, I took the card with the grief counselor's name that the cop gave me and tossed it into a recycling can. Then I got home and into bed and tried to get a decent night's sleep.

I had a lot to do tomorrow before killing myself.

. . .

I woke the next morning and listened for Angie, and for half a minute was amazed that she was still sleeping. I wondered why Kate, always a late riser, had gotten out of our bed so early.

Then the realization slammed into me like a high wave of water, and I lay there in a kind of shock, so devastated that I became jittery, eyeballs darting around, feeling confused and trying to convince myself that what had happened yesterday had been a dream I'd just awakened from. Soon, though, I had to force myself to understand that they were gone. When the emotions began to overwhelm me, I found consolation in the idea that my despair wouldn't last long. Make it through this morning, I told myself. Then you can end this life and all its pain.

I showered and made myself as presentable as possible, which for me was a pair of two-year-old jeans and a plain black T-shirt. I walked a few blocks over to Lombard Funeral Home, chosen because it was closest.

I stood on the porch, unsure of whether to knock or enter the place, and after a few moments of indecision was saved by a woman inside who must have seen me. She opened the front door.

"Good morning," she said. She was maybe sixty, her hair gray and well styled, and, like me, in jeans and a shirt, though she carried an air of respectability and professional friendliness that I'd never had. She looked me right in the eye. I glanced elsewhere, embarrassed that mine were so bloodshot.

"Are you . . . open?"

"Yes. My husband had to step out on an errand, but I can help you. Would you like to come in?"

I followed her to a small office to the right, close to the front door. She offered me a heavy wooden chair; then she moved to the business side of the desk.

"I shoulda called, I guess, but uh, you know . . ." I was reverting to Philly-speak, and I willed myself to slow down. My city accent occasionally baffled Locksburg listeners—I often can't help cutting the *g* from *ing*-ended words, and my vocabulary choices sometimes run counter to townsfolk-language. I'll say, "Can I get a soda?" and be asked, "You'nz want a pop?" with a bewildered look.

I stopped to collect myself. She saved me with: "You're fine. How about a cup of coffee?"

"No. I mean, unless you've got some made."

"It will take one minute. I've got one of those new Keurig makers. Tell you the truth, I'd like a cup too. I'll be right back."

I scanned the office: plaques on the wall, framed certifications, photographs. The place was so silent I could hear the coffee streaming into the cup in the next room. She popped back in. "How would you like yours?"

"Milk, no sugar, please." I might have asked for some whiskey in it had it not been so early in the morning, and had I not been here on such a task.

She returned with the coffee, then retook her seat.

"Oh, I'm sorry—I'm Carol Lombard. And you're . . . ?"

"Andy Devon."

"How can I help you, Andy?" she asked.

"I, uh, I . . . my wife. And my daughter . . ."

Just saying those words aloud made my bottom lip tremble. I stared at the floor and resigned myself to pushing the information out of my mouth, reminding myself to get this done, finish this part, and later, all will be over.

I began again. "I'm guessing you already heard. Everyone knows everything in this town, it seems."

"I had heard something, yes, about a mother and daughter. I'm so sorry."

"I'd like to have them both cremated. No ceremony or anything."

She surprised me by asking, "How long were you married?"

"Ten years. My daughter, she had Down syndrome. We used to take a lot of walks. Sometimes we'd walk by here. You probably saw us."

"Yes, I remember you."

The woman didn't appear especially familiar, but I knew she'd remember us. You don't forget a crew like Kate, Angie, and me and how we walked the streets, happier than anyone else around us, surely. And I will say this for myself: even with a miserable early life, I knew that I had experienced real happiness later on. I had the kind of pride that comes from surviving a terrible time and still finding love, a love that was powerful and . . .

"Dear?"

I had faded away. I swallowed hot coffee to burn me to attention.

"Sorry. What did you say?"

"I asked, where are they now? Are they at . . . ?"

"At Locksburg General. I really don't know . . . how this works. If I need to call there or . . ."

"We'll take care of everything." I got the feeling that if I were sitting there next to her, she would have touched my hand in sympathy.

"So, like, how much will this cost?"

She tapped a few numbers into a desk calculator, then wrote a total on a piece of paper and handed it to me. The price was higher than I expected.

"And that's . . . no ceremony or anything, right? I'm really sorry if I sound stupid. I've never done this before. Obviously."

"Don't apologize. Yes. Only the cremations. Andy, are you sure you don't want to go home and rest? I could have my husband stop by later today. Or tomorrow. Take some time. You can—"

"No. I need to get this done now. Can I pay by check?"

"Yes. That's fine."

"There's one other thing," I said. "I've . . . This may sound . . . but, um. When I die . . . See, it's only me now. And I'm afraid, if I go. You know, die. No one will take care of me. What I want to do is leave instructions for when I go. To have me cremated too. And have all our ashes put together and scattered. So . . . do people, like, pay ahead of time?"

"Some do. But as I said, Andy, you should take some time to think about—"

"I don't need any more time," I said. It was blunter than I wanted it to sound to this nice woman. But I had to plow through, in case my resolve began to wane. "I just want to get all this done right now. Please."

A half hour later I walked out with a receipt in my pocket for three cremations, totaling a mere fourteen dollars less than the balance of my savings account.

Pretty good, I told myself. *There's not much left to leave to any-one.*

...

I considered doing something darkly romantic, like surrounding myself with the hundreds of photographs that Kate, Angie, and I had taken over the years, or playing the children's records that we'd listen and sing along to together. But then I thought of Kate, who wasn't one for sentimentality. If she wanted to do something, she did it, no frills. Her favorite phrase wasn't anything dreamy or clever or cute. It was: "I get shit done."

"Then let's get this shit done, motherfucker!" I shouted inside my empty house. Punched the door frame for good measure.

From behind the needlepoint I took the remainder of the bag-gie that Kate had used. As I cooked it up in the spoon, I couldn't help thinking back on my life, which I often considered in chapters: the first, as a kid growing up in Northeast Philadelphia, wild as a street rat, with parents who didn't care much about themselves, and less about me. Then the next chapter was tougher, and began the night my dad beat my mother into a pulp then never returned, leaving her permanently changed and distracted, not even notic-ing when I dropped out of high school in tenth grade. The heroin chapter followed that, when I hit the junk hard and eventually met Kate, and we'd shoot up side by side and live together on and off the streets. Finally, the only good section, when Kate and I had Angie, and we cleaned ourselves up and lived our best lives.

That's the last memory I wanted in my mind.

I sucked up the juice from the spoon then steadied the over-filled syringe. Yanked the belt tight and tapped a vein in my arm. Felt the pinch as the needle went in. Then shot hard.

A second later, the overdose hit my heart.

I gasped.

My eyelids weighed two hundred pounds each. They dropped and put me into blackness, then my neck weakened and my head . . . felt . . .

so
unimaginably
heavy
that
it
bobbed
and
I
couldn't
lift
it
at
all.

I mumbled as I fell away into something infinitely dark and bottomlessly deep. I don't know if I said the words, though I know I felt them. The words were:

Kate.
Angie.
Here I come.

NATHAN

When Paula and I started dating, her cheerfulness was uplifting: she'd knit me things, like a cheesy, tasseled winter hat, and hide smiley-faced notes in my pockets for me to discover later. Her decency was still more moving and filled me with admiration: she'd forgive the drunks who came in and upchucked on the hospital floor, and she always bent down to talk to the little girl with Down syndrome who we'd sometimes see when we walked around town. Most of all, Paula held no grudges, and her forgiveness seemed never-ending. While our later disappointments had embittered me, her compassion had only deepened.

More and more, that compassion finds its way under my skin, and when we spoke in the morning, I wanted to punch a wall. I felt as if I were explaining a situation to a child who not only didn't understand the world but had no desire to learn its ways. Paula appeared haggard, having woken early from a restless sleep. We argued through breakfast, where she pleaded again and again for me to return the money.

"If I do that, I'll never be able to show my face around here."

"Then we'll move."

"See? This is what I'm saying, Paula! I want to take the *money* and move! But you only want to move if I'm humiliated."

"That's not true. I know you. I don't think you really want to keep that money. You made a mistake . . ."

"That's exactly what I didn't do. All these damn years, working, keeping my head down. It's gotten me nowhere. It's time to take a chance for once. I'm tired of being broke . . ."

"We're not broke."

"We got loans on both cars. This house needs cement work and a new roof. We have, what, fifteen years left on the mortgage? Then all the doctor bills we're still paying . . ."

I trailed off and left it at that. My god, the things we couldn't say to each other. That was a wound we tried not to touch, and we talked about fertility issues only when we absolutely had to. But rounds and rounds of IVF and the tests and the trips to specialists in Baltimore and Philadelphia, most not covered by our paltry insurance, had sunk us deep, with nothing to show for it. Each time the treatments failed, it broke us in ways that hadn't mended, made worse by having us delay any ideas of adoption, until we were now perhaps too old to apply.

"We're fine," she said.

"I want to be better than fine. I want my life to be something other than settling for almost good enough."

Twice she put a hand on my arm. Twice I shrugged her off. She tried it a third time, and I stormed out to my truck and drove off. I saw her in the rearview, holding my lunch bag high. I kept driving.

Paula came into the shop at noon with my food. I took it, mumbled a thank-you, and shot her a look that said: *Don't talk about this here.*

"I'm working a four-o'clock shift today," she reminded me.

"I know."

"So I'll see you tonight. Will you be up?"

"I guess."

She went to kiss me on the cheek. The only reason I didn't pull away was because others might notice.

"You're a good man, Nathan," she whispered after her lips touched me. "We both know that."

...

Her words stuck inside my head and made me furious throughout the rest of the workday: I was pissed that Paula would try to manipulate me. Angry that she was unable to see my side. Frustrated that she couldn't understand what I wanted, or grasp my reasoning.

She was working the evening shift at the hospital all week, so I went to Maxie's for a beer and a sandwich after my own shift ended at five. There, I could sit alone, and in my mind rehearse what to say to her. I've never been good at speaking, and I was even less articulate when put on the spot. So I wanted to be ready.

"Paula, listen to me," I'd start when we talked later that night. I'd try to summon a kind of rationalization and wrap my words in that, like a lawyer convincing a jury. "I'm not stupid. I understand what you're saying. I do. But this is drug money and no one will miss it. Do you realize we're over forty now? Why are we waiting to live? What are we going to do, die here in Locksburg, having seen and done nothing of any substance? I can't do that, Paula. This is our chance."

It seemed like a good claim until I began to imagine her responses, like those she'd used that morning: "What more do we need, Nathan? If we take that money we'll always feel guilty about what we've done. We'd be paranoid all the time. I can see that you're already getting consumed by this."

When I thought of how she'd try to argue, I'd sip my beer and attempt to craft a comeback line. Soon, five pints were in me. I'd be walking home and picking up my truck tomorrow morning. If that was the case, there was nothing wrong with having a sixth. I ordered and kept arguing with my wife inside my head, until the emotions and the alcohol and the anger swirled into something acidic: an infuriation with her.

"There's a guy we don't see a lot of."

I turned to see LeeLee Roland, then glanced over my other shoulder. No one else was with her.

"Who's we?" I said.

"Only me, Mister Literal. Mind if I sit down?"

She didn't wait for an answer as she took the stool next to me. She had to hop up to get there. LeeLee was barely over five feet and the kind of woman who was proud of being short. It made people call her cute or pixieish or adorable, and gave her license to say things like "Big things come in small packages!" or "It's not the size of the girl in the fight, it's the size of the fight in the girl!" with a smile that she probably figured was no less appealing for being so well practiced.

LeeLee said, "Don't see you in here much."

I shrugged.

"Don't hear you much either."

I had no answer. Just finished the pint and slid it forward for a refill.

"So how ya been?" she asked. It was a standard and useless question: everyone knows how everyone is in Locksburg. But she sounded interested enough and having her sit next to me wasn't unpleasant, even considering our history. After her abortion, we avoided each other throughout the rest of high school. She later moved in with one of the Tate brothers and pumped out a couple quick kids, then left Jimmy Tate, who three months later drunk-drove himself into a tree on Route 54. The tree still stands. Tate is six feet under at Locksburg Cemetery, and both their kids have joined the military and sailed off for elsewhere, happy to be away from her and from this town, or so I've heard. LeeLee and I would nod or say hi here and there at the supermarket or on the sidewalk or any other place we ran into each other, all of it perfunctory. Lately I'd seen her hanging around Orky's or Maxie's. Age-wise, she was in that strange place—none of the twentysomethings were eager to hang with someone who was pushing forty, and most everyone her own age was married and at home with children.

"I'm good. You?"

"Eh, you know."

"I hear that."

She ordered a beer. When it arrived, I pushed forward two dollars from my change on the bar.

"Aw, thank you, Nate."

She gave my shoulder a squeeze and shifted in her seat to get comfortable. I caught sight of a bit of leg and a denim skirt. Above that, a tight, short-sleeved top that her body had a year or two left of wearing before heads stopped turning to watch her walk past. I couldn't tell if her hair was a natural dirty blond or a dye job—I've never known how to figure that out—but I could see that she took care with that and with her makeup, which tended toward the bright on her cheeks and the glossy on her lips.

After LeeLee sipped her beer, she said, "So what's on your mind? You're sitting there like you're thinking some deep thoughts."

Fuck it, I thought. She wanted words, I'd give her a few, well-oiled by six beers.

"Want to know what I'm really thinking, LeeLee?"

"Yeah. Tell me."

"I'm thinking of getting out of this shithole."

"Aw, come on. Maxie's is the best bar around."

I snorted.

"I don't mean this shithole. I meant this Locksburg shithole. The whole town."

"Ohhh! Duhh!" She laughed, and I followed along. It was the first time that a laugh had left my mouth all day. All week, maybe. She became excited when she understood what I'd meant.

"Oh man, Nate, you must be psychic! I'm always saying I should get out of this place!" Then she called out: "Nicky!"

The bartender broke his conversation and glanced over.

"C'mere!" she said when he appeared reluctant to move.

He approached us, ready to pour a drink.

"What can I get ya?"

"Don't I always say I should get out of this shithole?" LeeLee said.

"This bar?"

"No! Locksburg!"

"Yeah. You never shut up about it."

"See? There you go!" she said, and eyeballed me, as if this proved something profound.

Nicky walked away with a slight shake of his head, that he'd been called over only for that question.

LeeLee said, "I say it to everyone. I swear I'm getting out of here, the sooner the better. And everyone says the same thing: they're going to move away too."

"Then why don't they?"

"Because they don't really want to. This town's full of talkers."

"True."

"I'm surprised to hear it from you, though. I always had you pegged as a lifer."

She might have said it with humor, but I didn't take it that way.

"Da hell you mean by that, LeeLee?"

"Don't get mad! I mean, you were born here. You're from here. You know?"

I knew. It was something that, in my most pissed-off moments, I berated myself for.

After a while she said, "Where you thinking of going?"

"I dunno. Florida, I guess. Hate these winters. Want to feel the sun. Fish off the beach."

"That sounds real nice. I'd do that in a second."

"Why haven't you gone?"

"With what? I'm a secretary for the mayor, the police chief, the fire chief, and three others. My one job is six jobs. I stay late every night and work my little tail off, and still get paid nothin'."

I nodded in agreement, though she was, to put it mildly, exaggerating. Sure, she worked as the town hall secretary, but none of those officials got many calls or held a lot of meetings, and the few times I'd been there, LeeLee had been painting her nails at her desk or texting away on her cell phone. She was flirty, though, and looked pretty sitting at her desk wearing V-cut tops, so no one complained, at least none of the men.

"And it's expensive to move," she added.

I thought of the money in my attic and couldn't trap the guffaw that escaped my mouth.

"What? You win the lottery?"

"I got enough to move."

"You got enough to buy a girl another beer?"

We both refilled, and she set about recalling high school classmates who'd moved away, teachers too. The names seemed familiar, though cloudy and indistinct in my memory. I don't like to think about the past, but she focused on it as if she thought of those people, jealously, every day.

After an hour, the bar cleared out to maybe a half-dozen weeknighters. The bartender realized this was a lost cause for big profits and rang the bell at nine fifteen for last call.

LeeLee said, "I hope you ain't driving."

"Nope. Gonna hoof it."

My house was a mile and a half away, far enough that I was sometimes jokingly called an edge-of-towner. I thought the air might clear my head, though, and I didn't want to drive any distance drunk in this town. With two million dollars in my attic, I didn't want to see a cop anywhere near me.

"Well, walk a girl home," LeeLee said, and hopped off her seat. Her feet hit the floor, and her first step was a stagger that she tried to cover up by acting like she tripped. "It's on the way, right?" she said, as if I knew where she lived.

As we walked, she talked about leaving Locksburg and told a tale of how she once went looking for an apartment in Maryland and somehow bounced a check or didn't have enough for the security deposit or whatever. I'd lost the thread of the story. I mmm-hmmed a few times to make it sound like I was listening. But what I was really doing was thinking about Paula and the money. What would happen if we couldn't agree? Could I move and hope that Paula followed? I'd think she would. She was loyal, I'd give her that. She'd forgive me for anything. And that realization began to intensify my anger—even Paula's forgiveness could feel stifling and belittling, as if I *needed* to be forgiven. The embers of anger were still red-hot when I thought of her and all her damn goodness and her oh-so-right way of thinking, which made me feel worse for wanting to keep what I'd found. And I shouldn't have felt guilty at all. It was mine. That was for damn sure.

"Here we are," LeeLee said.

We'd gone down an alley between two houses. At the back of one was a set of steps that led to a second-floor apartment.

"Another dumb thing keeping me here—wastin' my pay on renting this place when I should have bought, you know?"

I nodded, though she probably didn't notice in the dark.

We stood there.

"C'mere," she said. "You been so nice to me."

I tried to lie to myself. It didn't work. Though half drunk, I had known where this was leading from the moment we met in the bar. Somewhere underneath my other worries and ideas, I understood where talking to LeeLee could end up, and when she stepped forward and kissed me, I wasn't surprised in the least.

Nor was I surprised when, a few minutes later, we were in her bedroom.

...

I'd never been unfaithful to Paula before, and I wondered if I'd feel worse later. Now it was just something that had happened, and I was numb, nothing more. LeeLee and I lay there afterward and I tried not to let her see me stretch over to glance at the bedside clock: 11:19. I had less than an hour to leave and get home before Paula returned from her shift, which ended at midnight.

"What are you thinking?" LeeLee asked.

How to answer that? I was thinking that I was a goddamn cliché, a forty-one-year-old guy who had cheated on his wife. And with a woman he first slept with when he was seventeen. I was thinking about the bag with two million dollars that was sitting in my gun cabinet. I was thinking about Paula's insistence on returning the money. Words, always so useless to me, were laughable to try to employ now, with all that was in my mind. But I guessed I had to give LeeLee something.

"Thinkin' that was real nice."

"I was thinking the same," she said.

Then, a moment before I got up and went home, LeeLee said: "I was also thinking, are you really serious about leaving town?"

CALLIE

"I don't know if you're going to die soon," I told Gabriella. "And that's the truth. No one knows for sure."

"It's bad, though, isn't it?"

"It's not great. But remissions can happen."

"What are my chances?"

Misleading the sick is against my personal and professional code, but I also didn't have to volunteer too much information, especially not to a sixteen-year-old. It's usually best to sidestep.

"I'm no doctor, and I don't know your case history," I said.

"My dad says God will heal me. Do you think that's true?"

"Now we're getting deep, aren't we?"

"Is that a no?"

"Your dad believes it. That's his prerogative. I try to respect that."

"But do *you* think it's true?"

Not in the least. Even in a small hospital, I'd seen far too much pointless tragedy—child abuse, car wrecks, and the like—to believe a loving god could be watching over anyone. Yet how to say that to a dying sixteen-year-old? Answer: You don't. Ever.

"I don't lie to patients. But I also don't have to talk about everything they want to."

"So you avoid the subject."

"Correct. Or I use some expert misdirection."

"Like how?"

"So, what grade are you in?"

"I'm homeschooled. I guess I'd be in tenth grade."

"What's your favorite subject?"

"Wait. Do you really care? Or is this the misdirection you were talking about?"

"Yes to both. So what's your favorite subject?"

"Biology. What was yours?"

"The same. I was the only girl in class who liked dissecting a frog."

"Did you have a lot of boyfriends in high school?"

"No."

"Oh, I don't believe you. Are you married?"

"No."

"Were you ever married?"

"So many questions."

"Sorry."

"No. Never married."

"Why not? Are you gay?"

"I'm not gay. It's just that the average quality of men in Locksburg is somewhat suboptimal."

That cracked her up, and her laughing led me to do the same.

"Seriously!" she said. "You're so pretty. Why not?"

"I'm not so pretty under this mask. I've got a scar, from a condition I was born with. So it's tough to meet people. Romantically, I mean."

We were both quiet for a bit.

Then I took off my mask to show her.

"That's not so bad. You're pretty."

"Thank you for saying so."

"It's true," she said. "I wouldn't lie to you."

...

Locksburg General is one of the newest buildings within town limits. It was built on a weedy lot at the farthest end of Archer Avenue when the previous hospital was condemned and torn down. The place remains a work in process. Construction of an MRI room was recently begun at the back of the building, and if the funds are ever raised—and that's a five-hundred-thousand-dollar *if*—perhaps we'll see the machine that the space was planned for. I'm not overly optimistic. We're a nonprofit and mostly an afterthought to the town's residents, when we're not serving as the butt of their jokes. There's an often-told story about a carpenter from nearby Greenbriar who got three of his fingers sliced off clean by an industrial band saw. He wrapped his belt around his wrist to stanch the bleeding, plopped his severed digits into a Tupperware bowl, and sped to Northumberland Memorial Hospital.

The doctor there managed to take good care of the fingers, then race them and the carpenter to Harrisburg via ambulance, where two were successfully reattached. When all was said and done, the doctor asked the carpenter: "You were bleeding like a stuck pig and had three fingers on the seat next to you. Locksburg General was fifteen minutes closer than Northumberland. Why didn't you go there instead?" The carpenter said, "I considered it. But, well, you know, it's Locksburg." The doctor replied: "Oh yeah. I would have done the same."

That tale is thirty years old, and Locksburg General has come a very long way—I've put in plenty of unpaid overtime to make sure of it. But bad reputations die hard, and ours sends most residents elsewhere if it's not a dire emergency.

One good thing about the hospital's lack of patients is its

resulting quietness. Gabriella and I talked uninterrupted for hours. I'd periodically step out into the lobby to check on things—and to wake our receptionist, who kept nodding off behind the front desk—then return to Gabriella's room, where she'd say something like, "Oh, here's another thing I forgot to say to you!" in reference to a story she'd shared earlier, or, "Wait, you never told me about your Christmases when you were a kid!" after a talk we had about my growing up. We spent the morning together, and I stayed there after my shift ended to have dinner with Gabriella before the cancer pain bit into her again, and the doctor sedated her to help her sleep through the night.

The next morning, she was rested and smiled brightly when I opened the door to her room.

"Good morning," she said.

"Hi. How are you feeling?"

"Not bad," she said. "How much longer will I be here?"

"How much longer do you want to be here?"

"Another day, maybe? It's always so loud at my house, and I've been having a lot of trouble sleeping."

She had four brothers and three sisters, she'd told me earlier. And the youngest two had more energy than most power plants.

"The younger two—they're boys, right?"

"Yeah. They're especially annoying."

"That's their job. If you think they're bad now, wait till you get older. They'll be worse."

"If I get older," she said.

I tried to salvage my choice of words.

"Oh. See that?"

"What?"

"You're older. By three seconds. Oh, look, it happened again!"

I made a motion with my hand, as if time were flittering by.

Gabriella said, "Wave your hand. Make a year go by."

"Whoosh. There ya go. It's a year later."

"Am I alive?"

"You're here right now, honey. That's all that matters."

"So can I stay for another day?"

It seemed to me a sad question, a girl who wanted to remain in an empty hospital rather than return to her home.

"If you feel you need it. But I can't lie to your father."

"Are you afraid of God?"

"I'm not religious, so I guess that's a no."

"Then why are you so afraid to lie to someone?"

"You don't need religion to be a good person. Or to know that lying is not such a good thing to do."

"I know that. But are you afraid to lie?"

"No. It's like this: though the truth is hard, it's almost always better. When I was growing up, the doctors, they were always saying to me: 'You're going to be so beautiful. We're going to fix you right up!' They did everything to convince me. And I'd believe them. Then when it didn't happen, they'd talk me back into hoping again. It was . . . horrible to do to a kid. You build yourself up with false optimism, and it hurts more later. And I guess it made me bitter in some ways. So I promised I'd never do that to anyone else."

I left it at that, as poor an explanation as it was. How could I even convey the nights I'd cry over and over, and the long days of pain? How could I describe the feeling of seeing a doctor's eyes as he'd remove the bandages and couldn't hide his disappointment? Or the sense of failure when he'd pat me on the head and use phrases like, "It's all right, honey," when it wasn't, or, "Next time will be better," before the nurse would come in and give me a stronger dose of antibiotics to fight off an infection that almost killed me? How to explain the stitches and the agony of trying to chew or speak or not to cry, because to frown would hurt so much.

"I guess that's good, then," Gabriella said.

"It's the best I got. How about you? Are you afraid of god?"

"I don't know if I should be. Don't tell my father that. But I don't know."

"It's OK not to know."

"Did your parents believe?"

"My father . . . I don't really know what he believed. We went to church here and there. But he and my mom were always busy working. So we didn't talk about it much. We didn't talk about anything much. That was just the way they were."

"Did they take you places, when you were growing up?"

"Knoebels, a couple times," I said.

"The amusement park?"

"Yeah."

"Anywhere else?"

"Harrisburg, sometimes. My dad had a farm about ten miles from here, so we went to the farm show. My medical bills . . . after my dad paid those, there wasn't much left over."

"Did he take you to the ocean?"

"No. We never had time, with the farm and all."

"Have you seen it?"

"The ocean? I never have, no."

"Oh my gosh, why not?"

"I made plans a few times after college, but they always fell through. I might go next summer, though."

"I want to see it. It's like the biggest dream I have. I mean that—I literally dream about seeing the ocean."

"Maybe your mom and dad will take you there. Do you want me to ask them?"

"I already did. Like five times. They say I can see it when I get older. I said to them, what if I don't get older? And they say it's a sin, to doubt God like that. If I don't believe, I won't get better."

I stayed silent.

After a while she turned her head to the window.

"How long does it take to get there?" Gabriella asked.

"The ocean? I guess you could drive there in four hours or so."

"I want to see it."

"I don't know what to tell you, honey."

"I might sneak out of here one night and try to go."

There was little chance of that, I think we both knew. Yet people have tried stranger things, and I was obligated to convince her not to attempt something so foolish.

"Gabriella, please don't do anything like that. You could get hurt . . ."

"Well, that would be terrible, wouldn't it? I wouldn't want to get hurt, since I'm going to die soon."

"Or you could get someone else hurt. And I know you don't want that."

She frowned. And after a moment she said:

"Can you take me to the ocean?"

The question caught me by surprise, and I sputtered a bit before slapping together an answer that sounded like a poor excuse.

"Your mother and father have to make those decisions."

"I'll never see it, then, will I?"

She looked at me. We both knew the odds, and the answer.

She said, "We could drive there and come back, and no one would know. I won't tell. I promise."

"I can't do that."

She was quiet. Her chin trembled.

"I could get in an immense amount of trouble," I said.

Silence settled into the room. And in it, I was embarrassed and angry at her parents, at the world, at any god who would make a sixteen-year-old girl suffer like this.

"Please?" she said. "Take me to the ocean, just to see it once?"

I judge people way too much.

And when I find that I'm judging, I ask myself: *Who are you to judge them? You don't know how they think, or what they've been through, or who they really are. You simply don't.*

So I try and I try and I try never to judge others.

But I think I can say this with certainty: if you can look at a girl with an illness like that, sitting in a hospital like this, who has parents like hers, and you can tell that girl that you won't give her the one small thing that may just be her last wish in life . . .

Well, then I'd judge you to be some kind of soulless prick.

ANDY

Whoever hit me with the first shot of Narcan slammed the needle in so hard that it later felt as if a piece of the metal had scraped against a bone and snapped off inside. When that didn't wake me, I'm told, the EMT rolled me to the side and stuck me with a second dose in my other thigh. When that drug, which almost instantly reverses opioid overdoses, ran through my veins, I remember sitting up, spewing whatever was in my stomach onto the front of my shirt, then falling back and clunking my head on the wooden floor. The damn EMT should have placed a pillow back there in case that happened.

I didn't realize I'd mumbled the thought aloud.

"Don't blame him," said Chief Kriner, who was standing there watching the action. "You put yourself in this situation."

A few minutes later, I was in the ambulance to Locksburg General, where they hoisted me onto a bed. I lay there sober and drained, gazing up at the florescent ceiling lights and blinking. Narcan immediately neutralizes heroin, but the price is shivering cold and extreme exhaustion. I wrapped myself in blankets that wouldn't warm me and trembled until I finally slept, then woke at ten the next morning. I pulled the pulse monitor from my finger and tried to climb from the bed. A nurse marched into the room.

"Back in bed," she ordered. "Now."

"I gotta get outta here."

"What you gotta do is listen to what I say."

Her tone was a plate of no nonsense, served with a side of disgust. I sat back down on the bed and wondered what I must look like, even without the overdose. Long after kicking the habit, I've remained thin and awkward. Well, that's being kind. I'm only a few pounds past scrawny, and have always been as graceless as a three-legged horse. When my long hair would stick out in all directions in the morning, Kate would laugh and say that I was the human equivalent of a mop.

The nurse said, "I'll be back. When I am, your feet will be under that sheet."

She stepped outside. Barely a minute later, she pushed the door open again. Her other hand was placing a cell phone into the pocket of her scrubs.

"That was speedy."

She reattached my pulse monitor.

"Where did you go?" I asked, to no response. "I guess you called the cops."

All at once I was ravenously thirsty. I felt like I could chug a bucket of water and not have enough. I searched around for a cup. She saw me and thrust one into my hand. If it hadn't had a lid, it would have soaked me.

"Your bedside manner is somewhat deficient." I read her name-tag and added, "Callie."

"If you need something, ring the bell. Do not get out of bed. The police chief said that if you leave before he gets here, he'll arrest you."

"I was groggy when I got here yesterday. If I said something to offend you, it was the drugs talking. I'm sorry."

"You didn't say anything to me."

"So you're always this pleasant to patients?"

"I'm pleasant to patients who need it. I've got a sixteen-year-old girl with cancer in the next room who'd love to have the life you tried to throw away. She needs it. You just need to shut up."

She walked out in a huff.

I finished my cup of water and was about to refill it from the pitcher, then decided to guzzle water straight from there.

Chief Kriner arrived ten minutes later.

"Do you remember me finding you?" he asked.

"Not really."

"I knocked, then walked around to the bedroom window. Saw you on the floor. Went back and kicked the door in." He studied me, as if I should be impressed. "I don't get a thanks?"

"Do you want one?"

"Not if I have to ask for it."

"Am I under arrest?"

"Want to be?"

I had plenty of replies to offer, none of which would leave my lips. The years had taught me never to mouth off to the police if I wanted to keep my teeth intact.

The chief said, "I know you're going through an incredibly hard time. I ain't even gonna try to imagine what it's like for you. But I can't let you leave if you're going to attempt to kill yourself again. Will you?"

"No," I said. I didn't have to think of the answer—you always give a cop what he wants. The only thing I was thinking of was a spot in the forest that I knew, right near the state game lands. I'd go there the next time I overdosed. No one would be around to stop me. My body would likely lie there for weeks.

"I can't be sure you're telling the truth."

"I bet that undertaker lady called you."

"Let's just say others noticed that you were distraught."

I sniffed at that. Thought again of that nice area in the forest, and how I'd dose so hard that a gallon of Narcan wouldn't be able to wake me.

"I gave you Father Glynn's number before. Do you have it?"

"I've . . . misplaced it."

"Threw it away, huh?"

"More or less."

"That's not a more-or-less kind of question."

He took another card from his wallet. "Here's his number. Again. He's only in town another day, I think, but he can talk to you on the phone. Or he'll be back in two weeks. He splits his duties between churches here and in Lock Haven. You can trust him."

I took the card he offered and nodded along with everything he said. When he asked, "Do I have your word that you won't try anything like this again?" I gave it with no pause. If he was a cop with any kind of sense, he'd know better than to believe me.

"OK, then. I'll send the nurse in. You can go if she says it's OK."

I nodded again, silently hating his guts for keeping me alive.

. . .

The nurse checked some vital signs, then said, "You can leave."

I wasn't going to waste words on her, not after her last show of attitude. I got up and went to the door. Before I could leave she called:

"Hey."

I turned around.

The nurse said, "Chief Kriner told me. About your wife and daughter. I received them, when the ambulance brought them in the other day. I didn't know they were your family."

I nodded, suddenly sad at how they must have appeared to her.

"I'm sorry about what happened to them."

"Thank you, Callie."

"And I'm sorry that you're here. And sorry about what you're doing to yourself. So stop it. Don't be a damn idiot."

"There's the nurse I know and love."

"Go," she said. "Throw away your life, then, if you want to."

"Thank you for your permission," I said.

"Wait. Hey. I . . . You know I don't mean that. Don't do anything to yourself. OK?"

I couldn't lie to her, so I didn't. Instead, I just offered a bit of a smile as a thank-you. She returned the same.

From the bedside table she picked up the card that the cop had given me.

"You forgot something."

"No I didn't," I said.

She examined it. "He wants you to talk to Father Glynn?" She gave a sourpuss expression and we shared a smirk. Then she dropped the card into the trash can.

She wasn't so bad after all.

. . .

I went home and pushed open the front door. The frame was split from where the cop had kicked it in. Someone else—I'd bet anything it was one of the Boyd clan, who lived the next block over and supplemented their welfare checks with friendly neighborhood theft—had come in overnight and stolen the TV set, a cheap watch that I had bought Kate years ago, and probably a few other things that I didn't immediately notice. I might have been bothered if I'd owned anything of real value, or if I was planning to stay on this earth much longer. But I didn't, and I wasn't. I had fucked up my overdose once. That wouldn't happen again.

I got my checkbook, then walked to the other side of town to the State Store. Picked out the cheapest fifth of vodka, Majorska, and a two-liter bottle of ginger ale.

"Before you ring it up, can I pay by check?" I asked the clerk.

"If you've got ID."

"I do. Give me the total."

"Thirteen twenty-two."

That left my bank account with seventy-eight cents more than I needed to cremate the three of us. I should have been a mathematician instead of a junkie.

Behind the building, I spilled out half the ginger ale, where it bubbled and hissed on the asphalt, then poured the entire fifth of vodka into the soda bottle. The first swallow went down tough; I had to force it. The second and third were somewhat smoother. After thirty minutes, the bottle was half gone. Ten minutes beyond that and I burped and saw that it was three-quarters empty. When the bottle slipped from my hand and hit the ground, I didn't bother reaching for it. I was so plastered that I stumbled against the dumpster, then kicked the damn thing. With that, I recognized the anger that alcohol would sometimes bring out in me.

Now I had the drunk courage to go find some money to steal.

I needed a few bags of heroin and some supplies. I had no cash, and even if I had anything at home worth selling that hadn't been stolen by the Boyds, I wouldn't know who to sell it to. Back in Philly I used to scavenge copper pipes and wires from empty buildings to cash in at a scrapyard. Locksburg had plenty of abandoned houses. Maybe I'd give one of those a shot tomorrow, I figured, if I couldn't find any cash tonight. I'd given up thievery when I quit heroin, and I grew to hate myself for the life I'd lived then. If I wanted to be a thief again, I'd have to be wasted, and I sure was.

I staggered a few blocks and became disoriented. After ten or twenty minutes my feet took me down a street that looked like every other one in Locksburg: brick houses with small porches and older cars parked out front.

About a hundred yards away, someone was packing a few bags into a dark sedan. The guy was huge, six feet six or more, which would normally have had me second-guessing stealing from him. But he was fat, one hundred pounds overweight at least, and had either a limp or a waddle. I could outrun him by walking.

The guy closed the trunk with one hand. In the other he held a double-thick briefcase, the kind that locked. And when you locked something, you had something worth locking up. Money, I'd bet, or at least jewelry.

He put the briefcase through the open window and onto the passenger-side front seat. Then the phone rang in the house, surprising him. He hurried inside, giving me an opportunity. I jogged over, reached through the open car window, and took the briefcase.

I scurried away, holding it close to my chest, and quickly turned the corner. I walk-ran another block, my head spinning, then made my way down a one-way street. I may have taken another turn or two. Who knows. I was drunk, I was a thief, I was dizzy, and I also had to piss real bad. The walk sobered me some and made me realize that I shouldn't be hurrying along carrying something that was so clearly not mine. Best to take out anything of value and ditch the briefcase.

Like most streets in Locksburg, there were several abandoned row houses on the block. I went to the nearest and pushed in the front door with little effort. Ducked inside.

Stairs were to be feared in places like this. In Philly, a fellow scavenger fell straight through a set and lay there for half a day with two busted feet, until I wandered in and discovered him by accident. Yet now I wanted to get up high, peer out the top window, and keep watch over the street. I kept close to the sides of the steps and took every second one. They creaked as if they were just a pound of pressure away from splitting. On the second floor, I went into the bedroom overlooking the block. Out there, the car I'd stolen the briefcase from was moving along slowly, surveying the streets. He must really want back what I now had.

Sorry, fuckface.

The car cruised on.

The bedroom was empty except for some fallen plaster on the floor and a rusted bedframe. I unhooked one side of the frame and used the metal bar to pry up the briefcase locks and snap them. Easy enough.

Inside were two photo albums. Underneath them, some kind of cloths or rags. I was drunk and mumbling in anger at not finding any cash.

I opened one of the albums. The dying day provided barely enough light to make out what was in the photos, so I put my face closer.

Then I pulled back fast, more horrified than if a giant spider or a roach had crawled out and jumped onto my cheek.

I convinced myself I hadn't seen what was there, and inspected it again, then flipped through a few more pages. Opened the other album and found the same: dozens of photos of children, naked and in stomach-turning poses, sometimes alone, sometimes with what appeared to be a grown man—his image had been cut out of the pictures, obviously to save him from prosecution should the photos ever be found. But the pieces that were removed suggested a larger adult, no doubt the guy who had put the briefcase in the car.

The children's eyes shook me to my core: the pain and confusion and fear of what was being done to them. I threw both albums across the floor, as if their vileness could rub off or slither onto me. Inside the briefcase, what I'd thought were rags were instead a few pairs of children's underwear, some sick kind of keepsake.

I flung those away too.

I began to get to my feet. Fell on all fours. Then threw up everything I'd drunk an hour earlier, spitting strings of thick puke onto the floor.

And suddenly, terror infected me.

If anyone came here and saw me with those albums, I'd be branded as a child molester and pornographer and arrested. I wanted to get out of the house immediately. That rabid fear, combined with the repulsion and the alcohol, powered a panic that had me leaping up then racing down the creaking steps. I held on to the wall to guide myself, then bolted out onto the sidewalk.

Where the hell was I? No clue. I kept walking, five, six, seven blocks and a few turns until a street seemed familiar, then another, and somehow found my way home. I curled up in bed and cried for all the pain in this world. Not just mine, but also the children's in those pictures. My stomach retched, with nothing left to come up.

What I didn't want to admit to myself was this: one of those pictures was of a kid with Down syndrome. A boy of perhaps fourteen. Maybe he was a friend of Angie's at the day camp she once went to. I cried more. That guy with the pictures had hurt someone like my own child.

The images seared into my mind, and I thought, *Another good reason to be dead. I'll never have to remember or see those photos again.*

But for the first time, my plan felt cowardly to me. Not because it was suicide. I had no problem with that. Rather, to kill myself while a loathsome guy like that lived and kept on damaging children seemed selfish.

And meaningless.

And wrong.

He had hurt so many kids.

He was surely going to harm more of them.

And the ultimate sin in my book, none worse: he had harmed someone like Angie.

That was something I couldn't forgive and couldn't let go.

After I stopped sobbing, I told myself: *Sure, Andy, if you want to kill yourself, go ahead, no fuckin' problem, be my guest. Go straight to hell, if you want.*

But if you're going to hell, you gotta take that guy with you.

NATHAN

"What did you do tonight?"

Paula asked that question every time she came home from an evening shift. But now I parsed her words for tone, for implication, dead sure that she somehow knew about LeeLee. Then I examined the silence that followed. I read into it, doubted myself, worried more.

I had left LeeLee's apartment then hurried back to Maxie's, gotten my car, and returned with enough time to wash up and change clothes in case the smell of LeeLee was sticking to me. Paula walked in fifteen minutes later to find me kicked back on the sofa in a pose I hoped suggested I'd been sitting there for hours.

"Nothing," I said.

She made some sound.

"Oh!" I said, much too loud. "I went to Maxie's for dinner. For a hamburger. After work."

"Good," she said. "And a beer too, I bet."

"Right! Only one." Then I thought, wait, I've covered my bases, in case anyone told her they saw me there. But I had several beers. Best to tell the truth about that.

"Well, maybe two or three."

"OK," she said. Which I overthought again, until I told myself to shut up. My nerves were jumping. Best to sit in silence rather than open my mouth and risk making mistakes.

"I couldn't stop thinking about the money today," Paula said. "There's still a way to make this all better. We could throw the bag in the woods, then make an anonymous call. Or—"

I said, "I'm exhausted. I'm going to bed. I'll sleep in the guest room."

We had five of those, since no other bedroom in the house was occupied except for our own. I went into the first one I passed, then collapsed onto the bed and lay in the dark, eyes wide, listening to Paula go into our bedroom. About twenty minutes later the door opened, and she came in and lay beside me.

"I don't want us to go to bed mad."

"Fine," I said. "Then let's not be mad. Let's just go to sleep."

I heard her prepare to say something, then stop, maybe waiting for me to ask her what it was. I didn't. Instead, I lay there next to my wife, thinking about the other woman I'd been with two hours earlier, a memory that had me feeling equal measures of excitement and shame.

...

At work the next day, my cell phone sounded in my pocket.

Hey, hope you don't mind me texting.

I stood on the shop floor. The phone number was unfamiliar, though I knew who it had to be. I texted back: *Hi.*

Going to be at Maxie's again tonight?

Maybe.

Or you could come right over to my place. It's LeeLee by the way, lol.

The text was like a shot of adrenaline pumped directly into my veins. I hadn't felt a rush like that in so long, which, I guess, showed me how uneventful my life had been. There I was, standing on the shop-room floor like some teenager, smiling at a handful of electronic words from a woman who wanted me. Then my mind flashed to Paula. Sure, I could forgive myself for a one-night stand, brush it off with the easy excuses: I was drunk. She meant nothing. I'll never do it again. But these texts were bringing it into another realm. If this went further, it would be an affair.

I figured it was you. How did you get my number?

I added one of those smiley faces, to make it look flirty instead of sounding accusatory. In truth, I didn't care how she got my number. I only wanted to keep the conversation going.

Uh, I work at City Hall? I can get anything.

Good deal.

So. Five thirty at my place?

Someone across the shop floor said my name. I practically jumped out of my skin. I shoved the phone into my pocket and felt it there, like a ticking bomb that could explode at any moment, as I walked over to discuss some minor problem. When the phone vibrated, I could barely pay attention to what one of the workers was saying.

After a five-minute eternity I went to the bathroom and locked the stall, then took the phone back out. LeeLee had written:

Is that a no? :(

The excitement of the texts was more than the expectation of sleeping with her again. It was that the texts felt forbidden and thrilling, and had me smiling until embarrassment came around to remind me that I was sitting on a toilet, debating whether to cheat on my wife. Again.

I reread the entire text thread twice.

This was the moment, the decision, that I realized could change so much. I should tell LeeLee no, this had all been a mistake.

I fully understood that's what I should do.

Deep down I knew what the right thing was.

...

LeeLee and I lay in bed.

It was light outside, and the curtains were closed, leaving the cheap, paneled room in shadows. Before going up to her apartment I'd scanned the alley like a thief to make sure no one was watching me, and that guiltiness seemed to fuel my desire once I stepped inside. I practically charged at her from the moment the front door clicked shut, and she met me with the same hunger. Afterward we were catching our breath, which was the only sound in the room other than the rattling refrigerator, which seemed about a week away from breaking a belt and going warm.

"You still thinking of moving?" she asked after a few minutes.

"I am." When I didn't say anything more, she reached over and stroked my chest.

"Florida?"

"Yeah. I went to Gossling's today."

Gossling's was what passed for a travel agency in this town. The slapdash storefront served as a combination UPS store, lottery agent, and stationery shop, with old Mrs. Gossling—and we called her old Mrs. Gossling even when I was a boy—sitting behind a computer on which she could sell you a bus ticket or book you a flight reservation. I went in and bought stamps that I didn't need, and with a fake nonchalance picked up some flyers with covers of sunny skies and sandy shores, geared toward the brave few Locksburg residents who wanted to vacation down south. Only difference is, wherever I went, I wasn't coming back.

"You made reservations?" LeeLee asked.

"No. Just picked up some info."

"You're serious about this."

"Guess so."

"You got the money?"

"What money?" I said.

"I mean, money. Enough money. What money do you mean?"

I didn't want to get tangled in the words, so I went slower. "It's cheap down there. I won't need much. That's what I'm trying to say."

"It's not cheap anywhere anymore."

"True enough."

"Can I ask you a question?"

What do you say to that? No? Then the unasked question sits there, like a weight between both people. It's a question that must be answered yes, and one that usually ushers in a still more uncomfortable question.

"G'head."

"Are you and Paula . . . are you going to Florida together?"

I'm not sure how long I lay there, thinking over the answer. Two minutes, maybe? Which can be a near eternity between a couple of people in a quiet room. After all the options clogged my head, I started to think that maybe an honest answer wasn't possible at that moment. There was too much to consider, not the least of which was the bag stuffed with cash in my attic.

"That remains to be seen" is what I finally said.

LeeLee leaned over and flicked her tongue out, licking my neck. She purred, then slid on top of me, rubbing herself against my leg and letting out moans that made me feel like some kind of powerful animal. I put my hands back on her naked ass and pulled her toward me. By the time we finished again, it was fully dark in the room.

LeeLee lay beside me. Her breathing changed, and I could tell she was about to speak.

"Nate?"

"Hmmm."

"I'll only say this now, one time. OK?"

"'K."

She put her face close to my neck and kissed again. She then pulled back and whispered very quietly:

"I imagined you today, on that beach in Florida, fishing."

"Mmm-hmm."

"I didn't imagine only you there, though."

I knew what she would say next. Or at least I thought I did.

"I imagined you were on the beach, fishing, with someone else."

"Who's that?"

"Your kid," she said. "Let's get out of Locksburg. Take me to Florida with you. When we get there . . . I just turned thirty-nine . . . We could start our lives over. We could have a baby."

She propped her head up on her bent arm and kissed my lips this time.

Then LeeLee whispered: "I could give you a son."

CALLIE

Because of two square inches, I practically bankrupted my family. Because of my scar, I had few close friends, never went to my prom, cried gallons of tears over years of nights. I had once imagined that college would be my salvation; I'd read that the attitude there was accepting. After the second or third house party where frat boys snickered behind my back and a few treacly sorority do-gooders came up to me, unbidden, to attempt a look-how-brave-I-am conversation, I stuck my head in my books and got out of Mansfield State University a year early with my degree. It's fascinating, in a morbid kind of way, how something as small as a scar can radically change the entire course of one's life.

But if I'm honest, I'm to blame, too, for at least some of the fear I've felt and the cynicism I've cultivated. And it seems to be getting worse. I'm worried that I'm growing more scared of life, rather than learning to be fearless and surging ahead. I shy away from conflict, then curse others inside my head and pretend that that's a kind of personal victory.

After I told Gabriella that I'd take her to the ocean, I went home and second-guessed my decision. What I initially thought to be a *fuck you* moment to the world morphed into a mess of second guesses: *Do you want to lose your nursing license? You could get arrested too. What will you do if that happens? Who will bail you out?*

Then I wondered if this was about the girl at all. Or was it about me and the overwhelming sadness I'd been feeling, and the growing realization that if I kept going on as I'd been going on, I was destined to grow old alone in this town, and at the end of my life have an obituary printed in *The Locksburg Leader* with a last line that read: *Never married, no survivors.* Far worse than that, I'd have to look back and know that I'd taken no risks, and that my own fear had beaten me down. I'd have to admit that those people who had looked at me with pity my whole life were right when they thought: *That poor Callie, she'll never do anything, not with a face like that.*

So yeah, maybe this was as much about me as it was about Gabriella.

Maybe more.

. . .

I spent most of my shift the next day sitting with Gabriella.

"Please tell me you haven't changed your mind" was the first thing she said when I came into her room.

"No. But you need to rest and stay strong, so we don't have any problems on the ride."

"I will! I will!" she said, anything but relaxed. We both couldn't help smiling at the craziness of the plan.

"Here's the thing. Your parents. I never want you to lie to them. I mean that."

"I don't have to! I know how to talk around everything! It's like an art form! They'll never find out, I promise."

"I'm going to ask them again, though. Maybe they'll change their minds."

Gabriella snorted at that.

A white passenger van pulled up a few minutes after noon, with the words *Shepard's Staff Tabernacle* painted onto the side and bookended by crucifixes. Gabriella's mother and father filed out with Gabriella's siblings. Inside, they formed a semicircle around Gabriella's bed and held hands as the father led a prayer to which the rest of them murmured pious responses.

After an hour, they readied to leave, without asking to see the doctor. The kids walked outside to the van while Gabriella's father went to the restroom. I said to her mother: "Hi. Do you have a moment?"

Her hair was pulled into a thick braid that went halfway down her back, and she wore a plain, light yellow dress that looked as if it had been washed so often it might fall apart if someone touched it or its wearer.

"Of course," she said. "Just wait for my husband."

"Gabriella and I have talked a lot," I said as if I hadn't heard her. "She'd really like to see the ocean. I think that would make her feel better. Happier."

It was a simple word chosen for maximum effect. Who wouldn't want their child to be happier?

"Thank you," she said, though I didn't know what she was thanking me for. "My husband will only be a minute."

"What do you think?" I asked. I held her to the question, even stepped forward a little as if requesting an answer. I expected—and wanted—a kind of meek agreement. Instead, she sneered, as if trapped.

"I said, we'll wait for my husband. Nurse."

"Gabriella's mentioned the beach before," the father said. He'd appeared from behind me. I tried not to show my surprise.

"Oh, you're taking her?"

"Maybe someday," he said. "After all this is over."

"Good, good. But . . . she was thinking, maybe she'd go now. To give her some comfort. As she battles this."

"She has all the comfort she needs. In her family, and in God."

I looked to the mother, whose self-righteous grin made her the very definition of a German word that my father was fond of: *Backpfeifengesicht*. A face that could use a smack.

As for her husband, it would have been better for me if he was a Snidely Whiplash kind of guy, someone so despicable or argumentative that he was a formidable and angry opponent. Instead, he was bland to the point of dismissive, always ready to abandon the conversation, as he was now. It was like playing a game of catch with someone who never went for the ball, or tug-of-war with someone who let go of the rope.

"Is there any way you can take her soon?" When no one replied, I said, "Or maybe someone else can drive her there? I'm sure someone would . . ."

"Listen, please," he said, as if dropping any pretense. "We think we know best how to take care of our child. You can make decisions for your own children." His eyes flicked to my face and the scar there. Then he added: "If you have any."

. . .

At the end of my shift I led Paula and Dr. Willis into an empty room and directed them to two chairs. I shut the door behind us and sat on the bed. Earlier I'd practiced a speech. It fell apart immediately. I ummed a few times, OKed at least thrice, then decided to go for it off the cuff.

"I need to talk to you two about something, and I need to know it's just between us. Whatever I say can't leave this room. Are you both OK with that?"

They nodded. So did I for some reason.

"It's about Gabriella. See . . . I know you shouldn't get too close to a patient . . . and I haven't! I swear! This isn't some weird . . . well, it may sound weird. Jeez, I need to stay on the topic . . ."

"Please do," Dr. Willis said, and gave me a grin to let me know that all was well. He reached and turned his hearing aid higher. Apparently I was mumbling as well as babbling.

I said, "This girl . . . we know her prognosis. She knows it too. And she wants only one thing out of life: she wants to see the ocean. I'm going to take her there."

"That's really nice of you," Paula said. "Are her parents coming too? If so, that's going to be one long, boring drive."

"Her parents don't know about this. No one knows about this. Except Gabriella and me. And now you."

"Did you ask her father to take her?" Paula said.

"Yes."

"What did he say?"

"You want the short version or the long?"

"Make it short."

"He said no."

"What's the long version?"

"He said no way."

"See, that's a problem," Paula said, as close to sarcastic as she got these days. She'd been quiet lately, and that worried me a little. Last year, she confided that after she gave up trying to have a child, her doctor said she had signs of depression—not a rare happening for those grappling with IVF failure and with the feeling that they've let down their spouse. Paula had been seeing a psychologist in Harrisburg since, and I covered her shifts for a few hours when she went. She kept it all a secret. I tried to convince her to at least tell her husband, Nathan, but she'd say she didn't want to worry him or remind him of their disappointments. Then she'd smile and tell me that everything would be fine. I hoped she was right. I hoped she was not hiding too much sadness behind that smile.

I said, "Tomorrow afternoon I am going to drive Gabriella to the beach, see it, then come back, and no one will be the wiser. I need to tell you two because you're on shift, so, of course, you'll notice she's not here."

"And if she has visitors?" Paula asked.

"Her family came this afternoon and left by one. If they do the same tomorrow, we'll leave at one thirty, get to the beach by six, then head back and be here before midnight. Gabriella told me the parents will be holding some long monthly prayer event tomorrow night, so it should be fine."

"You think it's going to be that easy?"

"It's a drive to the beach. My car is in good shape. It should be simple."

"And if her parents call or stop by?"

"I don't know—you could say she needed some late tests in Harrisburg? Or that . . . I dunno. I was hoping maybe you could help me with that."

Dr. Willis, who had sat in silence so long that I had to keep glancing over to check that he wasn't taking one of his unscheduled naps, was in fact paying great attention. He leaned forward, fingertips together, head cocked slightly to hear everything. When he considered me and saw that I'd run out of words, he turned to Paula, who shrugged. Then he began.

"So you want to kidnap a child—"

"I'm not kidnapping—"

"Yes. That's what this is. Even if she wants to go where you're taking her—if you remove her from this hospital, against the wishes of her legal guardians—"

"Listen—"

He held up a finger, which stopped me. He continued.

"If you do that, you'll be kidnapping the girl. You, who have known her for, what? A few days? You think you can make these decisions better than her parents. This minor, who has terminal cancer, who herself may not be thinking clearly."

"She's thinking fine."

"Imagine how this will sound to the jury who will be hearing your case. Because if something were to go wrong—"

"Nothing will! It's just a quick drive to the beach and back! People do it every day! What could go wrong?"

"May I continue, please? Thank you. If something were to go wrong, this girl could be in terrible pain. As for you—pish!— you would lose your nursing license so fast your head would spin off your neck. Do you want to take that chance? Think very, very carefully before you answer."

I already had. But I thought it through again, as he instructed.

I said, "This girl has been fucked over her whole life. Now she's going to die. And no one is going to remember her. The next day, after she's gone, it's going to be as if she never existed. All she wants is one thing. One easy, simple little thing. And I'm going to give it to her. I'd take that chance. Yes. I know it sounds insane. But it means everything to her. And now it means everything to me."

Somewhere around that point I could feel my tears threatening to flow. I slammed them back with the fury that I felt over Gabriella's condition. Though maybe I was also using my own anger at my life.

I said, "I could lose a lot. But if I don't do this, I'll never forgive myself."

"So this is for you, and not entirely for her."

"It doesn't matter who it's for. It needs to be done."

Dr. Willis checked his watch. "I've got to go. I've got a conference call on the new MRI room down the hall."

I couldn't do this without him, and as I saw my plan crumble, I became incensed.

"Paula?" I asked. "Are you with me on this?"

"I . . ." She looked to each of us, back and forth.

I said, "You'd have no risk. I'd lie to you, say that Dr. Willis told me to take her to Harrisburg. So that way, if someone were to find out, you both could say that I misled you. You'd have plausible deniability. You wouldn't get in trouble if the shit hit the fan."

"If you put it like that, yes. I'd do it. To help the girl."

"Ladies, I have my MRI meeting."

"How can you talk about an MRI meeting when this girl—"

"Nurse Hoffmann!" he barked, shutting me down immediately and silencing me with the use of my last name, which he never employed. "You asked me to listen to you in confidence, and I've listened to you in confidence. Yes?"

"Yes."

"Now. If there's nothing else, I have to go discuss the new MRI room. You know it's still under construction down the hall, yes?"

I didn't answer.

"You know it's still under construction down the hall, yes?" he asked again. This was becoming bizarre.

"Of course I know that."

"Of course you know that," he practically mocked. "The room is nearly complete. But as usual around this hospital, and in this town, they've left a lot unfinished. They haven't gotten around to installing the security cameras yet. Did you know that, Nurse Hoffmann?"

I stared at him, perplexed, and shook my head.

"So it's the only room in this place," he said, "where you could enter or exit without being videotaped."

"Oh."

"They're putting in the cameras next week. So if one were to use that back door, say, tomorrow afternoon, one could do so without detection."

"Yeah, one could," I said. A grin grew on my face.

Dr. Willis had his hand on the doorknob. He turned around to look at me. "Tomorrow I'll be attending to private patients, then going home to sleep, as I am on call for this hospital. So I'm afraid I won't be aware of what happens around here."

"Everything is going to work out. I swear . . ."

He dropped all pretense. "Don't swear. Just show the girl the beach, turn around, and get back here as soon as possible." Then to Paula and to me he said: "We were never in this room together. And if something goes wrong, Callie, we can't be with you on this."

ANDY

I woke hungover and before long started cursing myself for what I'd done. Or more accurately, what I'd failed to do. By botching my suicide plan, I'd gone on to leave the hospital and steal two vile photo albums whose images turned my stomach and had me sobbing half the night. When I did sleep, it barely counted. I tossed and was mired in dark dreams.

After a shower and some watery instant coffee, I decided my first step would be to locate the guy who owned the briefcase. I had a good recollection of his appearance, but no real idea of where his house had been.

Fuck it, the best way to find his place was to go search for it.

I stepped outside my own house, shock-squinted at the bright sun, and slunk back inside to vomit the morning coffee and a heel of stale toast into the kitchen sink. Then I returned to the streets, attempting to retrace my steps from the day before. Within five minutes, it was clear the effort was futile. I'd been blind drunk the previous day, and now I had no clue of which streets I'd taken.

Locksburg has two main drags, both equally functional and each perfectly bland. Archer Ave. runs north-south and is cut in half by Queen Street, which travels east-west. There are about ten bars and restaurants currently operating in Locksburg, and most can be found around that intersection, along with the usual businesses that keep a small town running: a laundromat, two banks, an Elks Lodge, a consignment shop, a VFW Post, and the like. It's the kind of place that generous people would call quaint, dismissive ones would call the boondocks, and smart-ass ones would call Pennsyltucky.

It's also a town defined by what it doesn't have, as much as what it does: no movie theater, no nightclubs, and no museums, art or otherwise. There has been frenzied speculation that a Starbucks will open in one of the empty storefronts. Until that thrilling day arrives, Creamy Bros. Ice Cream and Coffee, with its handprinted sign announcing FREE "WI-FI" FOR PAYING CUSTOMERS, will have to do. Those unnecessary quotation marks grate my eyes the same way fingernails on a chalkboard do my ears, and I'm a high school dropout who, even when he found his way into a classroom, failed English.

A few dozen streets branch off each side of Archer and Queen, and run for six or seven blocks. Those are lined mostly with mind-numbingly identical three-bedroom brick row houses, hastily built in the 1930s for the coal miners and steelworkers who flocked here, ready to work, and turned Locksburg into a relatively bustling town of twenty thousand, spread across a space some two miles wide and three miles long.

The coal mines in the hills that surround the town have been closed since the early seventies, and the smelting plant folded around the same time. Within a decade, three quarters of the population had packed up and hightailed it out of Locksburg. They left behind the houses, of course, and hundreds of them now stand empty, a blight that the remaining five thousand residents are happy to bitch about whenever they're given the chance.

It took me half an hour to cross Locksburg to begin again at the State Store, where I'd gotten drunk. Along the way I talked to Kate and Angie inside my head, recalling our lives together, reminding them and me of all those good times the three of us had. At the store I scanned the street to try to remember which way I'd gone. When I couldn't recall, I walked up Verrick then down the other side to see it from another angle, then turned left and walked up and down Keefer, trying to scrape together a memory of the night before. Nothing seemed familiar. Or rather, everything did. I'd been on most every street in town at one time or another over the past few years. I just didn't know where I'd been last night.

At the corner I turned again and decided that random searching wasn't getting me anywhere. I'd have to walk the entire town, examine every house.

That realization pissed me off.

But these days, what else did I have to do?

· · ·

The June sun had me sweating through my T-shirt as I cursed myself for wearing a black one on a hot day. Twice, I'd stopped at hose spigots, opened them with squeaky turns, then cupped my hands to drink. Once, I ducked into an alleyway to piss.

Yet the walk sobered me and had me sweating out any heroin and vodka that may have been lingering in my system. I examined everyone who passed. Several people tried to smile, then looked away, probably because of my appearance: that of a guy who had overdosed some forty-eight hours earlier, then twelve hours ago guzzled nearly an entire fifth of vodka. My red eyes felt as if someone had scrubbed a pound of dry sand into each.

I walked by the Locksburg public library and decided, three birds, one stone: I'd go in to use the bathroom, cool down in the air-conditioning, and check out the town map that hung on the inside wall to better guide my search.

The library is housed on the first floor of a long-closed department store that sat empty for decades before being converted. The large windows let in plenty of light for the ten or so people, usually retirees, who haunt the place during the days. Kate, Angie, and I were regulars there. Several times each week we'd set out on a walk then stop in for a reading break. When we'd enter, you could feel the average patron age freefall. The very first time we were there, the librarian, Jane Kimmel—her name helpfully supplied by an etched nameplate on the front desk—came over and coughed twice, *eh-em*, to alert Kate that she had become too loud and animated when reading a book to Angie.

As a rule, we took shit from no one, and Jane Kimmel was the exception that proved it: seeing her walk our way gave Kate and me a bit of a comic fright. When she passed us, we would look at each other, lips squeezed shut and eyebrows raised high.

The librarian was rail-thin and pale, with sharp features and white-gray hair that waved down to her shoulders like she was some aging and disenchanted starlet. Yet her tone conveyed an unwavering authority. In Jane Kimmel, Kate and I met our match in attitude, and at home we joked about her often. Once, as Kate, Angie, and I were watching *The Wizard of Oz*, Kate whispered to me, "Jane Kimmel!" when the green-faced Wicked Witch of the West flew on-screen. Her name became our synonym for the *motherfucker*s and *son of a bitch*es that we didn't want to say aloud around Angie. If I cut a finger while cooking, I would bark: "Jane Kimmel!" When, a couple months back, our seventeen-year-old clunker finally stopped running for good, the first thing Kate said was "Frickin' Jane Kimmel!" after turning the ignition key and hearing nothing from the engine. Still, we kept such jokes at home and stayed mouse-quiet in the library.

I entered the place. Jane Kimmel was over in Adult Nonfiction, frowning at a patron who was shelving a book. She watched the guy finish, then pulled the book off the shelf where he had just slid it in and carried it over to a cart clearly marked BOOKS TO RESHELVE. She placed the book there and looked back at that patron with an expression that said, *See? That is how we do things here.* The grown man stared at the floor in embarrassment. His shoulders slumped.

Jane Kimmel glanced over to see who had come in the front door. She couldn't make out who I was, however—the sunlight coming through the front windows was too strong. I went to the bathroom, then came out to check the town map on the wall. Locksburg's streets were in a grid, and I could split the town into quadrants to search. After five minutes at the map the most efficient paths to take became clear, and that would save me effort. When I was done I moved past the Children's Books section as fast as possible to avoid triggering any memories and had a hand on the door when Jane Kimmel said, "Excuse me."

She was sitting high on her chair at the front desk, surveying the place like a pissed-off hawk on its perch. And for the first time since coming to this library years ago, I saw a change in her expression. Her mouth parted slightly when she looked at me. That was it. But that was all I needed, to know that she had heard about Angie and Kate.

"Mr. Devon," Jane Kimmel said.

I turned and nodded, and hoped that was all she'd say and that I could go, feeling like some schoolboy overeager to escape a classroom and the clutches of his stern teacher.

"May I speak with you outside?" she said. I nodded again and went through the door onto the sidewalk.

I thought maybe she'd stand to my right, but when she came out she positioned herself in front of me, as if I were about to be disciplined. I looked around a little before saying, "Yeah? What's up?"

"I heard about your family."

I stared into the street. Not a single car drove by. I had nothing to reply.

"I've been thinking of them all morning," the librarian said.

That surprised me. She was a woman with a complete lack of

bullshit—I could tell that she really had been thinking of them, and that had me wondering why.

She said, "Your daughter. Angela . . ."

"We called her Angie."

"Yes. Angie. You'd come in two or three times a week and . . . in retrospect . . . I realize now that I should have been . . . less strict. More . . . indulgent. This pains me, to think that now. But my pain means nothing in this case. I want to apologize to you, if I was sometimes gruff with her. And also if I was that way with you and your wife. I offer my condolences. And my apology. I hope you can accept them. If not, I completely understand. Perhaps I wouldn't either."

It was the most sustained stream of words that I'd ever heard leave her mouth, this woman who needed only a "Quiet, please" to shush a rowdy pack of high-school boys or "This material is overdue" to convince you to never return a book late again.

I said to her, "When we'd leave the house to go on our walks, Angie would say, 'Can we go see Miss Kimmel today?' And when Kate would tuck Angie into bed, she'd ask her, 'What was the best part of your day today?' Angie would sometimes say, 'Seeing Miss Kimmel at the library!' And I gotta tell you, for years Kate and I would wonder why. Like, why was Angie so happy to see you, more than anyone? And you know what I finally figured out? I think she liked you so much because . . . because you didn't treat her any different than anyone else. You treated her like a person. No more. No less. And even this little kid with Down syndrome, she could sense that."

Jane Kimmel said, "I . . . perhaps I could have been . . ."

"You are who you are, Jane Kimmel. That's who you should be. Don't let anyone give you shit for that."

"I won't," she said.

"Oh, I know you won't."

"I hope you do the same, Mr. Devon. And I hope you keep coming to the library."

"Thanks again. Thanks for being you with Angie."

We both smiled a little. I was tempted, just for the hell of it, to give her a hug and see how she reacted. But I wasn't a hugger, and she sure didn't seem like one either, so we only nodded a few times.

Then Jane Kimmel went back inside her library.

And I set out again on my search.

...

A welcome breeze came off the hills at about three o'clock, and by four I'd walked both sides of every street west of Queen. It had taken hours. I'd found nothing, and uncovered no clues as to where I had been the day before.

At around five I was famished and walked the forty-five minutes home. There I found some canned goods pushed back in a cupboard. With a moist *thwick* the contents plopped into the pot: some kind of spaghetti and two vegetables whose labels had fallen off, though they appeared to be green beans and yams. I mixed all three together and after five minutes of high heat, began chowing down with a plastic fork, eating straight from the pot.

I smelled myself and almost gagged, and I didn't need a reflection to know that my hair was sweaty and my skin sunburned. I kicked off my shoes and felt a pinching kind of pain: my feet were blistered and bloody from hours of walking, in which I tried to solve something that I had so totally fucked up.

A voice said: *You're feeling like shit. You're eating slop. You've lost everything you've loved. Maybe you should turn on the oven, let the gas fill the room, and this time get it done for good. You could sleep. You could forget.*

But though I held no belief in an afterlife, what about Kate and Angie? If by chance I were to see them again, how would I face them, knowing I let this pervert live to torment children?

I rushed over to the sink and hurled everything I'd eaten. It tasted about as good coming up as it did going down.

I laughed a little at that.

Because I was so witty.

What I wanted more than anything was another hit of heroin. A taste would be heavenly. But what held that craving at bay, at least for a short while, was a thought of the guy who owned the briefcase. The guy who was surely wishing that someone had thrown away his photos, or who was holding out hope that the albums would turn up, or who was convinced that no one would know that they were his.

I spit out a string of whatever was left in my mouth when I imagined that guy.

Then I cackled at him.

If he was hoping that no one was searching for him, he was worse than wrong: he was fucking doomed.

This one is for my daughter, and for others like her.

I will not give up.

I.

Get.

Shit.

Done.

NATHAN

There was a time when I thought I was going to own the company I work for. Sure, it's only a metal fabrication and assembly outfit, but I figured if I worked hard and was duly promoted, I could take the place over, or even start my own plant. Maybe use it to get me out of Locksburg, since my earlier escape plans had never materialized.

How dumb we are when we're young.

The first time I came up with an idea to cut costs, the manager said, "Yeah, that sounds great." I mentioned the idea again, months later, when it hadn't been implemented. "You said that before," the manager muttered, and told me to get back to work, we were behind schedule. Soon after, the place went through a series of owners, and the resulting job cuts shrunk us from one hundred and fifty to ninety workers. From then on I kept my head down and my mouth closed, in case they were searching for an excuse to fire someone else.

I was working in my usual self-imposed silence this morning when the floor supervisor called, "Hey, Nathan," and waved me over. He pointed to the private room.

"Someone's in there, wants to see you."

"Who?"

"A cop."

The bottom of my stomach froze.

It was a windowless conference room, though no conferences were held there, and it was too small to seat everyone for lunch. So we called it the private room, the place you'd make a call if you needed to talk to your doctor, or if your wife was screaming her head off and you didn't want anyone else to hear. When I stepped inside, a guy rose to his feet and thrust out a hand.

"There's the town hero," he said with a smile full of big teeth. After an extra-firm double-pump he let go of my hand and motioned to a chair across the table from him.

"So do you feel any different?" he asked. We both hadn't taken a seat.

I must have appeared confused.

"For saving a man's life!" the guy said. "You're Nathan Stultz, right? The volunteer fireman?"

"Yeah."

"So you saved that guy's life."

"I just, you know, helped him out of the place."

"That's not what I heard! I heard he would have burned to death."

"Where'd you hear that?"

"I was talking to Jack Naugle, the fire chief."

"And you are?"

"Excuse me?"

"I don't know who you are."

"Oh! Jeez! Henry Janson. Pennsylvania State Police. Investigations."

The only troopers I'd had contact with were outfitted in pressed and belted uniforms, with hats with tight chin straps perched atop crew-cut heads that looked down at you as they handed over a speeding ticket. He wore none of that, but he came equipped with the hard-ass appearance: the high-and-tight haircut, the sharp shave. Straining against his suit jacket was a chest that could pass for a piece of granite.

"Have a seat."

"I've got to get back to work. We have a project due . . ."

"I talked to them about that. It's cool. I told them it's about the fire. I'm tying up loose ends. Everything is . . . What do they say? Hunky-dorky? Isn't that what the kids say? My daughter says it all the time. You got any kids?"

"No."

"Ah. OK. So you were first on the scene, right? At the fire?"

"Right. What's this about? Is the guy . . . is he OK?"

"We hope he's getting better."

"I hope so too."

"'Course you do."

"I've fought a few fires before. I never had someone, you know, interested."

"I'll be your first, then."

I couldn't get a bead on what he was saying. The words themselves were easy enough. Yet the manner walked a tightrope between serious and sarcastic. It was hard to figure out how he wanted to be heard.

"So tell me what happened."

"I went fishing up at Laurel Lake. Got the call on the way back. Saw that the place was in flames. Ran in, started screaming. The guy came running at me, on fire. I extinguished the flames, then carried him to the front lawn."

"Mmm-hmm."

"That's it."

"Did you see anyone else inside?"

"No."

"Or outside?"

"No."

"Did you see anything else?"

"Like what?"

"Like anything else. Let me rephrase. Did you see anything out of the ordinary?"

"Smoke."

"Ha-ha! There you got me, bro. That sure is out of the ordinary. But besides that."

"No."

"Think. Take your time."

"I didn't see anything."

"So you say. But sometimes people remember things, if they give it a few minutes. No need to be in a hurry, Nathan. Do you go by Nate?"

"No."

"Got it. So go ahead, Nathan, take a minute. Think about if you saw anything out of the ordinary. Imagine yourself there in the house."

I stared at the ceiling, counted to five. Then I decided that wouldn't be long enough, so I counted five more before saying no in a way that I hoped sounded bewildered.

"So you had your car there, right?"

"My truck. Yes."

"What kind of truck?"

"F-150. Pickup."

"Same as everyone around here, huh?"

"Guess so."

He let a long silence languish, one I wasn't about to fill.

"Then what?"

"What?"

"What did you do?"

"I went home."

"Why not to the hospital?"

"I felt fine. I wasn't hurt."

"Oh? I was talking to Chief Naugle. He said that's where you were going afterward. Your hands were singed. But you didn't go?"

"I didn't feel the need."

The detective sat with hands folded. Nodding. I thought it a good thing that he wasn't taking notes. Or maybe that was bad. Maybe he'd already made up his mind.

"So why did you tell him you were going to the hospital?"

"I was thinking of going. Then changed my mind."

"But he ordered you to?"

"I didn't feel the need."

Another round of silence.

"So where'd you go?"

"Home."

"Where do you live?"

I gave him the address, which he didn't write down. He probably had it already. Then why was he asking? To hear me talk, apparently.

He continued: "And you didn't see anything else inside the house. Besides smoke and the man."

"No. Why, were there drugs in there or something?"

"Drugs?"

"Yeah."

"What kind?"

"That's your job."

"What kind would you think?"

"Meth, I guess."

"Why would you guess that?"

"Because that's what some guys do around here."

"Do you know any guys like that around here?"

"No."

"Did you see any drugs inside?"

"No. I mean, I wouldn't . . . I never even smoked pot. So I wouldn't know what to look for."

"And you didn't see anything else in there? Any equipment, or anything like that?"

"I didn't. I was taking care of the guy, you know?"

"Right. Did you put anything in your truck?"

"No. Like what?"

"I don't know. You tell me."

"Like drugs?"

"Like anything."

I caught myself a split second before going on the defensive. I was thinking of announcing something like: "I was risking my life in that building, what are you trying to say?" But instead, I did what I do well. I kept quiet, except for a single no. Then shook my head. Added a shrug for good measure.

The silence that followed clocked in a whole revolution of the second hand on the wall clock. Then he said:

"OK."

"Can I go?"

"Yeah."

I stood and wasn't surprised when, as my hand grasped the door handle, he spoke again.

"Did you catch anything?"

"Huh?"

"Fishing. At Laurel Lake."

"No. Struck out."

"Sorry to hear," he said.

Again, I couldn't tell how to take it.

• • •

I watched the conference room door out of the corner of my eye. A long ten minutes later the trooper left.

For hours afterward I was struggling not to get sucked into a panic. I wondered what the cop wanted. Wondered if he could get a warrant to search my house. Wondered what would happen if I tried to take the money elsewhere. Maybe he was watching me. My house sat far apart from any other; we had a few acres. It would be easy to spy on my house from a distance and not be seen.

But isn't it irrational to suspect that you're being watched? That had me worrying about me, on top of my worries about him.

That afternoon I chewed through two packs of gum and bummed a cigarette so I could take a break and smoke it and hopefully calm myself some. When I knew that Paula's shift had started, I called her at the hospital.

"Hey."

"Hey. I can't remember the last time you called me at work. Everything all right?"

"Yeah. Just . . . saying hi."

"You sound . . . different."

"How?"

"Shaky or something. Everything OK at work?"

"Fine."

"You sure?"

"I just said it was fine, Paula."

"All right."

"So how's that guy been. The burn victim?"

"They're thinking of transferring him. They say he's going to make it."

I had to take a long moment, grit my teeth so I wouldn't yell at her. Tried for three deep breaths but only got two in and out before saying: "When were you going to tell me this?"

"I heard it a half hour ago."

"So what else?"

"They didn't say much more."

"Who's 'they'?"

"Doctor Lennard. And these two other men who came in to see the patient."

"Cops?"

"One was a state trooper. The other was, I think he said, Secret Service or FBI or something."

"What the fuck, Paula. He can't be Secret Service. They—"

"I thought that was what he said. Please don't curse at me."

"You're nervous. You're not hearing right."

All at once I wondered: *Should I be talking like this? Can they tap your phone? Wait, isn't that crazy to think that? Unless they are . . .*

"Of course I'm nervous," Paula said, getting me out of my head. "Aren't you?"

"No. I'm not nervous. Not at all."

I wasn't in the mood for anything funny. Yet I smirked at how blatant that lie was.

I was on the verge of panic, and was as scared as I'd ever been. Or at least as scared as I'd been since I was seventeen.

CALLIE

The cat circled my legs, pining for a petting that I was too busy to give. Instead, I sat at the kitchen table, using one hand to drink from a coffee cup and the other to scribble notes to ensure that nothing would be overlooked: park my car around the side of the hospital, get Gabriella out of there at about one thirty in the afternoon, remember to bring along her painkillers and prescriptions, make it to the beach at about six, watch the ocean for an hour, then hightail it back home and get her in bed before midnight.

Easy as pie.

Then I got into the hospital and the best-laid plans were shot to shit.

At about ten that morning, Doctor Yellen from Pine Hill stopped in to visit Gabriella. She stayed for over an hour, and when she left Gabriella's room, she beelined to the lavatory. From inside I heard a sudden and deep sob, that of a woman who had bottled up her emotions and now let the cap pop off in private. Her eyes were wet when she came out ten minutes later. She didn't try to hide them as she walked over to me.

"Send her home to her parents," the doctor said. "I don't like them. But at this point it doesn't matter. It should happen at home instead of here."

"Is there anything left to try?"

"It's too late. The cancer's spread all over. I explained it to her. She understands. Discharge her."

"When her parents come today, I'll tell them she can leave tomorrow."

"They can take her now."

"Gabriella wants to stay another night. We've got . . . something special planned."

The doctor only raised an eyebrow over a watery eye.

"OK, I'll call her father and tell him to take her home tomorrow."

I patted her shoulder. She mumbled a thank-you then wandered around the lobby for a few minutes—checking her phone, staring out the window—as if she could somehow figure out a way to save the girl if only she thought about it long enough. After a while, though, she found only the strength to leave.

Gabriella's family showed up at one o'clock for their prayers, an hour later than the day before. I saw that a few of the older kids were affected by how weak Gabriella had gotten over the course of only one day. Her father, though, didn't appear to have noticed. He continued in the same droning voice that I'd loathed from his first "Let us pray."

At two thirty I started to drum my fingers on the nurses' station, then exhaled hard in impatience, willing the family to leave. At three fifteen I entered her room with some made-up excuse about checking Gabriella's blood pressure. The prayer session was still going strong.

I hung around after my shift ended, periodically calculating how much time we'd have at the beach, then recalculating the longer the family remained. Long before five, when they prepared to leave, I'd resigned myself to the fact that Gabriella and I wouldn't be seeing the ocean that day. I started to think of other ways to get her there—I could have someone call the family and say she'd won a trip, or I could sneak her out of their house or something.

Then I remembered who I was and where I lived. This was Central Pennsylvania. We don't mire ourselves in complex plans here. Around here we farm and manufacture and work, then drink and sleep and wake up like we did the previous day and month and year, then start all over again. We like things straightforward. We don't have time for convolution.

There was only one way left to take Gabriella to see the ocean, and that was by taking Gabriella to see the ocean.

. . .

"Mr. Stanhope," I said when he stepped out of Gabriella's room.

"You can call me Pastor," he said.

"I can also call you asshole," I didn't say.

Instead, I said, "Doctor Yellen was here today. She said—"

"Yes. She left a message for me. I haven't called her back."

"A real concerned dickhead you are" was another thing that didn't leave my mouth.

I said, "Gabriella can go home tomorrow."

"Fine."

"She'll be ready at one. We're going to give her something to sleep and—"

"We'll be here then."

I had so much I felt like saying to him, but nothing worth jeopardizing my plan for. Before I could turn away he said, "I know you don't believe it, but we do. God will cure her."

"And if he doesn't?"

"Then it's his will."

"Heads he wins, tails you lose?"

"Haven't you ever believed in anything?"

"Not blindly."

"Then I feel sorry for you," he said, and I could see that he really did.

. . .

I went to Gabriella's room.

"I tried to get them to leave!" she said, breathless. "We—"

"Shhhh. Don't worry about it."

"We can go now."

"We'll never make it."

"What do you mean? It'll still be there!"

"But . . . if you want to see the ocean, you have to see it in the light."

"Says who?"

"Says me."

"Can we go tomorrow?"

"Your parents are picking you up at one."

"What can we do?"

"The only way is if we leave late tonight. Get down there at first light, then come back. I figure if we leave the beach at eight in the morning, we can get back here by noon."

"Oh yes. Please. We have to."

"Only if you sleep. I'll go home and come back later tonight. You need to rest, though, OK?"

"I will," she said, though it was obvious she wouldn't.

Neither would I.

. . .

I returned to the hospital at about ten o'clock that night. I hadn't rested. Only wandered around my house, picking up books to read that were put down five minutes later and staring at the television but watching nothing.

When I got to Locksburg General I parked my car at the back, near the MRI room, then went around and entered through the front door. There I nodded to Paula, who sat at the receptionist's desk, preoccupied.

"Good luck, Callie," she said.

"You OK?"

She gave me a look that could have meant anything. Maybe she was concerned for me.

I figured I'd say the lie out loud, for the sake of formality: "I'm taking Gabriella to Harrisburg. Doctor Willis told me to."

She nodded. I'd have to talk with her when this was over, maybe take her out for a drink if we could work it into our schedules. I'd owe it to her for this.

I entered Gabriella's room. She was sitting in a chair, wearing the summer sundress that she'd arrived at the hospital in. Her hair was pulled back and her shoes were on.

"Let's go!" she said.

"Did you sleep?"

"Yes."

"Are you lying?"

"Yes."

"Well, at least you're honest. Listen. We're too early. If we leave now it'll be dark when we get there."

"Then we can watch the sun rise! Please?"

I'd considered that already and figured it wouldn't hurt. Nancy, a temp nurse from Shamokin who was working the overnight, would fill in for me until I got back. I told her Gabriella was staying a night in Harrisburg, and Nancy barely seemed to listen: she was more interested in picking up extra pay and hopefully sleeping through her shift. I'd be back to take over from her long before Gabriella's parents arrived.

"OK. We'll take our time. You can sleep in the car," I told Gabriella.

I got her a wheelchair, and when I came back to her room she was standing. "Nope. Get in this."

"I don't need it!"

"Get in. My car, my rules."

"I hope you have a cool car."

"A four-door Ford."

"So that's a no."

She sat in the wheelchair. My idea had been to quietly scoot her out the back door, a plan immediately ruined by a squeaky wheel on the chair. Nothing around the hospital ever seemed to work right, and this was yet another example. It squeaked so loudly that we could do nothing but laugh at it.

"Sounds like a thousand mice," I said.

"Being chased by a thousand rats," she said.

"Remind me, when we stop somewhere, to get oil. We'll need it when we wheel you back in."

I opened the MRI room exit and practically shoved her outside, all while holding the door open so it wouldn't lock me out.

"Stay right here," I said. Then I went down the hall, nodded to Paula, and left the hospital through the front doors. If anyone were to view the video, it would appear as if I'd entered and left that way.

Gabriella saw my unstylish sedan and said, "Well, I hope it's got a good radio."

"It works. Now get your butt in."

"Butt's in," she said as I folded the wheelchair and put it in the back seat, along with a zippered case of syringes and vials of hydromorphone, in case Gabriella needed it for pain. Then I laid down some rules.

"This is just going to be a ride to the beach. Nice and easy. But it's a four-hour drive. So if you feel nauseous or hungry or dizzy, let me know. Promise?"

"I promise."

"No lying."

"Right. This is a lie-free cruise."

We rolled out of the hospital lot and she cheered a "Yay!" when we were on the road.

"Exciting, huh?"

"It is."

"Can't believe we're driving all this way for one look at the ocean," I said.

"But you'll remember that one look for the rest of your life."

"I guess that's true."

"So will I."

"Let's hope that will be when you're one hundred."

"Yeah, but probably not."

I didn't have a response for that, so I drove on, past the closed Coal Miner Diner, which marked the last business inside Locksburg limits. You had to be a local to know that you were now outside of town: the YOU ARE LEAVING LOCKSBURG sign had been toppled by a drunk driver a few years ago and never replaced.

"You don't really think I'll make it to a hundred, do you?" Gabriella asked.

"What did the doctor tell you?"

"She said to prepare myself. It might be soon."

"I hope she's wrong."

"Why won't you say it?"

"Let's drive. Don't get worked up, honey."

"I just want to be honest. Both of us."

"I am honest. I'm not about bullshit."

She snorted. "Silence can be worse than bullshit. There's this prayer, it asks God to forgive the things I've said, and the things I failed to say. So it means, even silence can be really wrong."

Yet again, she had me reconsidering myself, this sixteen-year-old. It almost annoyed me. I've always thought of my silence as defiance, and here she was, proving to me that it could be weakness. Or worse, spinelessness.

We drove on, and I could sense her waiting for me to say

something. After a while I went with: "You're right. Your condition is dire. And yes, you might die. Soon. But I truly hope that doesn't happen."

"At least not until I've seen the ocean," she said.

· · ·

After nearly an hour we pulled off the highway and into an armpit of a town called New Rhineland that made Locksburg look like Monaco. The loss of coal and steel had crippled Locksburg, but it had amputated the legs right out from under this place—signs pleading FOR SALE OR RENT hung in eight of the twelve storefronts on what passed for a Main Street.

As we approached the gas station at the end of the block, the lights shut off and I prepared to howl at our bad luck. Then the lights flickered back on. Then off again. Faulty wiring or bad bulbs or both, it appeared. The light inside the store revealed someone behind the counter, though luckily I wouldn't have to go in—I could pay with a credit card at the pump.

In the near corner of the lot, thirty yards from the pumps, a dozen teenagers argued loudly in tones that matched their town: bitter, defeated, angry. I was almost finished pumping the gas when one girl in the group pushed another. The pushed girl staggered back five feet. The rest of the group roared, egging the aggressor on. The girl rushed forward and pushed again, and her victim got caught in her own feet, stepped into a pothole, and went down hard on the ground. All at once, three girls rushed forward to kick at her, and she covered up.

"Callie!" Gabriella said through the window, and pointed at them. If I had had time to think, I would have put the pump back and driven the hell out of there. But the simple unfairness of three girls ganging up on a fallen and defenseless one spurred me on without a thought.

"Hey!" I shouted. Two of the girls stopped. One kept kicking. "Hey! You don't kick someone when they're down! What's wrong with you?"

The girl on the ground labored to get up. She slipped and fell back, and a couple of the boys cracked up. I stepped over and hooked a hand under one of the girl's armpits to help her to her feet.

"Come with me," I said, and led her to my car.

"She's a thief!" some guy called out.

"Goddamn liar!" the girl hollered over her shoulder.

"Fuck you, dirtbag," one of them called out. Then another said, "Fuck you too, lady. Why you helping that thief?"

I opened a back door of my car and helped the girl inside. Half-way, she stopped. "I don't need no help," she said, and tried to get out.

"Get in, I'm driving you home."

"Let her back out!" someone in the crowd screamed. "She don't want to be there, with your ugly-ass face!"

They laughed. I had plenty of comebacks to cracks like that: "I'd rather be fuckin' ugly than a fuckin' idiot," or "Bend over, let me see your better side," or just a blunt "Pal, I'm not pretty, but your face looks like a can of smashed assholes." But I swallowed every insult. I was a woman in a rough and unfamiliar town, in the dark, and I knew that even a raised middle finger might cause an offense that could lead one of those losers to run after us, or to get in a nearby car for a chase. I got the girl into the back seat, slammed the door shut, and drove out of the lot as the crowd jeered.

"You coulda left me," the girl said from the back seat when we were on the road. She was eighteen or so and had an unpleasant countenance that I could tell was there long before she was pushed to the ground.

"Yeah. You seemed like you were handling yourself with Olympic skill back there."

"Fuck them," she said. "I hate them all."

"What did you steal?" Gabriella said.

"Nothin'! I never stole nothin' in my life! That little bitch Heather thinks . . . ah, never mind." She pointed ahead. "I live another mile away."

That mile turned into four. Her sense of distance was off either by nature or by one of the kicks to the head that she'd gotten. We moved into an adjoining town, Lee Mountain, which seemed to have a bit more promise than New Rhineland.

"That's the thing," the girl said out of nowhere. "They hate that I live in Lee Mountain. They're all jealous."

"Well, if I were you, I wouldn't go back there," I said.

"I ain't. I got better things to do."

I was tempted to ask, just for fun, what those better things might be, when Gabriella said:

"What's your name?"

"Kelsey. With a *K*," she said, as if there could be another lead letter.

"Have you ever seen the ocean, Kelsey?"

"No. Why?"

"That's where we're going. Want to come?"

If Gabriella were my own kid, I may have been tempted to flick a hand out and rap her on the shoulder just for asking that.

"Naw," the girl said, completely incurious. "I gotta get home."

"Awww, too bad," I said, and shot Gabriella a side glance that she grinned at.

"Right up here," Kelsey said.

"Right up here" turned out to be yet another mile away, the turn marked by a large sign that read LEE MOUNTAIN TRAILER PARK. I pulled into the entrance to find that the place opened up into an expansive lot that held over a hundred trailers, many now lit from inside by the blue glow of televisions.

"This place is big," I said. "You'll have to guide me to yours."

"No," Kelsey said. "Let me off here."

"We can't let you out in the dark," Gabriella said.

"I need to walk some before I go in. Think about a couple things. It's really safe. Hell, you can't get attacked. Just scream. There's people all around."

Before I could argue, she opened the back door.

"Thanks for the ride," she said, and shut the door without waiting for a response.

I took a wide turn at the entrance and pulled out of the trailer park.

"'We're going to the ocean, Kelsey. Do you want to come?'" I mimicked to Gabriella, with more humor than I actually felt. "Are you insane?"

"I thought we could all have an adventure!" she said.

I couldn't help cracking up, and Gabriella joined in. That went on for almost a mile until I had a sudden and unwelcome notion. I quickly steered the car onto a turnoff on the dark road. I flicked the interior lights on, unbuckled, and got out. Opened the back door.

The wheelchair was still there, of course, pushed to one side.

But the zippered case that held Gabriella's drugs was missing.

ANDY

Here's a list of the stuff I gave up on before I met Kate and we had Angie:

1. Everything.

That's the concise version. The detailed list would include at least four decent jobs, two attempts at obtaining a GED (I didn't show for the test either time, too strung out), a book on addiction that I was going to self-publish (I wrote sixteen really good pages before losing them in some drug house and never writing again), dozens of friendships, and hundreds of promises to swear off heroin. If I wasn't a quitter by nature, I sure grew into it.

Then Angie was born, and she and Kate forced me to get my shit together. Angie's eyes were enough to keep me pushing brooms and pumping gas and uncurling my fist when I longed to coldcock some shithead boss. Kate was more blunt—she threatened to take a baseball bat to my head if I didn't wise up or if I dosed again. All my love, along with a large measure of husbandly fear, combined to give me enough strength to suffer through anything.

Now that my wife and child were gone, though, the old quitter began to creep back.

My second day of searching started out as miserable as the first, then grew exhausting. After a while I was walking the same blocks twice and thrice, and everything began to seem familiar, though not in the way that I wanted. Thin worms of doubt burrowed into my mind, hollowing out my resolve. I'd prepared better for this day's search—short pants and a light T-shirt, chosen to help save me from overheating. But the quitter in me was still there, trying to take control.

After hours of wandering and sweating and bitching and moaning, I knew I wasn't going to find that pervert's home or the abandoned house where I'd left the photo albums. There had to be another way. But it's no crime to say it—I wasn't smart enough to figure it out.

So what would Kate do?

She'd focus on the things she did have rather than on those she didn't. And the only thing I had was a mental picture of the guy—six feet six or thereabouts. Two seventy-five, at least. A waddle or a limp. Pockmarked face. Balding, I think.

Inside my head, Kate said: *OK, so you've got something, at least. Now what?*

I had no answer.

She said: *Don't be stupid all your life. Sit down for a few minutes. If walking hasn't helped you yet, it's not going to. Concentrate.*

I strode along Pulaski Street, head down, and almost tripped over the wide front steps of Saint Stanislaus Church. Maybe I could rest inside and gather my thoughts in the quiet. But some guy was locking the two wide front doors.

He had his back to me and was bending down to fit a key into the lock. After turning it, he stood to full height.

Six foot six.

A head with a few wispy hairs.

Then he faced me.

Two hundred seventy-five pounds, at least.

Pockmarked face.

He wore all black. Except for the white clerical collar.

He stared at me for a moment. Then gave a dismissive half nod of acknowledgment.

My mouth, dry, failed at first. Finally, I was able to spit out some words.

"Are you Father Glynn?"

"I am."

"The police chief, Joe Kriner, told me to get in touch with you. I, uh, overdosed. He said that you did counseling. Can we talk?"

"I'm very busy tonight. You can call the church phone and leave a message, and we can schedule something later."

"But see, Father, I'm thinkin' of using again and, uh, you know, I need help."

"I'm sorry. But like I just told you, I need to go home now."

"That's not very Christlike, Father."

He seemed to have doubts about me from the start. It was evident in his curt dismissal. But my response tripped his radar, and he flashed a bemused smile, as if his doubts were now justified.

"I'll be the judge of what's Christlike, son. Now good evening."

"I'd like to make a confession. Can you at least do that? I heard it's good for the soul."

He sighed, as if talking to a persistent idiot. "Confessions are heard every other Saturday between one and three in the afternoon."

"But what if I die before then? Like, I need to get rid of these sins now."

"Son, I don't think you're serious. Now, if you'd like me to call Chief Kriner, I can do that too. It's your choice."

He reached into his pocket and took out a phone.

"No, Father, no need to call the police. But I'm not kidding you. I've done some bad stuff."

"We can talk about it the Saturday after next."

"See, I stole a briefcase from someone's car."

The weather had been sunny all day and now hovered in the low eighties, but I could see his blood chill after that sentence left my lips. I let the silence sink in for a moment, savoring the expression on his pasty face.

"Is that so," he said.

"That's so," I said. "Broke the briefcase open. No money in there. Not even a dime. There was some other stuff, though."

"What's your name?" he asked.

"My name is Mister Fuck You, Father. Now, will you hear my confession, or do you want me to leave and come back in two Saturdays?"

He unlocked the doors. I'll give the bastard this—he regained his composure fast. The hand holding the key didn't miss its target or shake in nervousness. He stepped forward and I followed. Inside, the church was cool, and our footsteps echoed. Red-glass candles flickered on the altar, leaving the rest of the gothic space in shadows.

The priest stood between the rows of pews, and motioned for me to take a seat. Instead, I moved over to the confession box. My knees popped as I went down to the kneeler. A moment later he entered the other side and slid the window up, leaving only a screen between us.

"Bless me, Father, for I have sinned. It has been . . . oh, fuck me, what, seventeen years since my last confession? Give or take."

"I won't have this sacrament ridiculed by—"

"It has been seventeen years since my last confession." I talked over him. "Since then I have done things that should and will send me to hell, if there is one, though I don't think there is. Before I got straight, I stole from everyone when I lived in Philadelphia. I spent whole days scammin' to buy drugs. I paid for whores and fucked them before I met my wife. I lied pretty much every day. I was a repulsive person and I deeply regret it, but I know, without a doubt, that I'd do it again if I were usin'. So, well, for these and all my sins I am truly sorry."

"You're forgiven," he mumbled.

"What? No penance? Not even ten Hail Marys?"

"Tell me what you want. Now."

"I want my penance."

"Fine. Say the rosary."

"I will. Wait. That's a lie. I won't say the rosary. Hell, I wouldn't know how."

Silence.

"Aren't you supposed to say a prayer now, Father?"

He said it then. The prayer of absolution, which he knew by rote and I recognized from my childhood days at a Philadelphia church where my mother sometimes brought me. The priest raised two fingers and made a sign of the cross as he said:

"God, the Father of mercies, through the death and resurrection of his Son has reconciled the world to himself and sent the Holy Spirit among us for the forgiveness of sins; through the ministry of the Church, may God give you pardon and peace, and I absolve you from your sins in the name of the Father, and of the Son, and of the Holy Spirit. Amen."

"Amen," I said. Blessed myself, too, for good measure.

"Enough mockery," the priest said. "Get on with it."

"I wasn't mocking. I'm a sinful man, Father. But at least I don't fuck little boys and girls and take pictures of it."

He was cagey enough not to admit anything with words in case he was being set up, but his eyes and his manner said enough: he was desperate, a position guys like him are rarely in.

"So you have pictures of me?" he asked.

"No. You cut yourself out of them. But are you really so stupid to think they won't be able to find some way to figure out it's you in those pictures? If their photo labs can't do it, they'll just track down the kids, and they'll tell who was in the picture. Your fingerprints are probably on them too. So you're fucked if I hand those pictures over to the police. No pun intended."

"Return those things you stole to their rightful owner. And I will give you whatever money I have. And we'll both go on our own way."

I picked a number out of the air. "Ten grand."

"And where do you expect me to get that much money?"

"Turn some water into wine, then sell it."

"This is what you'll do: You'll give me what you have stolen. Then—"

"This is what *you'll* do: Shut your face, fatso."

He was one of those men unaccustomed to being challenged, and it showed. Through the screen I saw his jaw tighten.

"Then how do I know you have what you stole?"

"Of course I have it."

He saw something in me. Maybe a poker-like tell had appeared on my face, triggered by the frustration that had built up over the past two days of walking. He was good—he definitely had training in therapy—and he homed in on my weakness like a snake approaching prey.

"You don't have the things anymore, do you? Did you burn them? Or sell them to someone else?"

Damn it. He flustered me, and I went defensive.

"Who would I know, to sell that shit to? I don't deal with—"

"Then where are they?"

"Hidden."

"Where?"

"If I had my way, they'd be shoved up your asshole. Sideways."

He studied me, and if only in my mind, I could feel him getting the upper hand. Authority figures could do that to me.

"Bring them to me. And you'll get your money."

"You'll get them."

"When? I was supposed to leave town and go to my other parish. I had to reschedule."

"Wow. It's like you think I care. Don't worry, I'll find you."

I got up from the kneeler. Knees cracked again. Walked to the front doors. They were locked, sealing me in this church with him. I stepped to the side and waited for the priest to come over and unlock them, far enough away to stay out of his reach. The guy had already done the most evil things you could do. No telling what else he might try. I searched around for something to hit him with in case he went for me.

"Let's talk tomorrow," he said in a voice I'd heard before: from city cops who got off on bashing your head in with billy clubs until both the club and your skull broke. From strung-out junkies growling at each other over the last ten-dollar baggie. From dealers who delighted in holding off handing over their product, a callous form of torture that some of them savored. That was the kind of voice the priest had, and one I knew better than to trust.

"Open those doors," I said.

He unlocked them. I darted out cat-fast, half expecting a hand to reach out and grab my neck and pull me back inside the hellhole that was his church.

NATHAN

I hated myself for being with LeeLee, but not enough to stop seeing her. Or maybe I disliked the idea of what I was doing, but the reality excited me. And after the visit by the detective earlier in the day, and hearing from Paula that the police were sniffing around the hospital, I needed LeeLee, if only to lose myself when my hand would slide under her denim skirt and feel what she had on underneath. In those moments, as my fingers caressed the smooth silk on her ass, all my other worries subsided.

Yet the respite was short-lived. A minute after we fell into bed, she paused the action and rolled onto her back. The mood immediately stalled.

"The mayor had a meeting today," she said.

I made some sound of assent, and she continued:

"A couple of cops."

"What kind of cops?"

"One was a state trooper, I know that. He was assisting an investigation, with some federal guy."

"What was the meeting about?"

"I was hoping you'd tell me that."

"What does that mean?"

"What do you think it means?"

I said, "If you don't want to tell me, don't tell me."

"The mayor wouldn't say anything at first, but I have ways of finding out."

"What ways?"

She put on a girlish, seductive voice. "Oh, Mr. Mayor! What was happening today in that meeting? You're so important!"

She found it amusing, that she had flirted with a man to get what she wanted. I found it sneaky. Or maybe I was jealous. How absurd for a guy who was cheating on his wife to be jealous of his . . . What was LeeLee? A mistress? Lover? Whatever she was, I didn't like the game she was playing, though I needed to find out what she'd learned.

"That's funny," I said. "And what did the mayor say?"

"That fire up at Michaux. There was something in that house that the cops are very interested in."

"What are they interested in?"

"That's what I'm trying to find out."

She was good at using the silence. I was better. We lay there for a few minutes until LeeLee broke it by saying: "So are you going to tell me?"

"Tell you what?"

"Now who's playing games? Tell me what happened in that house."

"I got there when the house was burning. I dragged a guy out. Then the place collapsed."

"Well, here's what the mayor said: the cops want him to keep an eye out in case anyone starts spending a lot of money. Or if anyone packs up like they're moving out of town or acting different."

"OK."

"When the mayor said that, so much stuff started coming

together in my head. I thought: You've been talking about leaving town, Nate. You've been talking about it a lot."

"That's not a crime."

"And you've been acting different too."

"I'm not."

"Says the married guy I'm in bed with. A guy who's practically been a monk all his life."

"What else did the mayor say?"

"The cops may announce a big reward for information."

I said, "That house . . . they were probably meth cookers and the cops are interested because of the drugs. I wouldn't get too—"

"Tell me the truth, Nate. You've never been like the rest of the guys in Locksburg. You've always been straight-up."

She moved her hand over and caressed my crotch when she said that. Her type of humor.

"I've got nothing to tell you."

"So if I went to those cops and said: 'Hey, I know a guy who's leaving town, after living here his whole life. A guy who told me that suddenly he has the money to go. And that guy was the first one in that burning house.' What do you think the cops would think?"

"I don't care what the cops would think."

"All right, then. I'll tell them."

She waited a minute. When I didn't say anything, she said, "The cops are coming back in tomorrow, the mayor said. Maybe I'll talk to them then."

"Don't do that."

"Why not? Maybe I could help the investigation. Get that reward and use the money to move my ass outta Locksburg."

"Don't talk to the police."

"I don't understand, Nate," she said, in a voice I didn't like at all. "You've got nothing to hide."

She was tying me up in words. And then she worked the silence better than me. Shrewder. She didn't have all the pieces of the puzzle, but she had enough to start seeing some parts of the picture.

I said, "Why would you do something like that, LeeLee? Are you trying to get me in trouble?"

"No! But I've always hated secrets, Nate. I hate that you'd be keeping something from me. I mean, come on—if I wanted to get you in trouble, I could march over to your wife and tell her about us. But I'd never do that. I can keep a secret. That's proof, right?"

"Right."

"So why can't you tell me what the cops are going all bugshit for? Since you know I'd never tell."

"I got nothing to say, LeeLee."

She inhaled. Then: "Go home."

"Don't be like that."

"I'm not being like anything. I'm just saying, leave. We shouldn't see each other anymore. Especially since I don't know what you're up to."

She had that one card to play, and she was going all in on it. I fast considered my options: either tell her about the money, or risk her going to the police and fueling their suspicions. Maybe they'd get a search warrant on the house. If they started to question Paula, her honesty would lead her to confess my secret in minutes. But maybe I could split the difference: tell LeeLee just enough to keep her quiet, and get her to back off. I'd be doing it for me, and for Paula.

"I need your word, LeeLee, that if I told you something, you'd never whisper it again."

"Nate. I would never say anything."

A pause as I approached a line that I didn't want to cross.

"Maybe there was something in that house. And maybe I'm thinking, if it was once a drug dealer's, now it's mine."

"I totally agree with that! Finders keepers!" she said, egging me on. "Of course it's yours. You deserve it for risking your life! I'd do the same thing. The *exact* same thing!"

I couldn't shake the feeling that she was manipulating me like she'd manipulated the mayor. I heard what she was saying but couldn't feel the emotions. It sounded like just words to me.

"So let's leave it at that, LeeLee."

"What was it? What was in that house?"

"Give me another day or two. I need to figure some things out."

She went quiet, maybe weighing her own options. I waited, and when she began rubbing against me, I knew I'd bought myself a little time.

"Or maybe you could tell me in Florida," she said.

I didn't want to lead her on anymore. But I did need her to keep quiet, at least until the cops got out of town.

"Yeah, sure, Florida," I said, with no real intent of being there with her.

Those were just words to me.

CALLIE

I turned the car around and sped back to the trailer park.

"I don't need any medicine or painkillers," Gabriella said. "I feel good enough."

"You might feel bad later. And here's the thing—that stuff is high-powered. If she or anyone else takes those drugs, they're liable to kill themselves. If that happens, they'll find the labels and trace them back to the hospital. I'll be on the hook for accessory to murder."

We got to the front entrance. A large wooden sign illustrated a grid of the park and marked out the lots for nearly two hundred trailer homes. I groaned. And cursed. A lot. Gabriella pointed at a trailer with a small sign by the door: PARK MANAGER.

"Stay here," I said.

"Fat chance," she replied, and followed me to the front door of the trailer. I knocked. From inside, a chest-heaving cough sounded out, ending ten seconds later with a hock-spit. I dreaded to think of where that loogie ended up.

The door opened, and a tall, rail-thin woman appeared. She was somewhere in her fifties or sixties. It was hard to tell. She wore a pink terrycloth bathrobe and had her hair in overnight curlers. Her eyes widened in question, with an expression that said, *Well, this better be good.*

"Hi," I said. "I need to find someone who lives in this park."

A plucked eyebrow rose slightly. I waited, got no response, then soldiered on.

"I mean, someone specific. She . . . her name is Kelsey. I don't know her last name."

Another pause, one that had me wondering if the woman understood English.

"Any chance you know her?"

She grinned with no real humor behind it. "I'm the lot manager, honey. I'm not directory assistance."

"I'm sorry. I really hated to knock. But—"

"Why do you want Kelsey?"

"Do you know her?"

"I asked a question," she said, not without a drollness that implied she might be enjoying this conversation. "Now you answer it. That's how these things work."

"Right. Sorry . . ."

"You said that."

"Yes. Sorry."

"No need to apologize again. Go on."

"OK. I'm going to be flat-out honest here. We gave Kelsey a ride. And she took something that was ours. And we need to get it back."

The woman let out a chicken-like cackle, if that chicken had smoked a carton of unfiltered cigarettes and swilled a fifth of sloe gin. That led her to cough. When that was done, she cackled anew. I may have been tempted to laugh with her if Gabriella and I weren't in such a pinch.

The woman said: "Ha-ha! Why'd you give that twerp a ride? Everyone knows she's a thief!"

"Everyone except us," Gabriella chimed in.

"Right. Well, you learned your lesson, didn't ya?" Like her previous words, those came out sounding like a different version of the language I spoke, as if she had said: "Raht. Wull, yew learnt yer lessen, didn'tja?"

"Can you tell us . . . ?"

"I asked a question! Didn't we lay out the ground rules?"

She was apparently enjoying this now.

"Yes, we learned our lesson," I said.

"What'd she steal?"

"Gabriella here, she has medication. It was in the back seat. Kelsey must have—"

"No 'must have' about it. If it ain't nailed down, that girl will take it. Jesus. You think she'd steal some pimple cream or shampoo! Something she could use! But no, she's taking your medicine. Know what she once stole? She—"

"We—"

"Don't interrupt. This is a good story. She once stole a collar off a dog around here, then wore the damn thing around her neck like some fashion statement, except it smelled like a sweaty Rottweiler. When the owner saw her with the collar, he ripped it off Kelsey's neck so hard he almost took her head with it. He tried to put it back on the dog. But the dog refused to wear the collar again after Kelsey had worn it."

"That's funny," I said.

"Funny stupid," she replied. The woman brought her hand up halfway. Then she glanced down to realize there was no cigarette there. She sighed.

I said, "Could you tell us where she lives?"

"I could. But what country are we livin' in?"

"Huh?"

"Nope. Not the country of Huh. You lose." She eyeballed Gabriella, as if now it was the girl's golden opportunity to take a crack at the right answer.

"The United States of America," Gabriella said.

"Correct-a-moondo. So, as they say in the United States of America, what's in it for me?"

"C'mon," I said to Gabriella. This wasn't getting us anywhere.

"What are you gonna do?" she asked before we could walk away. "Knock on all one-hundred and sixty-eight doors around here? Go right ahead. But be careful—most of them got guns. You think they want you knocking on a dark night?"

"What do you want?"

"I was just about to get dressed and go down to Paul's store for some cigarettes. Could you go get them for me? I look like hell, I know, so I don't wanna embarrass myself. It's only a mile down the road. Get me two packs of Pall Malls. When you come back I'll tell you exactly where Kelsey lives. It'll take you a minute and save you hours."

"Only a mile?"

"Yeah! Right out on Route 5! You're not from around here, are you?"

"No."

"No shit. If you were, you wouldn't have given Kelsey a ride!" She cackle-coughed again at her own joke.

"Pall Malls at Paul's," the woman said. "Two packs. And make sure you go to Paul's—they're the only ones who sell 'em. Tell 'em they're for Wendy."

She pointed down the road, helpfully, then slammed her trailer door.

. . .

Only a mile, my ass.

After five minutes I was ready to turn around, until a small roadside store came into view. At least it was well lit, with a large front window that overlooked a clean lot with four gas pumps. I parked and told Gabriella to stay put. She snorted, the smart-ass, and followed me inside, as if she wasn't about to miss a moment of this. Behind the counter a twentysomething kid nodded at us, then went back to reading an *Autotrader* magazine.

"Might as well get some other stuff too, for the ride," I said to Gabriella, and minutes later we were back at the counter with a couple of Cokes and some granola bars.

"Can I get two packs of Pall Malls, please?"

"You getting 'em for Wendy?"

"She's the manager of the trailer park?"

"Wicked Wendy. That's her. Only one I ever met who smokes Pall Malls. Only one who ever asks for them. I was surprised to hear the two words come out of anyone else's mouth."

"Yeah, she asked us to get them."

The guy reached into the rack above his head. After a short search, his hand came back empty.

"Huh. No more here."

"Do you have a carton or something?"

"Cartons are locked up in the back after nine o'clock. Too many thieves in this town."

"So I hear. What else does Wendy smoke?"

"Nothin'. She won't touch anything else. She said her lungs are only made for Pall Malls. She never smoked any other kind of cigarette in her life."

"Are you shitting me?" I said.

"I shit you not."

Gabriella said, "Is there another store?"

"Nope," the guy said. "No one carries Pall Malls around here. We special-order them for Wendy."

"Can you open up a carton? Or go ahead and sell me the whole carton."

"I got no problem selling you a pack or a carton."

"Good."

"I do have a problem getting in the back room, though. It's locked up tight."

"You can't open it?"

"I usually have the key. But Paul, the owner, he forgot to leave it with me. Tell you what. If you really want the Pall Malls, you can ask him to open it."

"Is he here?"

"He's down at the Creekside Lounge."

"I can't go to some lounge."

"It's real close by."

"Can you call him?"

"I tried earlier. The Creekside has a live band tonight. He probably can't hear his cell phone."

"Do you know a girl named Kelsey?"

"Who doesn't know her? She steals everything around here."

"Do you know where she lives?"

"Sure do."

"Good! Where?"

"In the trailer park."

"Yeah, but which number?"

"That, I don't know. You'd have to ask Wendy."

I nearly walked out and left but remembered the drugs, and pictured a crew of teenagers lying on slabs in the morgue, dead from overdoses.

"Where's the Creekside Lounge?"

"Right down the road."

"Don't say a mile."

"It's not. It's two point seven miles exactly."

"Go in and ask for Paul?"

"Yeah. Tell him to give you the key. Tell him Randy told you he needed it. Then I'll get you the Pall Malls."

"How am I going to know who Paul is, in a crowded bar?"

"It's hard to miss Paul. He's only got one arm."

"Seriously?"

"You're supposed to say, 'Are you shittin' me?'"

"Are you shittin' me?"

"I shit you not. Yet again."

"OK, we'll go get the key."

From behind me, Gabriella gave a little clap.

The kid behind the counter said, "Just go in the Creekside Lounge. If you see a guy with one arm, that's probably Paul."

...

"This is absurd," I grumbled when we got back in the car.

"This is excellent!" Gabriella said.

When the odometer turned two point six miles, the Creekside Lounge, built to look like an oversize log cabin, came into view. The lot was full, and the runny words on a spray-painted sheet of plywood read THERE'S MORE PARKING OVER HERE, Y'ALL! with an arrow that pointed down toward the creek that no doubt gave the joint its name. The parking spots, though, were another hundred yards away. I wasn't going to be walking that far in the dark of night, not with a girl who had plenty of problems getting around. I went back to the front of the place and pulled into an empty handicapped spot.

"I'm not handicapped," Gabriella said, but there was no fight in her voice. I could see she was growing tired after the two previous stops.

"Shush," I said. "I guess I can't convince you to stay in the car?"

"And miss this? No way."

A chord of "Free Bird" sounded from inside the bar, and when I put my hand on the handle I could feel the vibration from the music. I opened the door to see about forty people holding lit cigarette lighters high and swaying to the tune. Another forty held up cell phones, their screens glowing in the dark. The singer wailed on, not half bad, then the lead guitarist went into a solo. I was glad that the crowd was focused on the band. Walking into a crowded place is a dreadful experience when you've got a disfigurement:

every eye seems to be watching your face, while some people nod your way and whisper to their friends: "Check that out."

Gabriella and I scanned the place. After a moment, she tapped my shoulder and raised a chin toward a small table at the far end. Only one of the four chairs was taken. Sitting in it was a guy in a pressed, blue button-down shirt with an unused sleeve pinned neatly to his side. With his one hand he picked up his mug of beer and sipped without taking his eyes off the band. He smiled but seemed melancholy, and his leather boot softly tapped the floor in time with the music. Gabriella and I weaved through the crowd. When we got to him, he stood and motioned to the chairs.

"Those seats are free if you want to sit," he said. "I'm not waiting for anybody."

Gabriella sat down and surveyed the bar, as fascinated by the place as if it were a great emperor's crystal ballroom.

"Are you Paul?" I asked.

"That's me. What's your name?"

"I'm Callie. This is Gabriella."

"How ya doin'?" He offered his hand to Gabriella, then to me. He shook with surprising gentleness for a guy who was well over six feet and held himself like the owner of a farm or a ranch rather than a convenience store.

"Let me get you drinks," he said.

"Whiskey," Gabriella piped up before I shut her down with a side look.

"Thanks, but we're not staying," I said to Paul. "We came for the key to the back room at your store. We wanted to buy a few packs of Pall Malls. Randy said they were locked in storage."

"Are you friends of Wendy's?"

"How'd you guess?" Gabriella said, and the three of us chuckled.

I said: "We told Wendy we'd get them for her, then the back room was locked, so Randy said to come here to ask you for the key. You can call him . . ."

"I trust you," he said. He reached deep into the pocket of his blue jeans, then handed over a single key on a single ring. "I'm sorry you had to run all the way down here. The two packs are on me. My fault."

"No. Please. We'll pay."

"Where're you from, Callie?" he asked.

"Locksburg."

"Nice town. Why are you here?"

"That's a really long story . . ."

"I got plenty of time." He smiled a genuine smile, full of welcome. I'd planned to rush in and out of this place, but I'll admit that I wasn't so eager to hurry now. He had that effect.

"The quick version is, we gave a girl by the name of Kelsey a ride . . ."

"Oh, watch your stuff around her. She's got some sticky fingers."

"Yeah, so we're told," Gabriella said.

"Anyway, we drove Kelsey to the trailer park, and that's how we ran into Wendy. We promised to get her cigarettes and . . . here we are."

"You sure I can't buy you both a drink?"

"That's really kind, but we've got a long drive ahead of us."

"You could ask Callie to dance, though!" Gabriella chimed in, oh so cheerily, as the band moved into some sad, soft country tune.

"I would love to," Paul said, and stood. "How about it, Callie? Would you like to dance?"

"No. Really. You don't . . ."

And somewhere in those excuses I wondered why I was saying that. I wanted to dance, and so did he. Then why was I defaulting to fear rather than doing what I wanted? And before I could overthink anymore, Gabriella kicked my chair and mouthed, *Go!* A moment later Paul and I were on the dance floor. He took one of my hands, and I placed the other on his waist.

"Sorry I can't hold you tighter," he said. I was nearly puzzled until he motioned to where his other arm should be.

"This is fine. This is real fine," I said, fighting and losing the battle not to blush.

"Thank you for dancing with me," he said.

"Thank you for asking."

"You almost said no."

"I was momentarily stupid."

"I'm glad the moment passed."

"So am I." Blushed again, damn it.

"I get momentarily stupid too sometimes. But tonight I did the smartest thing I ever did."

"What's that?"

"Asked you to dance."

"That's nice. Thank you."

"So where's your long drive to?"

"The beach."

"Vacation?"

"No. Gabriella wants to see it, so I'm taking her there."

"Is she your sister?"

"No. I'm a nurse. She's a patient of mine. It's kind of a long story."

"I love long stories. When can you tell it to me?"

"I have to get on the road. We're way behind schedule."

"I don't mean now. We can . . . you know . . . over dinner. If you want."

If the room had fallen in, or if I found the rest of the bar was populated with little green spacemen, I couldn't have been more flabbergasted. The synapses in my idiot brain had never fired in quite that way before, so it took a speechless half a minute to comprehend that he was asking me out.

And then I realized that this was the time to say something really confident or flirty or clever.

"Um . . . I . . ."

No words would follow. I was still stunned. Then I saw that, almost imperceptibly, he motioned to his empty sleeve.

"That's OK," he said. "Sorry to ask."

That was like a shot of energy to me: "No! I mean, I'd like to go. Dinner would be really, really fabulous. Really."

"Really?"

"Really! It's only, I live in Locksburg. It's a bit of a drive."

"It's not so bad. I like to drive. Put the radio on, you know."

I nodded, he did the same, and when the song was coming to an end, Paul made a head motion to the singer, who motioned back and went into another slow tune. Then Paul looked at me, and it was his turn to blush.

"Maybe I'm being momentarily stupid here, but . . . you said yes, right? To dinner?"

"Sure. Yes. I'd like to have dinner. With you."

"I just wanted to be sure that you're not married or got a boyfriend or anything?" His sincerity almost made me burst out laughing.

"Me?"

He looked me in the eye.

"Yeah, you."

"I don't get asked out much. You know, since I'm such a Marilyn Monroe look-alike. Guys get intimidated."

"You sound like you're making a joke, but I think any guy would go out with you in a heartbeat."

"Well. I mean, I'm not going to . . . I'll come right out and say it . . . I had this surgery when I was a kid. I mean, you can see it. And people . . ."

"I know what it's like to have people stare. Believe me."

"Right."

"That'll be another long story we can talk about."

"Deal."

"I'll take you to the best restaurant in Locksburg."

"Don't get your hopes up. Locksburg's not known for its cuisine."

"What is it known for? Besides nice people like you."

"It's got some really picturesque dead-end streets."

"Well, the food doesn't matter," he said. "I got big hopes for the company."

We moved closer then, and I put my cheek on his shoulder and breathed in. He smelled of warm cotton, of soap, and I tried to memorize the scent while we swayed to the music.

The dance ended, and I couldn't exactly say how I got back to the table. Yes I can. He took my hand and led me there, and I was sorry to let his hand go when we sat down. Gabriella squeezed my knee, eyes wide. I wanted to give her an annoyed expression but couldn't. I was feeling a little mesmerized.

Paul took out his cell phone. "Can I get your number?"

I said my phone number extra slowly, extra clearly, while chiding myself for acting like a sixteen-year-old who wanted to make sure there was no way she'd be misunderstood. A moment after I finished, my phone vibrated. I looked. His number was there, and a message:

Looking forward to dinner :)

I said, "Thanks so much for the key and . . . the dance. I really wish we didn't have to go but . . ."

"It's OK," he said. "Tell me about it all later. I'd go back to the store with you, but that's my cousin in the band. This is their first gig and he's really nervous. I told them I'd help them break it down afterward and load it into my truck, and they've only got five more minutes."

"No problem at all. Tell him I said they're great. I'll talk to you soon."

"She needs a hug too!" Gabriella announced.

"So do I," Paul said. When he hugged me I breathed his scent in again, and my head swam. Then Gabriella hugged him. He smiled over top of her at me. I smiled back.

We said a few too many start-and-stop goodbyes, see yas, and talk laters. Then Gabriella and I were weaving through the crowd toward the door.

"You're practically swooning!" Gabriella said, sticky sweet, in a singsong.

"You're practically shutting up!" I said in the same tone. But she was right. I felt as if I were a little drunk, and couldn't stop grinning.

That grin dropped, though, when we went outside to find an empty space where my car had been.

ANDY

I walked down the front steps of the church slowly, careful not to appear as creeped out as I was, then turned and trotted fifty yards before ducking behind a van. There I waited a few minutes until the priest left. Following him was easy: he'd gone only a block and a half before arriving at a house and going inside. I waited a while then strolled past.

Son.

Of.

A.

Bitch.

It was the house where I'd ripped him off, with his car parked there in front. I'd since passed it by at least once, clueless. Sober and clearheaded, it was recognizable. I mentally drew a map of how I'd arrived there after leaving the liquor store. Now it was time to figure out where I'd gone once I'd stolen the briefcase.

I put myself in the mindset of a drunk idiot—me, the other day—who had just stolen something. Which way would I have gone? I'd have hurried along the street and turned left, surely, to get out of sight of the house. Then I'd have ventured down the nearest one-way street to avoid being chased by a car. I did so again, and within minutes was in front of the abandoned row house.

The wood creaked as I bolted upstairs to the front bedroom. There on the floor was the broken briefcase and the two photo albums. I put the albums in the briefcase and hid them far back in the room's only closet. I loathed touching them; there was no way I'd carry them around or keep them in my house.

Now that I knew where they were, it was time to go home. A good night of sleep would help me figure out my next move. I shut the bedroom door and started down the steps. In the middle of the flight, a wicked *crack!* sounded as my foot broke through the rotted wood. My hand shot out for the railing, which ripped from the stairs when I grabbed it. That forced me to put more weight on my foot. I fell farther through the step, almost up to my knee, and my short pants offered no protection.

The first bolts of pain came when I saw the six-inch pieces of jagged wood stabbing into the muscle of my calf. I tried to free myself. The pieces were angled down, like barbs on a fishhook, and dug deeper into my skin the more I pulled up.

All kinds of shit left my mouth: spit, screams, curses, trailing off with "Oh my fucking god, Jesus fucking *Christ!*" My sneaker was filling with the blood that was spurting from my wounds.

I was stuck.

Could barely move.

Horrid thoughts began racing through my mind: What would happen if the entire staircase caved in? I'd be dead for sure, and my body wouldn't be found for months. Somewhere below, a rat skittered across the floor. He and his friends would feast on me, dead or alive.

I pulled my leg up again, then gasped at the pain and stopped. After a moment it became apparent that there was no real choice: the only way to free myself was to yank my leg upward, as fast as I could, and hope the rest of the stairs didn't give way.

Took a deep breath. Prepared.

Then stopped.

Fucking hell, I couldn't do it. The expectation of pain froze me.

Then I heard Kate's voice say, lovingly: *Don't be a pussy. Just get this shit done.*

Then I told myself: *Do it, damn it. Now!*

I screamed and wrenched my leg up hard. It caught and wouldn't come loose. I yanked and pulled again, felt my skin tear. Blood gushed from my cuts.

And all at once I was free.

I fell backward and, despite the pain, got up immediately and went down the rest of the stairs to the floor, to get off the staircase. I leaned against a wall, breathing heavily. I was cursing myself and the priest and the house, and after a few minutes got calm enough to go outside. As I walked, I left a trail of blood behind me on the sidewalk.

A white van with *D'Andrea's Plumbing* painted freehand on the hood sat half a block down the street. A guy closed the back doors and caught sight of me hobbling his way. He propped an elbow against the side of the truck, eyeing me up and chewing a hunk of tobacco as I came toward him.

"Y'all right?" he finally said, then spit.

"I'm all wrong."

"Appears that way. Hurt your leg, huh?"

"You're a regular Alvin Einstein."

"I thought his name was Arthur?"

"That's his smarter cousin."

"I knew it was one of them."

We both looked down at my wounds. My once-white sock was now entirely soaked red.

"Got any duct tape?" I asked.

"Every plumber has duct tape."

"Well, start actin' like every plumber and lend me some, will ya?"

He reopened the back doors, got a roll of tape, and handed it over. I sat on the curb and wrapped the tape around my lower leg. There were three main gashes, each eight inches long and so deep I could see bloody muscle. Inside one of the cuts was a two-inch piece of rotten wood, which I picked out and flicked onto the sidewalk. I kept wrapping the tape. It would be hell to remove later, when it would surely attach to the wounds and rip them open wider. But for now I needed them closed to stop the bleeding.

I tossed the roll of tape back to the guy. He nodded at the length around my leg.

"You can keep that."

"Huh?"

"You asked me to lend you some. But I don't want that part back."

I couldn't tell if he was kidding.

"Uh, thanks. Great gift."

"Need a ride to the hospital?" he asked.

"For what?"

"Suit yerself."

He offered me a hand and got me to my feet.

"That's gonna get infected," he said.

"How long do you think that'll take?"

He eyed up my leg like a field surgeon, stroking his goatee as if considering his vast knowledge of physiology and bacteriology. Then he nodded sagely.

"Three or four days."

"No problem, then," I told him, and started my limp down the block toward home. "I won't be around much longer than that."

. . .

The duct tape gave me some support, and by the time I reached my front door I'd perfected a shuffle-walk-limp that I convinced myself would seem at least half normal to a three-quarter-blind viewer, and would appear somewhat better once I found the old set of crutches that were collecting dust in my basement.

I went to the first-floor bathroom to get some aspirin. The medicine cabinet held only the pills that Kate had used for her menstrual cramps. I shook out four of those and swallowed them with the water I cupped in my filthy hands.

I shambled out of the bathroom and stopped cold.

Something was off.

I couldn't immediately put a finger on what it was.

I didn't have to wait long to find out—a fist that felt like it was made of concrete slammed into the side of my face. I saw black, then stars. Another brutal, rock-strong punch to my cheek sent me staggering across the room, where I collapsed.

When I could finally open my eyes, the priest was standing over me.

"Where are my things?" he growled.

"I don't have them here!"

"I'll only ask you once more: Where are my things?"

"I told you!"

He stared down at me, sprawled on the floor, my leg exposed and wrapped tight in duct tape.

Then he put the heel of his shoe on my calf.

He brought his weight down.

NATHAN

I'd showered and lain in bed before Paula returned home, hoping to be asleep before she arrived. No such luck. My mind hadn't shut off since the moment I found the money, and she saw my open eyes when she entered the bedroom. Paula got into bed and put her head on my chest in silence.

"How're you?" I asked.

"Do you really want to know?"

"Of course," I said, not really wanting to know.

"I can't concentrate. I don't sleep well. The police showed up again. The doctor says the guy is pulling through. They're planning to transfer him out."

I kept quiet, thinking it through.

Then Paula said, "After you left for work this morning, I went up to the attic."

I must have tensed, and she felt it.

"Don't worry. I would never touch anything that's yours. I went up there to find my old journals."

"You don't write in one anymore, do you?"

"No. I gave it up a couple years ago."

I didn't ask why, though I could guess. That was about the time the resignation started to set in, that we'd never have children.

"So why were you searching for them?"

"Because I was thinking of leaving you."

I tensed again. Not many men I knew trusted their wives as much as I did Paula. She was a bedrock, something I took for granted, like air or the ground under my feet. To hear her say such a thing threw me.

"I went to read what I'd written about our marriage, back in the old days," she said. "Then I went down a rabbit hole. Spent four or five hours up there, reading over everything. I was almost late for work. And I'm never late for work. I'm going to tell you a secret now. It's probably the biggest secret I have."

She took her head off my chest, positioned her pillow against the headboard, and sat up. I reached over for the lamp. "No," she said. "Keep it off."

So we stayed in the dark, and she began: "Before I met you I was dating Robert."

"You told me that, a long time ago. The doctor."

"Back then, I told you that he and I had been out on a few dates. But we were more serious than that. He and I dated for a while. You didn't know him, except for one time he stitched you up, but he was really ambitious. Always sending out letters, trying to move to a better hospital. And finally, it happened. A big research hospital in Los Angeles flew him out there twice for interviews. And when they called to offer it to him, after he said yes, he put down the phone and started packing his bags, right then. He and I were at that weird point—we were dating and serious, but not overly serious, you know? Eventually he left for LA. Then you and I started dating, and after six months or so you started hinting around at marriage. Remember that? How you'd casually mention it, to see what I'd say?"

I recalled how dopey I must have sounded at the time. "I wasn't exactly slick."

"Slick as sandpaper."

"Of course I remember."

"So you and I had been dating. And then . . . I got a letter from Robert. He laid it all out. He said the job was secure and he couldn't stop thinking about me. And right in that letter he asked me to come there and marry him."

I'm glad I didn't speak. I might have said something weak like "I can't believe it." But I could believe it. Paula was easy to love, and I've seen plenty of guys in town flirt with her, their faces brightening when they catch sight of her smile.

"And, I have to be honest with you, Nathan. I didn't know what to do. I went back and forth for days. He called and left me messages. You and I went out one night and you asked if something was bothering me, because you could see that my head was just . . . everywhere. Then you asked me to go to Laurel Lake that weekend. To hike to the top of Rock Mountain. And I knew that's where you'd propose. So I had two days to make a decision. I remember writing in my journal for so long that my hand cramped. I made a list of the pros and cons of both of you. And when it came time to decide— well, you already know the end. But do you know why I chose you?"

"I don't." It came out almost as a whisper.

"I chose you . . . because I could talk to you. Oh, I know you don't say a lot. I know you like to keep to yourself sometimes. But I also know you listen to everything I say."

"I try to. I really do."

"So that's why I didn't go to LA. And that's why I married you. Because I can talk to you. And I'm telling you now, Nathan. Please give that money back. The longer you draw this out, the worse it's going to get."

· · ·

I woke early, slid out of bed, and left the house before Paula got up. After her story the night before, we lay there in the dark, quiet under some unsaid agreement. She soon fell into an exhausted sleep. I was awake for another hour, thinking about what she'd said, and knew that it applied to LeeLee too: the longer I saw her, the more trouble that would arrive when it ended. She was already getting too close to me, and that was dangerous. I had to break it off tonight. That led to another hour of no sleep, as I considered how to get it done.

At work, I watched the door each time it opened, nervous that the police would arrive. They didn't, and at exactly five o'clock I went out that same door to the parking lot.

LeeLee was sitting in the passenger seat of my pickup. She was leaning back, deep in the seat, apparently napping. Her eyes opened when I got in.

"Oh! Surprise!" she said.

"What are you . . . Did you drive here?"

"Uh. Nathan? I don't have a car. You don't even know that about me, do you? Anyway, no, I walked from City Hall. Been here a half hour already."

"Aren't you supposed to be working?"

"Eh, I don't know if I have a job anymore."

I started the truck and pulled out of the lot so we wouldn't be seen.

"What happened?"

"The mayor, giving me shit as always. He wants to get into my pants. And because I don't let him, he finds something to complain about. OK, I took a really long lunch today. I admit it. Like, there was nothing going on at the office. Nothing. And I had someone cover me in case the phone rang. So when I got back he was bitching. Saying I was drinking and . . ."

"Were you?"

". . . and I said, you know what, Mayor Fucknuts? I'm leaving early. Go ahead, fire me if you want. But if I were you, I'd start advertising for my replacement, because you're gonna be screwed when I leave."

"Why did you say that?"

"Why not? I'll write him hate mail from Florida."

She ran her hand over my crotch.

"Driver, take me home, then take me to bed," she said.

She took her phone and played with it for a moment, and didn't see that I'd passed her street. Instead, I drove to Dykeman Pond, a park about a mile away on the outskirts of town. It was fairly deserted at that time, and I pulled to the far end so we couldn't be seen.

"Why are we here?"

"To talk. Put your phone down, please."

She did, and I began.

"LeeLee, I've been thinking, and I know the longer I draw this out, the tougher it will get, so . . . I just want to be straight with you. I like you. A lot. You're fun . . ."

"This sounds like a hundred breakup speeches I heard before."

"It's true, though. You're great. But I can't . . . I don't think it's fair to have you waiting for me. I . . . I can't leave Paula."

"'Course not. Now that you went into that burning house and found whatever you found, you and her are gonna go away, right? And leave me here, after you fucked me."

"I don't know what I'm going to do. But this isn't about money. This—"

"So you found money there, huh?"

Fuck. I'd slipped up. The money was always on my mind, and the thought of it alone was causing me to make mistakes.

"Yeah, I did. And you're going to get some of it. So listen."

She put the phone on the seat. Stayed quiet.

"I found some cash in the house. I got scared and nervous, and then you and I met, and you helped me calm down. So thank you for that. And I think you should go to Florida. Get away from Locksburg. You're too smart for this town."

It was an exceptionally flattering version of reality. Though, really, I just needed LeeLee out of my life, and if giving her money would do that and keep her quiet, then I'd hand some of it over.

I said: "I'm going to give you enough to get you down there. But here's the thing: if and when I give you any money, that means you're complicit in all this. If you take what I give you, you're in on it too."

"How much?" she said. She slurred ever so slightly. Four or five beers at lunch, for sure.

"You understand that, right?"

"Yeah. How much?"

"I'll give you fifty thousand right now. Then, when you settle in, I'll send some more, once everything here blows over."

I might send her money, I might not. If I was lucky, I'd be long gone, far from Locksburg, with no forwarding address. And she'd have spent whatever I'd given her, leaving her with no way to say anything to the cops, lest she get busted too.

"Give me it now," she said.

"Let's wait a little bit."

"Fuck that. I'm practically out of a job. I got a cousin who lives down near Georgia. I'll move in with her. Get away from this place. And you. And the mayor too."

In the way she said that, I would wager that she'd bedded him as well, at least once.

"I'm sorry this happened," I said.

"I bet you are."

I was. LeeLee was going to be a fifty-thousand-dollar mistake. But many men have paid lots more for their bad decisions, so I considered myself lucky and would write this off as a cost of doing business.

"Let's wait until the end of the week."

"I don't know if you'll even be around. I don't know shit about you, Nate."

"First thing you should know is that I don't go by Nate. It's always been Nathan. Second thing is—"

"Second thing is, do you want to fight, or give me my money so I can get the hell away from you?"

"OK, then."

We drove to my house in silence.

"Stay here," I said when pulling into the driveway.

"I gotta pee. I been sitting in this truck for over an hour now."

"I'll take you home in five minutes."

"You're gonna have a puddle in your front seat, then."

"How much did you have to drink at lunch? Did you go to Maxie's?" I said it with a half smile, trying to act like we were in this together, attempting to lighten the mood. She was having none of it.

"Just let me use the toilet."

We went inside. I motioned to the hallway bathroom. When she went in, I bolted up the stairs, fooling myself that I could get to the attic, unlock the gun cabinet, and get her some money fast, without her looking up the staircase and seeing me. Yet by the time I had the pull cord in my hand to bring down the attic steps, she was coming upstairs and had probably not even used the bathroom. To heck with it. Later tonight, I'd find another place to stash the money. Somewhere outside the house where no one could find it, if the cops came. It didn't matter if she knew this hiding spot.

I climbed into the attic, went to the gun cabinet, and opened it. From the bag I pulled out five stacks of bills. Then I locked the metal doors, fast, right as LeeLee was scaling up the attic steps. When she got to the top, she saw the cash in my hands. Her eyes widened. I fed on her expression and her greed. Those would work in my favor.

"Oh yeah, boy," she said. "How much more you got?"

"About ten stacks like this," I lied. "You get these five. You're gonna be on the beach in Florida, fanning yourself with the bills."

"How much more you gonna give me?"

"Wait till you get down south. I'll send you two."

"Why should I believe you?"

"LeeLee, I've never lied to you. Now you've got something you can use against me, if you want. Please. Trust me."

I handed her the money.

She said, "No one's ever paid me this much for a couple of fucks before."

"I hope it was worth it." I forced a kind of lightheartedness into my voice. Anything to keep her somewhat happy and get her away from me. She shoved a stack into each pocket, front and back, then put the fifth in her waistband.

"For the money, it was worth it."

"Good."

"For free, though, it sucked."

"Fine."

"I never liked you anyway," she said. "Fucking you was a chore."

"Sorry to hear."

"Even the first time, when we were kids."

"Then why did you?"

"Peh. I needed the money."

She barked it out in disgust or anger or hurt feelings. Whatever it was, I saw that she immediately regretted what she'd said.

"What's that mean?"

"Nothin'."

"You want any more money? Tell me what that means. Or I'm taking it back."

Her hand went to her pocket, to feel the bills that she didn't want gone.

"Come on, Nate. You had to know. All these years? No one said shit to you?"

"Said what?"

"Like, ten of my friends knew. I figured you must have found out sometime."

"That you got pregnant?"

"I was never pregnant."

My face surely betrayed me. I couldn't stop staring at her. And I had to force my lips together, for my mouth was open in bewilderment. She saw that, and then she became the one trying to ease the mood, to keep me on an even keel.

"I needed the money. I was dumb. I wanted to tell you, that's the truth. I felt like shit about it. But then your mom died, and I figured, better to leave it be."

"You . . ."

"It don't matter now anyway, right? All this money, who cares about a thousand dollars?"

"You set me up?"

"I was a stupid kid."

"You weren't pregnant," I said.

She shrugged.

"Can you blame me, Nate? I was trying to get enough money to get outta Locksburg. Same thing you're doing now, isn't it? Ain't it the exact same thing?"

I saw her for what she was then: some made-up, small-town tramp. And I saw myself a little too: a damn idiot, pretty much all my life.

She must have recognized my anger. She stepped back toward the hole in the floor, ready to kneel to take the steps down.

Everything in me said to let her go, get her out of my life, stay quiet, let this part end.

Later on I'd debate myself, whether she fell entirely by accident, helped by the alcohol she'd had at lunch, or if, on purpose, I'd caused her fall by dekeing forward, a quick fake step as if I were charging at her in anger. I wouldn't have touched her, that much I would swear.

But she didn't know that.

LeeLee saw me lurch ahead.

Panicked, she jolted, tripped, and tumbled backward. At first, she fell across the hole in the floor, whacking her head on the side. And she would probably have been fine right there. But then the rest of her fell through the space, and she went down headfirst.

And even from up in the attic, I heard her neck snap when she hit the floor twelve feet below.

CALLIE

The tow truck was moving to the exit, pulling along my car, which had two wheels raised off the ground.

I flung my purse at Gabriella and dashed toward the truck.

"Wait wait wait wait!" I yelled, and waved my arms. There was a string of cars riding along Route 5, delaying the truck from leaving. When I got to my car, I could think of nothing to do other than dive up onto it. The driver heard the thump of my body hitting the hood. He put the truck in park and got out.

"Get the fuck offa there!" he screamed. "You're gonna get killed!"

"You can't take this car!"

"It was parked in a handicapped spot."

"I'm a nurse! I have a patient . . ."

"Where's your handicap tag?"

"I don't have one. Listen to me . . ."

"Law's the law. If you don't got a tag, I'm allowed to tow you."

"I don't have time for this!"

"Neither do I! I'm taking this to the yard. Pay your fine there and you can have the car back."

"I'm not going anywhere. And you can't move this car while I'm on it. That's a law too!"

"I'll call the cops. Somebody tried this on me last month. The cops automatically arrest you. Lady, you got one chance to get off there before you go to jail."

When I didn't move, he took a cell phone from his pocket.

I pleaded, "Listen to me! I need this car right now! Please don't take it!"

"I'm counting to three."

I had no idea what to do. But when he got to three, his cell phone rang in his hand. He sneered at me and turned away. He talked to someone for half a minute, hung up, then said to me: "All right, I'm gonna let you go! I'll bring the car down right here. Get off it."

"You promise?"

"Yeah. Now get off!"

"Say you promise!"

"I promise, ya frickin' nutter! Now go! I gotta hurry!"

I slid off the hood and sprinted around to the open driver's-side door of the tow truck, in case he tried to speed off. But he was keeping his word: he pulled a series of levers on the side of the truck. The winch lowered my car. Then he disconnected the hooks and the sling. I jogged back to the car and got in, but I needn't have hurried—he drove the tow truck out of the lot, pulled a hard left, and sped away.

I started the car and drove over to Gabriella, who was standing at the bar's front door. She got in the car, and we took off.

"Did you see that?" I said in a voice that was loud with victory. "I put him in his place! I always say that to myself: Be tenacious! Be bold! That's how you win in this world!" The energy was pulsing through me. "My god, I wish someone had videotaped it! Not that I'd have anyone to show it to. But I did it! I showed that fucker that I wasn't going to be pushed around!"

Gabriella sighed.

"See, you don't understand!" I said to her. "Tow truck drivers are notorious pricks. No one ever gets away from them without paying. But I did! You need to be impressed, Gabriella! Right now!"

"Oh, I am," she said, droll.

"I was up there on the hood! Am I totally crazy or what?"

Gabriella rolled her eyes.

"What?"

She opened my purse and took my cell phone out. Then she showed me a set of numbers from the recently dialed list.

"What's that?"

"The tow truck guy's number."

"Where'd you get it?"

"Uh, it was painted on the side of his truck?"

"Oh. Duh. Yeah. Are you planning to call him or something?" She shook her head, more annoyed at me.

"I did call him. While you were sprawled out on the hood of your car." She put on the voice of a very uptight woman: "Hi, Al's Towing? I'm broke down here, right at the exit to Route 61. I've got a really important event that I must get to. If you send someone out here in ten minutes, I'll give them a hundred-dollar tip. Hurry, please."

"Oh my god!"

"Yeah, it was divine inspiration."

"You brilliant little . . . liar!"

"OK. I lied. But we were in the right. I'm thinking God'll give us a pass."

"If there is a god, he's already got a thing against tow truck drivers. So we're good."

We arrived at Paul's convenience store as the lights were being switched off. I told Gabriella to wait in the car. She only nodded, visibly tired.

The kid, Randy, had locked the door to the store. I rapped on the window.

"No no no no! You're not closing up yet. Get me my Pall Malls!" I dangled the key. He frowned and let me in.

"Paul said it was OK, huh?"

"Either that, or I picked his pocket."

"Better his pocket than his nose," Randy said.

"Don't underestimate me."

"You can pick your friends . . ."

"But you can't pick your friend's nose. Heard that joke a thousand times. Now give me the damn cigarettes."

He brought out a carton from the back room and sold me two packs.

"Oh, look at this!" I said. In a display by the counter were cans of WD-40. "Give me a can of this stuff too. Need to stop some squeaks."

"Sounds like a personal problem."

After he rang it up and put it all in a paper sack, I said:

"Tell Paul I said thank you, again."

"I will."

"He's really nice."

"Yeah, he's a good boss."

"Is he, um . . . ? I never met him before. Is he, uh . . ."

"He ain't married."

"I wasn't going to ask that."

"Liar."

"Caught me," I said, and we both smiled. "Don't tell him I asked."

"You didn't ask it," Randy said. "Your eyes did, though."

"Are you shittin' me?" I said.

"I shit you snot," he said, and handed me the bag.

In the car, Gabriella was reclined, her head back on the headrest.

"You all right?"

"I'll be good," she said, and shifted in her seat, then grimaced, which I didn't like to see. "Get the cigarettes?"

"Yeah. Some WD-40 for the wheelchair wheels too."

I drove to the trailer park. Gabriella stayed in the car while I knocked on the manager's door.

"Took ya long enough," Wendy said, and reached for the Pall Malls that I held up for her to see.

I pulled them back.

"Where's Kelsey live?"

She pointed next door.

"You're shittin' me."

She grinned and shook her head. "Nope, I ain't a shitter. She's in trailer number two."

She snatched the cigarettes from my hand, cackled loudly, and slammed her front door hard enough so that the trailer's windows rattled. I could hear her chortling inside, before a round of coughing stopped her. Then yet another hock that preceded yet another thick spit.

Gabriella considered me through the open car window.

"Did you hear that?" I asked.

"The loogie?"

"No. Did you hear where Kelsey is?"

"Next door?"

"Right."

"Stay here," I told her. "I'll be back in a minute."

I didn't bother moving the car. It was barely a thirty-yard walk. Unlike the manager's trailer, this one was shoddy and blotched with green mold on the outside walls. I could hear the television inside. I knocked. The light changed in the peephole; someone had peered out. I knocked again.

"I saw that you saw me," I announced. "So open the door, Kelsey." Nothing.

"I can yell out here all night, until someone calls the cops. Is that what you want?"

"Go away!" she bellowed from inside. "I gotta get to sleep. I got a job interview tomorrow."

"Talk to me, please."

She opened the door a crack. I stood on a couple of cinder blocks that functioned as steps, and put a hand on the door.

"Kelsey, listen, Gabriella needs her medicine. You have to give it back to me."

"What medicine?"

"I can't play this game. I know you stole it from the back seat—"

"I ain't—!"

"And I need it now. Not just for her, but for you. That stuff is not your average painkiller. You could overdose."

"I don't know what you're talking about! I ain't no thief! So get the fuck out of here!"

Kelsey went to pull the door shut and missed the handle, probably half drunk already. I grabbed hold, flung it open, and pushed past her on my way inside, all while she repeated her claims of innocence.

The place stunk of mildewed carpet and cat shit and reeked of despair. Every piece of furniture was of a different variety: a soiled blue plush sofa, a ceramic table lamp, a second lamp, bare-bulbed, made of stainless steel, and two end tables that didn't match. The only thing they all had in common was they were all unclean. There was nothing on the paneled walls to indicate an interest in anything, and without looking, I would bet the sink was piled high with unwashed dishes.

On the sofa was the zippered case that held Gabriella's drugs. Kelsey saw what I was staring at. She tossed a stained throw pillow over top of the case, as if that would retroactively hide what we'd both already seen.

"I thought you said you didn't have it?"

"Get out before I call the cops on you!"

I made sure I paused and lowered my voice before saying: "Do it. Call the police. Now."

When she went quiet, I said, "Know what? I'll call them for you."

I can't say if I was going to call the police or not, though it didn't matter. Before I could do anything, a hand came from behind me and slapped the phone from my grip. I spun in anger, ready to ream out whoever did that. But when I turned, the barrel of a wicked, brushed-stainless-steel handgun—it was a .357 Magnum; I know because my dad used to own one—was about three inches away, aimed at my forehead.

The guy holding it pulled the hammer back.

"I don't know what you want," the guy said. "But I do know you really fucked up."

Then he slapped me across the face with the gun.

ANDY

When I was twenty-one I got into a fight with another junkie. We were both irritable and withdrawing and bad-tempered during a sticky Philadelphia summer heat wave that had dragged on for weeks and was exacerbated by a shortage of product on the streets. I wore no shirt, and when he pulled a kitchen knife and slashed me, he opened a nine-inch gash below my belly button. I looked down to see my own intestines about to slide out. Fearing that they might end up frying on the hot city sidewalk, I held a hand over the wound while speed-walking three blocks to the emergency room.

About a year later, I bit into a hidden fragment of chicken bone and cracked two rotten molars down to the exposed nerves, and felt electric anguish that made me breathless. I won't mention—all right, I will—the Doberman pinscher that once sank its slobber-dripping teeth through the flesh of my upper arm, or the cop who did his best Babe Ruth impression by swinging his billy club into my kneecap hard enough that my knee bent inward.

My point is, I'm no stranger to pain. But when that priest focused all two hundred and seventy-five pounds of himself onto only a few square inches of shoe heel and pressed directly into my ripped-open, taped-closed calf, I thought that the torture was going to explode my heart or burst a vein deep in the gray meat of my brain. Mercifully, I passed out.

It was probably only a minute or two later when I woke. The priest had gone into the kitchen, gotten the pot that had the remnants of the canned food I'd burnt the night before, and filled it with water from the tap. He splashed it on my face. I woke, then groaned, and wished I would pass out again.

"Would you like me to hurt you one more time?" he asked.

I had no desire to piss him off with a smart-ass answer. I just rolled my head back and forth on the floor.

"Good. You're learning. Now I'm going to ask you some questions. And you should know this: for twenty-some-odd years, I've been working with addicts and thieves and every kind of liar there is in this world. So if you tell me something that's not true, I will know it. Do you understand?"

"Yeah."

"And do you believe me?"

"I do," I said honestly. He was some kind of sick psycho. But he was some kind of shrewd one too.

"Very good. Now. Where did you take the photo albums?"

"I need somethin' to drink. Can you get me a cup of water? Please."

He stepped back into the kitchen. He half filled the dirty pot with tap water and brought it back to me. I took it and sipped despite the floating mess in there.

"You've had your water. Now, where are the things you stole?"

"I took them out of your car. Then I ran down the street and hid them in an abandoned house."

"Which street?"

"I don't know."

He picked up his foot, preparing to push it down on my wound, and I yelped like a dog, cowardly, wanting only not to be hurt again.

"Wait! It's true! I know where it is! I do! I just don't know the street name! I got them! I swear!"

He moved his foot back. "Continue."

I took the pot, gulped some more water.

"I sat in this abandoned house. And I kept them there. I didn't want to bring them here."

"So how are you going to get them back for me?"

"Tomorrow. When it's light out. I mean, I don't know if I could find the house now in the dark. Even if I could, there's no light in there, and the place is falling apart."

I knew I could find the house. But I needed some leeway. I gazed at him in fear, to see if he bought it, and he did.

"Go on."

"So when it's light, I'm going back there. I'll get the pictures and give them to you right away."

"Let's go tonight," he said.

"I can't walk! Look at my leg! I fell through the stairs. You wanna search through a dark abandoned house at night? You want people seeing you, a priest, going into one?"

He was debating the point with himself. I fed his thoughts, to get him to turn to my way of thinking. "I'm gonna get them first thing tomorrow. Leave your number here. I'll go there and get them and call you. I fuckin' swear."

"I have your number. I'll call you."

He looked at me, as if he were waiting for a question.

"What?" I said.

"Aren't you the least bit curious about how I got your phone number and your address?"

"Oh, I'm so sorry. But my curiosity is a bit dulled by some intense fucking pain at the moment. So, you know, my apologies for not asking. But I bet you're going to tell me."

"At the church you had said that Chief Kriner had referred you to me. He's a friend of mine. I called him and asked for your information, said I'd misplaced it."

"Ah. There's a good friend to have."

"While we were on the phone, I told the chief that he should be very concerned about you. I told him that you were a compulsive liar, and that you had violent thoughts about people in authority, me included. And that you'd admitted to me that you broke into houses in this town. My professional opinion was that you weren't to be trusted about anything, especially since you were an addict, and probably one with a long arrest record. So if you're thinking of going to the police, think again. And if you don't think I could kill you and get away with it, well, just try. I'd say you attacked me. It's time to realize that you've already lost this game."

"I'm not playing any games."

"That's good. So when do I get my photos?"

"Tomorrow."

"I'll call you early."

"Make it noon," I chanced. "You know, by the time I get over there and all."

He didn't have to say anything threatening or badass. Most guys who do, I've found, tend to be full of shit. It's the quiet ones who need to be watched the closest.

He put his hand on the door, and before he could turn it, I called out: "How about the money?"

"You'll get some," he said.

"How about a—you know, a down payment? In case I need to take a cab over there, with my leg like that, or buy food or something?"

He opened his wallet, took out what I later counted to be two hundred dollars, and let the bills flutter to the floor beside me. Then he opened the front door.

Before the priest left, he stared down at me, this battered, useless ex-junkie. I registered his disgust. His smug smile declared that he had won, and that he and his kind would always win, and that he would prove it to me over and over again if needed. It was that grin that had me giving up any idea of trying to get the police involved. Guys like him always found ways out of their crimes. No, he'd made it all unforgivable when I saw the pictures of the Down kid in his photo album. And he'd made it personal when he'd come into the house where my family had lived and touched things that they had once touched.

He left the house. A car started, then drove away.

After a few minutes I moved myself into a sitting position. The blood under the duct tape had loosened it, and some of the fluid leaked out; if the wound had begun to close, it had reopened when he stepped down on my calf. There was one good thing about this new injury, though: it was so agonizing that it stopped me from thinking of the pain in my face where he'd slugged me. I reached up and felt the tender swelling under two eyes that would turn them both black and blue tomorrow, if it hadn't already.

It took a half hour for me to stand. The first ten minutes were spent pulling myself up onto the sofa. Then another ten minutes for me to rise, fall, scream, then try and fail again. After I finally made it to my feet, I opened the front door to go on the small porch. The light breeze would feel good on my skin.

Outside, I didn't sit. I couldn't trust that I would be able to get up again. Instead, I leaned on the railing and stared out over the block. The streetlights hummed, and though I hadn't smoked in years, I would have huffed down a pack now if I'd had one.

Half a block away someone was shuffling along the street. The gait was recognizable before the face came into view. The guys at the gas station called him Brain Dead Brian. He was about thirty but moved like he was a sixty-year-old with flaming hemorrhoids. When he wasn't stoned or nearly blind drunk, he was offering to sell you something—Oxy, weed, a radio he swore he'd found—or just stopping to talk. I tried to keep away from him, to avoid temptation, but when he'd see Kate, Angie, and me walking, he'd turn into a bit of a kid himself, excited. He'd high-five Angie and ask her how she was, then give Kate and me the standard Locksburg greeting, "Hiya," before filling us in on local gossip. Some places had town drunks. Locksburg had Brain Dead Brian, the town's all-substance addict.

When Brain Dead Brian caught sight of me on the porch, he sauntered over.

"Hiya," he said.

"Yo," I said, sticking with the Philly tradition.

"'Sup?"

"Nada."

"What's wrong with your face?" He shifted his position and moved forward for a better angle. "Ho' shit, man. You get cold-cocked?"

"You should see the other guy."

"Yeah?" he said eagerly. "Bet you fucked him up, didn't you?"

"He's fucked up all right."

"I hear that, man, I hear that."

"Going home, Bri?"

"Yeah, yeah. You?"

"This is my home."

"Oh yeah. Duh. Heh."

We stood there—me on the porch, him on the sidewalk—in a not-uncomfortable silence.

"So, how's your little Angie Angel? Ain't seen you walking around in a while."

And all at once I felt sad not for me, not for Kate or Angie, but for Brian, who would now have to learn.

"Brian. She, uh . . . she died, man."

He looked away, then up the street, hiding his eyes from me.

"Hey, dude. Andy. Like, people fuck with me all the time.

I know they're only having fun but . . . I mean . . . you ain't fuckin' with me, are you?"

"I'm afraid I'm not. She had this heart problem that some Down kids have. We knew it was comin' but . . ." I stared up at the sky, checked out a couple of stars, found that appropriate.

Brian lifted his shirt, exposing a hairy belly, and used the bottom of the shirt to blow his nose and dab at his tears. Then he made his way up the front steps, walked over, and hugged me hard. I hugged back, wincing at the pain in my face and leg. Finally, I double-tapped his back and we moved apart.

"I'm so sorry, man. I, uh, I loved her."

"I know you did. She loved seeing you. You were nice to her."

"How's Kate holding up? Can I go inside and maybe say my condolences?"

"Brian . . . you know everything in this town. How come you don't know about what happened?"

"I been out of it for the past few days. You know how it is."

"Yeah, I know."

"You used to ride the horse too, didn't you?"

"Yeah. I rode for years."

"So you understand."

"I do. Brian . . . Kate is dead too. When Angie went . . . she decided to go with her."

"Oh."

"I'm sorry, man," I said. It seemed like the thing to say, though I didn't know who or what I was sorry for. Maybe everything in the world.

"I wish I knew," Brian said. "I wish I coulda helped you all or something."

"That's good of you. Thanks. Hey. I'm gonna go inside now, OK?"

He nodded. Moved off the porch, returned to the sidewalk.

"I'm sorry again," he said. "For your loss."

And as strange as it seemed, what happened next was a heart-felt move that touched me deeply. Brian again went up the three steps to my porch, walked over, and hugged me another time. Then he went back down.

"Bro. Andy. I mean, if you want a taste or anything, to help you through, let me know, OK?"

I wasn't offended. In the ways of junkies, it was perhaps the kindest thing he could have said. We both knew the lay of the land.

And my god, how exquisite a taste would be right now, I thought. Something to get rid of all the pain I had, in body and mind. And with the two hundred dollars from the priest, I could buy enough to end all my sufferings for good. I considered it, so seriously that I licked my lips and felt my arm tingle, as it used to in anticipation of a coming dose.

Then I recalled the priest. And his photos. And that smug smile he flashed on the way out of my house.

I said, "Thanks, Brian. But maybe another time."

"OK, man," he said. "Get some sleep, Andy."

Then Brain Dead Brian, who wore the same dirt-caked clothes for months on end, and hadn't cut his hair in years, and when he did bathe, soaked his body in shallow, algae-filled pools in the nearby Susquehanna River, said gently: "No offense, man, but you look like shit."

NATHAN

One day at work years ago, Chester Stanley hoisted a ten-foot-long, fifty-pound piece of iron bar onto his shoulder to move to a pile at the other end of the warehouse. Caught up in the work, he didn't notice I was standing to his side. He spun around fast, and the bar walloped me on the temple, hard enough to drop me to my knees. Most of the pain faded after an hour, but the blow left a faint, high-pitched whine behind everything I heard for the rest of the day, even later at Maxie's, where Chester had taken me to buy me beers as an apology.

The same kind of whine sounded in my ears the moment I scrambled down the attic steps to find LeeLee on the floor, her neck and head in a horrid contortion, her fall brutal though bloodless. From that moment on, my emotions weren't heightened. They were tamped down, and my mind buried most everything else but thoughts of what needed to be done to save myself. I don't know if that means I'm some kind of monster or merely a man of extreme focus. Maybe sometimes they're the same thing. What I understood was that if I dawdled, the rest of my life would be spent locked in a prison cell, and Paula would be ruined as well, shunned and shamed at the very minimum, perhaps arrested as an accessory to my theft.

I grabbed a tarp from the garage, one that we used as a drop cloth for painting, and brought it upstairs to wrap LeeLee in. Before covering her, I took the money and returned it to the gun cabinet, then emptied her pockets of everything else: apartment keys, three one-dollar bills, a credit card, and a cell phone. Then I checked her neck for a pulse that I knew I wouldn't find, as her skin was already growing cold. Nothing. I rolled her up in the tarp, then used packing tape to seal the tarp tight.

I carried her body down the steps and into the bed of my pickup, where I roped four cinder blocks to the tarp. Better to do it in my driveway where I was alone and shielded than at Laurel Lake, where anyone could come by without warning. I put my jon boat on top of the tarp. The boat stuck up over the closed tailgate and I tied it down to the bumper. Then I left my cell phone and LeeLee's in the garage and drove slowly, all the while thinking: *Don't dwell on what happened. Get this done right.*

To get to where I was going, I needed to drive across town, and I set out with care. Queen Street was as crowded as it got—two cars at the main intersection light. I stopped behind them just as Cigar John, a local retiree, lumbered out of Blake's News and Smoke Shop. He saw me, held up a hand.

"Goin' fishin'?" he called.

"Yep," I called back across the seat and out of the open passenger-side window. Then I looked back to the light, acting like a cautious driver.

He started to walk the twenty feet from sidewalk to street. Any other time, I'd think nothing of it. He probably wanted to tell a story or ask for fishing advice, and I'd double-park and talk, since there was no one behind me, and a summer evening in a small town made it nearly obligatory to stop and shoot the shit.

He closed the distance to ten feet.

I willed the light to change, and when it did, acted as if I hadn't seen Cigar John coming as I drove away, punching the gas far too fast for the middle of town. Four blocks and I was out of Locksburg, and a mile later the road started to rise into the hills.

My eyes flicked to the rearview, and I watched it almost as much as the windshield, worried that someone would follow, or that the truck gate would open and dump the jon boat and LeeLee's body onto the road. I drove as unhurriedly as possible and, when cresting a rise on Michaux Road, nearly pissed myself: two state police cars and two unmarkeds were parked ahead on the side of the road, at the remains of the burned house.

I checked the speedometer twice to make sure my speed was under the limit, and passed them by without a second glance, afraid that someone might call out and order me to stop. I got to Laurel Lake, five miles farther, and saw no other cars on the way.

It was after six on a weeknight, and the lake, always secluded, was deserted. After the boat went in the water, so much seemed to go wrong. Picking up LeeLee's body wasn't too difficult. Yet with the cinder blocks and rope, the unwieldiness had me tripping along the short dirt path from truck to water, all the while keeping an ear open for approaching cars. Finally, I got her into the boat and shoved off from the shore.

The trolling motor whirled steadily and moved us two hundred yards to the south center of the lake, the deepest section at thirty feet. There, I leaned back and to the left while pitching the tarp over the front right side. The boat rocked wildly twice before righting itself. In the water, bubbles rose for a minute before tailing off. LeeLee was now resting on the bottom. I looked around the lake to make sure no one was watching, and my eye caught the top of Rock Mountain, a mile in the distance, the place where I'd proposed to Paula. I imagined us there, looking down at the lake all those years ago, never imagining that I would be doing such a thing here. My ignorance must have been so blissful.

After a minute, I returned my attention to the water. I debated saying some type of prayer or a quiet apology. Yet, though I was sorry about what had happened, I now blamed LeeLee's lies for setting in motion, twenty-four years ago, what had brought us to this day.

How true all that was, I don't know. But I didn't need it to be true to at least believe it for a little while.

• • •

As I drove back to Locksburg, a state police car pulled out onto the road as I was about to pass the burned house. I slowed and the car left the lot, and another followed him. While I waited, I got a look at the place: it had been sifted through, and a couple of men were poking around in the middle of the mess.

It was dark by the time I returned home and unloaded the boat. I went back out and parked around the block from LeeLee's apartment, let myself in with her key, and began throwing things into two trash bags—jewelry, some of her clothes, all of her picture frames. The two bags went into the dumpster at work, along with her key. The only thing left to get rid of was her cell phone. I scrawled through her contacts, found one for the mayor, and typed and sent him a message: *OK then, I quit. Going south. Away from you, Dickhead.*

I taped the phone onto the underside of an eighteen-wheeler that was leaving the next morning to deliver metal shelving to a warehouse in Tennessee. Somewhere during the eight-hundred-mile drive, bumps and other movements would loosen the packing tape until the phone dropped off, hopefully onto the road where it would be crushed or simply run out of power.

But until then, the phone's location would ping as if LeeLee were traveling south and had left Locksburg behind, as she always told anyone who would listen that she one day would.

...

The shower steamed until the water ran cold. I stood under the spray, trying to stop thinking of what had happened to LeeLee. When I could get the images out of my head, questions arose to replace them, too many to answer: Was it really an accident? Was I a terrible person? Did I forget any evidence that would give me away? After the shower, I opened a bottle of Four Roses bourbon and tried to drink the questions away. Instead, the booze multiplied them.

On and on they went, and they had me examining every moment of my life, it seemed, even as I tried to tell myself that big questions weren't my strength. Such questions were for well-to-do people who lived in coastal cities and worked in offices and had more money and free time than I'd ever have.

No, I lived in Locksburg, where, most outsiders believed, nothing much happens and we don't think any kind of deep thoughts.

CALLIE

"That'll shut you up," the guy said after hitting me across the face with the gun. My hand went to my nose, came back with a smear of blood across my palm.

The guy said, "I was tryin' to chill the fuck out, and you come in here all screamin'."

"Who do you think you are?" I said. With no thought I reached out to try to slap the gun from his hand. A good way to get a bullet in the face. But being struck was so sudden and unexpected that I wasn't thinking straight.

"Don't do that, unless you want a hole in your forehead." He lowered the gun to his side and stepped in front of the door, blocking my way. "Now, who're you?"

Even if he wasn't holding a gun, the guy would have been terrifying. He had the jumpy, substance-fueled behavior that I'd seen in coke snorters and meth heads and hard-core alkies who found their way into the hospital. But he was young enough that his body hadn't yet been beaten down badly by the drugs. Despite the flaky skin and some angry acne, his arms were muscled and his chest was wide. After years of weighing patients, I can guess anyone's within a few pounds, and he was one seventy-five, five foot eleven. He might have been decent-looking had he changed out of a ripped Bon Jovi concert T-shirt and washed and cut his slimy hair, which was a half inch away from being officially deemed a mullet.

"Who the fuck are *you*?" I spat, with a weighty stress on the last word.

"I'm the guy who hit you. And I might be the guy who shoots you. So shut the fuck up and start talkin'."

"Well, which one do you want, you rocket scientist? Should I shut the fuck up or start talkin'?"

His other hand swung out with a short smack to my nose that upgraded my pain to agony. My eyes teared, though I wasn't going to cry in front of the bastard.

"I ain't askin' again."

I pointed to Kelsey. "I came here to get my stuff that she stole from me."

He smirked and said to Kelsey, "Ah, this is her?"

"Uh-huh," Kelsey said. "That's her, Lester."

"Why you carrying that juice around, hon?"

"I'm not your hon," I said to this guy, who was three or four years younger than me. "I'm a nurse. That stuff belongs to my patient."

"The other girl ain't no patient," Kelsey said. "She's fine."

"Thank you for your diagnosis, Doctor Kildare. You graduated from Harvard Medical, right?"

Lester said, "I googled that stuff. It looks tasty."

"Tasty enough to kill you. I want it back."

"You ain't getting shit. So leave here now."

He remained in the path to the door.

"Then move," I said.

He didn't, and something in the air changed.

"Or why don't you get us some more?" he said in a *just us* whisper that made my skin crawl.

"OK," I said. "Let me out. I'll go get plenty of it."

"She's lyin'!" Kelsey, Queen of Obvious, declared.

"You know, honey, I'd rap you again across the mouth if your face wasn't so fucked up already."

Kelsey haw-hawed, and I wasn't sure which one of them I hated more at that moment.

"How'd you get that, suckin' dick?" Lester said. He was the one haw-hawing this time until I said:

"Yeah, like your daddy used to do."

Both of them inhaled. If something in the air had changed before, now it was charged with fury.

"You gonna let him say that about Daddy, Lester?" Kelsey said.

Lester's hand darted out, fast as a cobra, and gripped my neck. I kept backing up until I fell onto the sofa. Lester stood above me.

"Oh, you just fucked up real bad."

"You did!" Kelsey said. "Talkin' about our family that way. You bitch."

Maybe it was a survival instinct, to keep my mind from going full panic, but all I could think of was how I would tell this story later. How I would recall it in detail during my talks with the police, or in court, or to the doctors who would patch me up, if I got out of there alive.

"Listen to me . . ." I croaked, my throat on fire even though Lester had let go.

"Get up," he said.

I didn't know if I should, though I hated being on the sofa in such a weak position. So I stood. Lester's voice went lower, and that made it more awful.

"Come on back in the bedroom with me."

"Listen . . ." I said.

"Go ahead, Lester," Kelsey spat. "Fuck her up."

"Oh, I'll do more than fuck her up. I'll see how good that ugly mouth works too."

"What are you going to do?" I pleaded. "Go to jail for the rest of your life? For me? That what you want? 'Cause they'll catch you."

"Hon, I'm already guaranteed a life sentence if they catch me," he said, with a tinge of evil pride. "I been running from them for a year now, and they ain't caught me yet. So anything I do to you is free."

"He already killed one guy who talked shit to him. You shoulda watched your disgusting mouth," Kelsey said. "Now you're gonna learn."

"Please think about this," I said weakly. "Please."

That only made him grin wider. He grabbed my wrist, twisted it, and began to pull me toward the back of the trailer.

Knock. Knock. Knock.

Three raps on the front door. Lester looked at Kelsey and raised his chin. Kelsey got the message and called out: "We're busy in here! Are we bein' too loud? We'll keep it down!"

"Is Callie in there?" Gabriella said.

"She left!" Kelsey said.

"Callie?" Gabriella said, loudly but not urgently. "Are you in there doing those drugs?"

Lester whispered in my ear, "Tell her to get lost."

"Go wait in the c-car, Gabriella," I said.

"Did you want me to bring in the rest of the stuff?" she said.

Lester gawked at Kelsey, who shrugged. To me he whispered, "What's she talkin' about?"

"Nothing. I don't know."

Gabriella called out, "Callie! The bag is heavy! You want the rest of this, or should I put it back in the car?"

Curiosity mixed with greed immediately got the best of Lester. He was done whispering.

"What're you talkin' about?" he said toward the door.

"Callie's got like fifty vials of that stuff she stole from the hospital!" Gabriella said.

"She's lying," I said.

"Are you gonna sell it to them or not, Callie?" Gabriella said with impatience.

"We're buying it!" Lester called. "Hold on."

He whispered in my ear, "You try anything, and I got nothin' to lose. Unnerstand? I'll put bullets in both of you if you fuck with me."

Lester tucked the gun into the waistband behind his back. He pushed me against the small counter that served as a kitchen. If I tried to run, the only way would be farther into the trailer. He unlocked the door. Gabriella was standing on the cinder-block steps holding a brown paper shopping bag, the one we got from Paul's barely half an hour ago.

"So are you guys buying this from Callie or not?"

"We are!" Lester said.

"Yeah, we'll buy it!" Kelsey added over him.

"So where's the money?" she asked. I had no clue what she was saying, or where she was going with this, but the performance was Oscar-worthy.

"We'll get it, we'll get it," Lester said. "You gotta show us the stuff first. That's the deal."

She stepped inside the trailer and stood in the center of the room.

I stared at Gabriella and only then saw that her hand was through the underside of the bag. She was short and Lester couldn't see it, not with his height and at his angle. But her hand was inside it, coming up from the bottom.

With her other hand, Gabriella parted the top of the bag, which she held up straight.

"There's like fifty vials in here," she said.

Lester stepped forward. He was so hungry for drugs that he even leaned down to put his face closer. One hand reached over and opened the bag wider.

When Lester's face was inches from the top, Gabriella moved it closer. Then a pressurized discharge—*Tsssss!*—like an over-inflated tire blasting air from a puncture sounded. A spray shot out of the bag and into Lester's eyes. He yowled and clawed at his face. Gabriella pulled her hand from the bottom of the bag, holding the can of WD-40, and kept spraying. Lester yowled. She shot it into his mouth, like one of those carnival water-pistol games. Lester inhaled it, gagged, and covered his eyes. He tried to turn away from her. Gabriella followed him around with the can just inches from his face. She had emptied enough of the oil and chemicals to blind him for hours. Still, she kept spraying.

With both of Lester's hands at his face, it was comically easy to snatch the gun from the waistband of his pants. I took it just as Gabriella stopped spraying and brought the edge of the can down on Lester's wrinkled forehead. That opened a cut that spewed blood, and that flowed into his eyes too. I swung the butt of the .357 onto the top of his head, and Lester dropped to the floor.

Kelsey was screaming all kinds of things—"Oh my god, Lester!" and "What did that bitch do?" and "Get the fuck outta here!"—and making up several new phrases until she saw that now I was the one with the gun. That shut her up instantly.

"Come on," I said to her, and motioned to the door.

"I don't wanna . . ."

"Now."

I pointed the .357 at her with authority. She moved toward the door.

Lester was on his knees, moaning and bleeding and coughing out a string of "Oh fuck oh fucks" that came out like "Urg feec! Urg feec!" I couldn't help calculating—that cut would take twelve stitches to close. You can never stop being a nurse.

When Gabriella and Kelsey busted out of the trailer, I lingered inside for only a moment, sizing Lester up. He may have other guns in the trailer, but his eyes wouldn't be functioning, at least not tonight. Yet I needed assurance that he would be incapacitated. OK, that's a lie. What I really wanted was revenge. So I prepared perfectly, like a football punter under no time pressure, and laid the hardest kick I could into his crotch. He wailed and keeled over onto the floor, where he wrapped himself in the fetal position.

I grabbed the zippered case with Gabriella's drugs from the sofa and checked it. Everything was there. Got my phone off the floor.

Then, still in kicking mode, I booted open the door of the trailer.

"You hurt my brother! You should be ashamed of yerself!" Kelsey was screaming outside, completely oblivious to the fact that her beloved sibling was, minutes earlier, ready to rape and perhaps kill me. It took a lot of willpower not to punt her in the crotch too.

"Go over to the car," I ordered, and pointed with the gun. She moved fast.

Gabriella got in. Before I did the same, I pushed Kelsey forward.

"Get in front," I said. "Sit down."

"You gonna run me over?" Kelsey's eyes went wide.

"Are you really that stupid? Sit!"

Kelsey lowered herself to the ground. I started the car. The headlights blinded her, and she appeared pathetic there, her mouth twisted in anger and hatred. I had half a mind to deliver a lecture, try to talk some sense into her. She was barely older than a girl and already a mess. But what to say? How to teach someone? How to explain to her where her life was headed? As I was considering it, Gabriella looked at her from the open car window.

"Deep down, you're the one who's ugly," she said to Kelsey.

That would work just fine.

I turned the car around and punched the gas. Gravel spun into the air and rained down on Kelsey as we sped away from the trailer park.

. . .

Gabriella and I were silent for nearly a minute as we drove. When we were certain that no one was following us, I exhaled air that felt like it had been in my lungs for an hour.

"Oh. My. God."

"Holy moly!" Gabriella's voice rang out. "That was . . . awesome!"

"Are you out of your—?"

"We rule!" she said, and put up her hand for a high five. It remained in the air until I had to take a hand off the steering wheel and slap.

I tried to speak, but when Gabriella laughed with delight, I couldn't help but let out a kind of "Huh! Huh!" that would have had me rolling my eyes if I hadn't been watching the road. Still, I managed to smile.

We were a mile from Route 61, and on the side of the road was an auto-parts store, closed, with a dark parking lot. When I examined it more closely, I saw what I'd hoped for: a pay phone. I pulled into the lot and got out of the car. With a section of my blouse, I wiped off the gun as best I could, then tossed the gun into the weeds behind the pay phone. Then I dialed three digits.

"Nine one one. What's your emergency?"

"Take this address: Lee Mountain Trailer Park. Trailer number two. There's a guy there, Lester, he's wanted by the police. I took his gun from him and threw it behind this pay phone. You can find that later when you trace this call. But for now, get to Lee Mountain Trailer Park, trailer number two. This Lester may have other guns, so be careful. He'll need medical attention too."

"Lee Mountain Trailer Park, trailer number two," the operator repeated.

"Correct."

"What's your name, ma'am?" was all the operator got out before I put the phone back on the hook.

We peeled out of the parking lot and, a mile down the road, saw the sign for the interstate.

As we took the exit, we passed the tow truck from earlier, parked on the shoulder, where the driver was searching for a broken-down car that he'd never find and a hundred-dollar tip that he'd never get.

ANDY

I woke to a suffering made no better by the fact that I had warned myself the night before to be prepared for the morning pain. My leg felt both incredibly tender and as heavy as a bag of wet cement. I knew I needed a few dozen stitches, not duct tape, to close the cut. The hurt had gotten so bad that I wondered if the wound might be deeper than I'd first guessed, and perhaps the muscle had been severely damaged. I cautiously moved my leg over the side of the bed. The clock read 8:07. By the time I rose to a sitting position and was ready to put some weight down, it was 8:21, and sweat was beading on my forehead and top lip.

All along, I bitched and mumbled and moaned and growled phrases like "That motherfucker is mine" and "Good day to die, isn't it, asshole?" and "Oh, I can't wait to fuck him up" and "That son of a bitch won't see tomorrow's sun." Those things were delivered under my breath in a voice that seethed with anger and menace.

And if I'm to be honest, they were bullshit, and maybe even borderline lies.

Could I murder a man? I don't know. I was trying to talk

myself into it while knowing how inept I was, even in simple situations, and how downright frightened I felt. Killing someone is simple in movies and television, where the hero rattles off some cool-sounding line then disposes of the villain without a second thought. That's all fake, insultingly so. To actually carry out a murder takes either blind courage or complete ignorance of what's required and the price it will cost the both of you.

I should know.

I tried to kill someone once.

• • •

I was nineteen and dumb as the day is long, though I don't beat myself up for that too much—being an idiot at that age is normal anywhere else, and practically required in Philadelphia. I'd been shooting up for a while but kept it mostly under control because of Danny Batista, my longtime best friend, whose awful life had made my wreck of an adolescence seem like I was raised on a meadow farm by a convent of cuddly nuns.

Danny and his younger sister, Sophie, grew up in a Kensington row house with a pair of loud and violent parents, who when they died in a drunk-driving accident on the Schuylkill Expressway led even their trashiest neighbors to breathe booze-scented sighs of relief. Danny, who was eighteen at the time, worked like a man twice his age to keep the house going and to raise fifteen-year-old Sophie until she could get away to college. Sometimes I'd stay at their house and wake to find Danny making her French toast. To see this stringy, streetwise guy with an apron around his waist, struggling to raise the both of them above the shit that they had been born into, astonished me. And watching Sophie come home with gold stars for perfect attendance and ribbons from a science fair seemed to lift me up too. They made me think that I could have a future.

The recession brought Philadelphia to its knees, and Danny was laid off from his construction job. He started to deal a bit of dope to make the mortgage payments on the row house and to save for Sophie's college and keep the braces on her teeth. He had discreet, steady customers, and we would dip into his stash only for an occasional taste. He stayed careful for Sophie's sake. He was far from being a saint, but I think he was closer than almost anyone I'd ever met.

I was at Danny's house one afternoon when someone knocked on the door. It was Slee, an oily addict who occasionally doubled as a dealer. We sometimes saw him around the way, and gave him no more than a nod. He was the type of guy you never felt comfortable around, and even the former convicts we knew who were serious bad news avoided him. Slee took that as a point of pride rather than an offense.

"Yo," he said to Danny, who stood at the front door.

"'Sup?"

"You in the market for anything?"

"I don't deal out of the house," Danny said. "Don't come by here. I'll give you my number, you can call, I'll meet you somewhere else."

"I hear ya," Slee said. "Thing is, I just came upon something real nice, and I need cash fast, or I'm gonna get my ass kicked."

Danny inspected the block, then let Slee in. There was reason to be less than wary of the police—the crack epidemic was making a resurgence on Philly's streets, and the cops were usually too mired in that mess to give low-level dealers like Danny much trouble as long as they kept their work from being a spectacle on the streets.

"Let's see," Danny said.

Slee reached into his underwear and took out a packet. "That's a half ounce, right there. Weigh it up. No one's stepped on that either. Uncut."

"How much you want?"

"How much you givin'?"

"I'm not here to play games, Slee. Tell me what you're asking."

"How's about . . . we all take a taste. And if you like it, then, say, a thousand dollars."

I raised my eyebrows. At that price, Danny could break it up and make close to eight grand.

"Where'd you get it?"

"Some ho, don't ask me how she got it." Then he added, with a leer that showed a gaudy gold tooth: "I took more than that from her, if you know what I'm sayin'."

"I don't keep any money here," Danny said. It was the line he gave everyone. He had a safe hidden in the kitchen behind the refrigerator and would take cash from there and hand it off to his suppliers later in a public place.

"That's OK," Slee said. "We'll take a taste, then you hit me after."

We went into Danny's basement and sat on a ratty sofa. Sophie wasn't due home for hours from a school event, and we calculated that we'd be straight again before she returned. Slee took a zipped case from behind his back in preparation to tie up, but Danny wanted to smoke instead; that way he could test the quality and regulate his intake.

We piped. When I inhaled, my eyes bugged out in unspeakable pleasure, and my mouth fell open. The stuff was as pure as I'd ever tasted.

"It's like . . . heaven," I breathed.

Danny snickered, just as high, before we both nodded off.

. . .

There are so many memories of my life that I long to erase from my mind, and that afternoon is among the worst. No horror film could ever shake me so much; few tragedies could bring me more tears.

After Danny and I smoked and passed out, I'd come to and worked my way upstairs to use the bathroom. There were smears of red on the kitchen floor, and a bloody handprint streaked on the wall, as if someone tried to hold on while being pulled away. Dumbly, I followed the trail upstairs and pushed open Sophie's bedroom door. She was on the bed, moaning quietly, naked and hideously bruised. I tried to speak with her. She only sobbed and shook her head. I hurried back to the basement to wake Danny.

When we went upstairs, Danny wrapped his sister in a sheet and held her. I stood leaning against the doorway.

Sophie told us.

The three of us cried.

● ● ●

As Danny and I sat in the hospital waiting room, we pieced together the entirety of what had happened. Slee had gotten us stoned, stayed sober himself, then tore apart the house, hunting for money. Sophie had come home unexpectedly early and surprised him, and he'd beaten then raped her.

All while we were nodding off downstairs, not thirty feet away.

● ● ●

Danny asked me to help him find Slee. I told him, give it a week. If the cops didn't get him, we'd do the job ourselves. Danny said no. He didn't want Sophie called in to ID the guy or have her testifying against him. That would only bring her further grief. I told him OK, then, of course I'd help, while secretly hoping that Slee would be caught before we could get to him.

One night, Slee called Sophie. He'd probably gotten her number from one of her school friends. He told her not to pursue charges, or he'd come after her. Then he fed her fear by recalling what he'd done to her and what he'd do again. She hung up and began to weep, and Slee called back twice more until Danny heard and took the phone. Slee laughed as Danny swore that he'd end Slee's life.

We found Slee two weeks later. Danny had talked to a streetwalker who knew most everyone in Kensington. Danny told her: "When you see Slee again, text me, then lead him into an abandoned house with the promise of drugs or sex. We'll come and take care of the rest."

I was at Danny's house when the text came. We were out the door in under a minute. The streetwalker had made the offer, and Slee agreed to take her up on it, right after he made another drug stop. By then we were already waiting in the dark house.

The streetwalker pushed open the front door. Slee was behind her and shoved her into the room, believing them to be alone. Danny had been standing to the side. He slammed the door shut. Slee saw him and darted for the back of the house, only to have me swing out a leg that he tripped over, and he face-planted on the floor. Danny gave him a ferocious kick to the ribs that momentarily paralyzed the guy with pain. Danny flipped the streetwalker a twenty-dollar bill and two hits.

"You see him push me?" she said. "He's a sadistic fucker. Hurt one of my girlfriends real bad a couple of months ago. Fuck him up." Then she was gone.

Slee lay on the floor, getting his breath back. Danny kicked him again, this time in the head, and I flinched at the sight. Even with what Slee had done, I didn't know if I could cross the line and murder him.

"Let's call the cops," I said, then tried to sound tougher. "Put his ass in jail. Let them—"

"We ain't callin' no cops," Danny said. "You cool or not?"

"Yeah, but—"

"If you can't be with me on this, go. Leave now."

I looked at Danny, the guy who let me crash at his house, and cooked for me, and whose beautiful sister was crying herself to sleep at nights, her tears rolling over the bruises that still ballooned under her eyes.

"I'm with you," I said.

We picked up Slee and shoved him into a chair.

I took a box cutter from my pocket, slid open the blade, and stood behind Slee. I pressed the point against his throat.

Danny took out a tie-up and wrapped it around Slee's arm to get a vein, or at least make it appear as if Slee had done so. Then Danny uncapped a syringe that he had filled at home. There was enough heroin inside it to kill Slee. But there was also a dose of battery acid that would sear Slee's brain before he died.

Danny smacked Slee across the face, bringing him to attention.

"Yo, Slee. I want you to think of my sister, OK?"

"I'm sorry," he muttered. "I was all hopped up. I didn't know what I was doin'."

"Well, that's neither here nor there, huh?"

"Just do it," Slee said. His head slumped down so far that I had to move the razor away when his chin hit his chest. "I want you to. I hate who I am. I deserve it. I got raped as a kid. Fucked by my dad. That's what made me this way."

He sounded resigned, pathetic. He said, "I got two kids. One's only a baby. Tell 'em I said I love 'em."

Danny prepared the injection.

I said, "We should beat his ass and call the police, Danny. C'mon."

Danny stared at me with disgust. Looked right in my eyes. When he did, Slee grabbed Danny's hand. He slammed it straight up until the needle was buried into Danny's neck. I hesitated. Then I dropped the razor and reached out to help Danny. But Slee had already pushed the plunger down and emptied the syringe into Danny.

Slee sprang out of the chair and bolted outside. Danny crumpled to the floor in convulsions. He forced a single word from his mouth, repeated three times, as one hand clawed at his skin and the other pointed at the door.

"Get . . . ! Get . . . ! Get . . . !"

I took off, out of the house and down the street. Slee was limping running, holding his side where he'd been kicked. I followed him along the block, maybe fifty yards behind, and kept running as he turned the corner. I tried to pace myself, realizing this could be a long haul and that I'd left the razor back at the house. But after another block I was tiring. All the shit I'd been putting into my body had ravaged it enough that I'd soon collapse from exhaustion. There was no way to keep up.

I was falling farther behind.

Slee glanced over his shoulder, still running faster than me. After fifty more yards, he turned around again to see that his lead had widened.

I saw him grin.

I saw him think that he had won.

I saw him pleased with himself, that his act had worked at the house, where he'd distracted us long enough to escape.

What he didn't see, though, was that he had sprinted out onto Frankford Avenue, where a speeding trash truck slammed into him. His body sailed into the air, thirty yards high and long. He may have been alive when he hit the ground face-first. But then the still-racing truck drove over Slee, crushing his head under the front then back wheels, before the tires screeched and the twenty-ton truck came to a stop.

. . .

With enough time and drugs, I think I could have blurred some of the memories of what had happened soon afterward: returning to the abandoned house to find Danny dead, going back to deliver the news to Sophie, watching her already-bruised heart break. But nothing will blot out what happened three years later. I've tried.

With Danny not around to keep me at least somewhat straight, I plummeted into addiction and was living full time without a home: sometimes under bridges, or in doorways, or, once, in a kid's plywood fort in a trash-strewn vacant lot. My life revolved around a single mission: to find enough money to score. Sometimes that money came through odd jobs, other times through panhandling or theft.

One winter night, I entered a vacant, half-burnt row house in North Philly. The floor crunched under my feet with used needles and broken glass. Some ten people were in various stages of nodding off or firing up. I leaned against a wall then slid down to my ass, ready to sleep.

Across the room a guy put his hand inside the jacket of a woman who was sitting on the floor. She was either sleeping or high, probably both, and had no awareness of what he was doing. He unzipped the jacket to get better access inside, then started to run his other hand along her leg.

"Don't do that shit," I said to him. It came out in a croak. I'd finished a quarter pint of Mad Dog that someone had given me an hour earlier, half of it spit and backwash, and my throat was seared from the cheap booze and from the hit I'd smoked an hour before that.

"Hear me?" I said when he didn't stop.

"Mind your own business," the guy spat. He unzipped the woman's pants.

An empty forty-ounce beer bottle was within reach. I picked it up and without a worry about missing swung it at him. If there had been a bull's-eye on his forehead, I'd have won a kewpie doll, made extra satisfying by the empty *thunk* that sounded on impact.

The guy yelped, and both of his hands went to his head. Then he scrambled to his feet.

"I'm gonna fuck you up!" he yelled. Most junkies are little more than tough talkers and this one was no exception. I didn't bother to stand.

"If you come near me," I said with a voice in complete control, "I'll gut you like a trout."

He huffed as if he weren't scared, but it was only for show. He staggered out the front door, declaring that he'd be back with friends he no doubt didn't have.

The woman sitting across the room shifted, awakened by what had happened. She zipped up the front of her pants.

"You're welcome," I said.

"What?"

"That guy was gonna rape you."

"What do you want, a reward? I don't have any money," she said. Even in the near dark I could see that her front teeth were rotted up to the gums and her hair had been unwashed for weeks, if not longer.

I shook my head and closed my eyes.

Then I opened them for a second glimpse.

"Hey. You. Hey."

She lifted her head. I flicked on a cigarette lighter and looked at her face in the light of a wavering flame.

"*Sophie?*"

"Who are you?"

"Andy. Andy Devon. Are you Sophie?"

"Yeah," she said. "I remember you, Andy."

"My god . . . what are you . . . what the . . . ?"

"Leave me alone," she said.

I moved over and sat by her. "Why are you . . . ?"

"What do you want?"

"Nothin'. Just . . . how ya doin'?"

"How do you think?"

"I remember you went to live with your cousin. After . . . Danny."

"Yeah. In Camden. They were dirtbags."

"Oh."

"And now I'm here. So what?"

I stared into hollow eyes that had once sparkled when she'd hand Danny a test paper that as always would be marked with an A plus. The only things on her face now were dirt and deep fatigue.

Her anger grew the more I spoke, and I was afraid she'd storm out, so I apologized and shut up, and decided to wait until morning to talk to her again, when we'd both be dried out. Once, a couple of hours later, I woke to find her leaning against me. She was asleep.

When the sun shined through the broken windows that morning, I awoke hoping that Sophie's head would still be on my shoulder.

But I felt nothing.

She had gone.

...

I searched for Sophie when I wandered the Philadelphia streets, and asked around for weeks. I sometimes wondered if she had been a drug hallucination. But I knew it was her. I look back at that time as my life's lowest point. Soon I was hitting twenty bags a day, and doing most anything to get the two hundred dollars I needed to buy them. When I would come down, I'd find myself shuffling along, mumbling to myself one moment, screaming aloud the next to drive out the thoughts of Sophie and Danny.

I was convinced then, and remain so today, that because I had hesitated and not cut Slee, I was responsible for Danny's death, which led to Sophie's fall. Because I'd fucked up, I'd destroyed the lives of two good people.

I guess I could say three people.

But I don't count me.

. . .

"So don't fuck this one up too," I said to myself while sitting in my house in Locksburg.

I stood, plopped back down on the bed, then did the same twice more before moving toward the wall to hold me up as I attempted to walk. After using the bathroom and taking another five minutes to raise myself from the toilet seat, I swallowed the last three menstrual cramp pills and washed them down with water.

I hobbled down four of the basement steps, then sat and scooched down the rest of them on my ass until I made it to the floor, where I limped around and found what I'd come for: an old set of crutches from the time when Kate had sprained an ankle. I tried them out, and they would definitely help me get around.

"Now we're cooking with motherfuckin' *gas*!" I cheered, then turned with the crutches and promptly tripped and fell on my face.

. . .

Eventually I made it back up the stairs, then went to my bedroom, found a pair of jeans, and gently pulled them on. They'd be unpleasant to wear in the June heat, but they'd hide my leg wound and were better to have on for the project that I was about to undertake. I scrubbed my face, put on a semi-clean T-shirt, then went into Angie's room. Her school backpack hung on a hook. The backpack was sparkly purple, with pictures of cartoon characters and rainbows. I didn't want to wear it, of course, but it was the only backpack in the house, and I needed one for this job. I put it on.

"Think you can do this?" I said to the living room mirror. "Don't bother leaving the house if you can't. Take the money the priest gave you, get high, and stay here if you can't get this shit done."

I didn't answer aloud. I didn't want to get too confident, or later prove myself to be a liar.

So instead I opened the door and crutched down the street and over to Keiser's Hardware Emporium.

NATHAN

Years of stoicism had me believing that I could withstand anything. Maybe that's true when you're talking about the disappointments of a childless marriage and the frustrations of a dead-end job, all spread out over time. But in less than a week I'd found millions of dollars, lied repeatedly to the police, learned a terrible truth of my youth, and, six hours earlier, sunk a dead body into a lake. It was too much too fast. I felt myself cracking up. Losing it. Going nuts. Any of those phrases we think are so funny as kids but are horrific when you're feeling that way.

I bit at my nails and ripped two of them off with my teeth, drawing blood, as I paced the living room for nearly an hour. When I stopped, I noticed that the rug had begun to wear a little diagonally where I'd walked. After pacing failed to calm me, I started on bourbon and was swilling my third large glass when Paula came in from her night shift at the hospital.

"Hello," she said, and glanced at the glass.

"Hello. How was, uh, work?"

"Fine."

"How's the guy?"

"Another two days to stabilize, then they've got the helicopter scheduled to take him to Philly."

"Is he up?"

"No. He's stirring, though. It'll be soon."

Paula went into the kitchen and I followed.

"Can we talk?"

"We can always talk, Nathan. All I want to do is talk to you. But you shut me down every time."

"I'm sorry. I realize I've been . . . I don't know the word to use. Jumpy. Nervous. But more than that."

"So give the money back."

I swallowed bourbon.

"Does that help?" she asked.

"No."

"So? Will you give it back?"

"No."

"Then this is what we do: burn the bills. Burn it all. That way there's no proof."

"I'm not burning two million dollars. No way. That money is mine. No way."

"So what's left to discuss?"

"Listen: let's go to Florida. Or anywhere else you want. We'll take the money. And . . . we mentioned adoption before. It was so expensive. Now it won't be."

"So that's what this is all about? Kids? You want to buy one with stolen money?"

"You don't want a child?"

"What kind of person asks me a question like that?"

"It was a bad choice of words. I'm sorry."

The kitchen went quiet. Paula pulled out a chair to sit down, thought the better of it, and stayed on her feet. She stared at me before turning away with grief on her face. Then she said words she'd probably had in her heart for a decade or more but never brought out.

"Every single night of every single week of every single year, I'd pray to god that I'd get pregnant. And when I'd see blood once a month I'd lock the bathroom door and sob into a bunched-up towel, then later act like it didn't matter that much when I told you we'd have to try again. But it did matter, Nathan. It mattered more than anything in my life, ever. Years and years of seeing everyone else pushing baby carriages, and of watching kids come into the hospital, some of them with shitty parents, and I'd ask god, Why do you give them children and not me? What's wrong with me? What did I do, god?"

"So maybe this is our answer."

"This is no answer. You asked me if I want a child? More than anything. Well, anything except that money. I won't do it. That's my answer."

"They're going to put me in a cell, Paula. In Carroll Valley prison. That's where I'll go. And I'll die in there."

"Then burn the money. Or throw it in the woods."

"When that guy gets better, he'll send some of his drug-dealing buddies to stick a knife in me."

"I told you what I thought. What else do you want?"

"Here's what I want: you said that Callie is taking that girl out of the hospital tomorrow night, the girl with cancer. They're using the MRI room door, where there's no camera."

"I told you that in confidence. Never tell anyone."

"I want you to open that door for me, after she goes."
"Why?"

"So I can go in and . . . talk to that guy."

"And what if you talk to him, and he doesn't listen?"

"I'll figure that out then."

"And what if someone sees you?"

"I'll say I wanted to check on the guy who I saved. It's understandable."

"And if he gets an infection, from your visit?"

"Know what? I hope he does. The guy should be dead. A god-damn drug dealer. Making meth, probably killing hundreds of kids. He would die, if this world were fair."

"Nathan? Where are you going with this?"

I couldn't say it to her. Couldn't admit it to myself either. The idea had started to form on the first day, I guess. But I refused to acknowledge that I was thinking it. Rather, it danced around the edges of my mind, where I could plausibly deny considering it. Paula kept staring at me. We both knew what I would do to him. Finally she said:

"I'd be afraid to let you into the hospital, the way you're acting. I'd be afraid of what you'd do to that man. You should see your eyes: they're darting all over the place. And your—"

"I'll be there at ten thirty. I'll knock on the door then."

"It's going to stay locked. I won't open it."

"Paula . . ."

"You aren't going to the hospital tomorrow night. And you won't knock on that door. I know who you are, Nathan Stultz. You're the guy who dressed up as Santa Claus to bring me break-fast in bed that year I had the flu at Christmas. That's the kind of man you are. But this money has poisoned your brain. All this pressure you're under? All this pressure you're putting on me? All these wild ideas—and I don't even want to know what you're thinking about doing to that burn patient—and all this paranoia and stress and anger are put there by greed. It's not who you really are. You don't know what you're doing. You can't see that. But I can."

"Just stop talking."

"What would your parents think?"

I can't say exactly which words came out of my mouth next. That would be like trying to count exactly how many shards of glass shattered when I threw my bourbon glass against the wall. Her words were the match that exploded what was in me right then. I merely needed an excuse, one she gave me by mentioning my dad and mom.

I was a wild animal at that moment.

I tore into her.

"My parents? Why the fuck would you bring them into this? You bitch. You think it's so easy to be good, don't you? You don't know shit. You're trying to make me someone I'm not. You don't know who I am! You've never known! You don't know how much I hate this town and this house! Who are *you*, Paula? Who the *fuck* are you?"

I charged forward as I screamed. Started yelling into her face. She stepped back, then again. I kept charging toward her, maybe three inches away, until she was against the wall and had no room to move.

"I'm asking you a question! Who do you think you are? Maybe you're the problem! Always so good! Always so nice! But no fuck-ing kids . . . !"

Her face dropped. As the words left my mouth, I knew they would open a wound that would never heal. To keep Paula from talking, or in disgust with myself, I grabbed her by the shoulders. Shook her.

"You're killing me, Paula! You're ruining my life!"

It was more violent than if I'd punched her a dozen times. Paula was too stunned to speak, and I shoved her away, against the wall. She slid down. Then she curled into a ball on the floor and began sobbing.

I took the bottle of bourbon and marched out to my truck, got in, and drove away from that house and from my wife.

CALLIE

Gabriella and I couldn't shut up.

We ran over every moment of the last two hours, from seeing Kelsey in peril at the gas station ("They were right after all, those jerks who were beating her up!" Gabriella said. I replied, "So it's OK to whack someone around?" Gabriella: "No! Well, maybe her! I don't know. What do you think?" That turned into a twenty-minute debate on crime and punishment), to getting the park manager's cigarettes, to meeting Paul at the Creekside, then to the gun and the menace in the trailer. ("That Lester is probably in jail now, and they're using the WD-40 on his face to grease the locks!" Gabriella cracked.) The smallest moments were magnified by our excitement too—"Remember? He was just about to close the store!"—and we recounted each at least twice. We talked through it while driving through Central Pennsylvania, then into the Lehigh Valley and along the lower range of the Pocono Mountains.

It took two hours of that before we both started to ease off the stories and stare out of the car windows in silence. The trip was nearly two hundred miles, most of it through forests and past farms. The land beyond the highway was often pitch dark and seemed to stretch out into some boundless distance. Occasionally we'd look down into a valley to see the few lights of a lonely town, then pass it, never to see that town again in our lives. That thought brought about a strange sadness in me, for all the things I'd never know or see or understand. Those tiny lights in the deep darkness made me feel so forlorn for those who lived there, and for those who were passing by Locksburg night after night and feeling the same about me. We were all more than lost to each other. We were never to be found, or even known, to nearly everyone else.

"This is the greatest adventure I've ever been on," Gabriella said as we took a bridge over the Delaware River, crossed the state line, and drove into New Jersey. There, at about four a.m., she cranked the radio and searched the dial for a Bruce Springsteen song, now that we were in his home state. One came on about a half hour later, and we sang along to "Thunder Road."

"Men aren't really like Bruce Springsteen, are they?" she asked after the song ended.

"Bruce Springsteen isn't like Bruce Springsteen," I said. "Everything gets romanticized. Even unromantic things. That's what art does."

"I'll never get laid," she said to shock me.

"Well, you ain't missing much," I countered instead of getting flustered.

"Really?"

It wasn't easy to collapse all the normal boundaries that I put up between myself and patients. At the hospital, with teenagers in particular, I'd hold my tongue or adjust my language or water down my comments. Why bother with that here? Nothing I said would be used against me later. No complaints would be filed. Being honest was something I could do for her. Maybe for myself too.

"Really," I said. "Only once. It wasn't . . . well, it wasn't something Springsteen will be singing about anytime soon."

"Tell me."

"Oh gosh, do I have to?"

"Now you're required to! Dish!"

I sighed, trying to be a little theatrical. But the memory was, to me, more melancholy than dramatic. I said:

"A year and a half ago. I started thinking, 'Thirty is on the way. And you'll still be a virgin.' I mean, not that there's anything wrong with that. No, wait, there is something wrong with that, if you don't want to be a virgin. There's something wrong about being a coward and being . . . lonely when you don't want to be."

"So you went for it."

"Yeah. I went for it."

"And . . . ? Don't be shy. I won't tell anyone. I promise. I mean, I won't live . . ."

"I'll tell you the story if you stop saying things like that."

"Deal. So . . . ?"

"I got it in my head that I wanted to have the experience . . ."

"The 'experience'!"

"OK. Sex. And . . . I had some time off work. So I went to Philadelphia for Christmas. Got a nice hotel, walked around the city, seeing all the lights. I told myself that I was just having a vacation. But I knew what I was there for. Near the hotel was this old pub, McGillin's. A little bigger than a bar, but not really a nightclub. A small dance floor. I started drinking. When you look like I do, you get used to men coming up to one side of you, starting to talk, and then when they see the other side of your face . . . I mean, I'm no longer offended."

I paused longer than I expected.

"What?"

"That's a lie. I mean, I thought it was the truth. But now that I said it, I know it's not. I do get offended. Still. These fuckers who think you look great from behind, or talk to you for a minute and call you brilliant, but when they see . . . when they'd see my lip . . . Gosh, it hurts. I can't lie to you and say it doesn't. Or lie to myself."

"It's OK," she said. "You can be mad around me."

"I don't want to be mad at all, to you or anyone."

"Just tell me the story."

"So anyway, the pub is known for its beer and I must have had four or five of them. And at a table behind me was a group of marines. They kept pushing the youngest one to go over and talk to me, this woman sitting alone at the bar. I watched them sometimes from the mirror behind the bar. I'd peek back and see them motioning to the young guy. And finally he comes over. He's so nervous, he keeps looking for the bartender as he starts talking to me. This marine with big ears. All of twenty-one, but looks like he's twelve. And he says:

"'Hi. Oh, and Merry Christmas.'

"'Merry Christmas to you.'

"'My name's Trevor. Can I buy you, like, a beer?' He was shy, and rubbernecking for the bartender.

"'You sure you want to do that?'

"'Yeah. I mean, why not?'

"'You still haven't looked at me.'

"He turned to me then, and I saw his eyes flick over my scar, and then he turned away like people do, to pretend they weren't looking.

"I said, 'So there ya go, Trevor. Have a good night.'

"He got drinks and took them to his buddies. Then he came back and said to me, 'Well, what can I get you?'

"I ordered a beer. Trevor sat down. And after a while his buddies got up to leave. They all slapped him on the back, like, you know, 'Don't do anything I wouldn't do! Huh-huh!' And he turned red as a fire hydrant. For an hour we talked about little things, you know? Like, he was from Arkansas, and how he missed his family, and he had four sisters who adored him because he was the youngest, and how he was nervous about being transferred to Asia but would never admit it to his buddies. He asked me how it was to be a nurse and how I liked living in Pennsylvania. After a while the bar closed and Trevor asked if I wanted to take a walk. So we did. Felt like we went all around the city that night. He saw me shiver and put his arm around me, and I . . . it was nice. And next thing I know we're at my hotel. He came up to my room and . . . well. It happened. I don't know if there's any other way to put it other than, we both liked it, but when I think back on that night, the most . . . I'm not sure of the word. Memorable, maybe? The most memorable thing was when he put his arm around me in the cold. To me, that was the most romantic, and the sex was just . . . the afterward."

"Did he stay over?"

"Yeah. He had to be back on base early, so we talked some and . . . I've never told this to anyone before. I mean, I never told any of this to anyone before, but if I did tell it to someone, I probably wouldn't tell them the final part. I feel like a stupid schoolgirl, doing what I did. But when Trevor was leaving, I took a pen and paper and wrote down my address and phone number. And I tried to be casual when I said, 'You know, if you ever come back into town, let me know. Or if you need someone to write to from Asia.' He took the paper and put it in his pocket. And we hugged and he left. Then . . . I was on the second floor of the hotel, and I went to the window and looked out over the street to watch him walk away. I still remember it—him with his hands in his pockets in the cold, his ears sticking out. And at the end of the block there was a trash can. I watched him stop and dig in his pocket. He took out the paper I gave him, with my phone number and address. He stared at it for . . . my god, it felt like minutes to me, watching. And he crumpled it up and tossed the paper in the trash. I stood there in that window, watching him in that morning sun, and then . . . this is the moment I won't forget . . . he took three steps and stopped, then turned around and picked the piece of paper out of the trash can. Stared at it, like he was rethinking . . . and he smiled and smoothed the paper, then folded it and put it in his wallet."

"Oh my gosh!" Gabriella said. "Did he ever write?"

"No. And he probably never will. But just the fact that . . . he thought of me for an extra couple of seconds and . . . I don't know what was going through his head. But the fact that he took the paper back. The fact that he would give me a second thought. Well, look, I don't need someone else to validate me. But we all want to be wanted. So I'll admit it—yeah, that meant something to me."

"I bet you he's going to write one day. You watch!"

"It's nice to think so," I said. "So how about you? Any boyfriends?"

"No. My dad. Well, you can imagine how he is."

"Is there anyone you like?"

"Ben Williamson. We were in Bible study. There's not much to tell. We'd usually find ways to sit next to each other and talk a little. His parents moved to Ohio and I never got a chance to say goodbye. The only thing that ever really happened was . . . we used to steal things from each other, to joke around, you know? If I went to the bathroom, I'd come back and my pencil would be gone. Or I'd turn the pages of his book and make him lose his place. And once, I went to take an eraser from his desk when I thought he wasn't looking. He grabbed it back and our hands touched and we stopped pulling it back and forth and . . ."

She paused for a moment in the memory, then said: "I think about that sometimes."

Gabriella took another moment, remembering. She stared out the car window.

"That's all."

"It sounds nice," I said.

"It was."

"It's always those little things, huh?"

"It always is."

We drove on, listening to the radio and singing along to the songs that we knew and faking the ones we didn't. After a while an excited exhaustion set in. The hours of travel and talk, not to mention all that had happened back at the town, were fueled by an elation that was tapering off. I could see Gabriella trying to sleep, though it wasn't working.

"You OK?" I asked, and waited for the usual "Yeah. I'm fine."

Instead, she said, "Can you pull over?"

I went to the side of the road. She opened the door and dry heaved. Some water came up and not much else. I went around to hold her hair back so it wouldn't get into the mess. After a minute she wiped her mouth.

"Are you in any pain?"

"It's all right."

"I didn't ask that. I asked if you were in any pain."

"Let's keep going," she said between clenched teeth.

We drove another ten minutes until a green sign appeared: CAYTON BEACH, 8 MILES. Two miles farther, a chrome-and-neon diner came into view, and the sight of that cheered Gabriella.

"Oh my gosh, I've heard of these. A twenty-four-hour diner! Nothing stays open past eight o'clock in Pine Hill."

"Same in Locksburg, except for the hospital. Let's go in the diner. There's about an hour until sunrise. You need something to eat."

We pulled into the parking lot, and when we got out of the car I didn't like the way Gabriella was walking: deliberate, occasionally cringing.

"You all right?"

"Besides the terminal cancer, I'm rockin' it."

We took a booth by the window and she stared out, amazed, as if a diner in New Jersey were the Taj Mahal, as seen from the Eiffel Tower.

"This is so cool," she said, astonished even at the long, plastic-coated menus and the lists of dishes.

A tired waitress took our orders—grilled cheese and fries, and glasses of water, for both of us—and we felt no need to talk much as we checked out this foreign world. She ate three fries before declaring that she wasn't hungry, and we had the rest wrapped to go. Gabriella then hobbled toward the bathroom. After fifteen minutes I went in to check on her. She was sitting on the toilet. I knocked a knuckle against the stall door.

"Can I help?"

"I'm not sure how to answer that."

"I mean, is there anything I can do to help?"

"No. Like . . . nothing is coming out. I'm a little crampy. I'll be OK, I think. Can we go now? Give me another minute in here and I'll be done."

I paid the check then went to the car, unfolded the wheelchair, and brought it inside as Gabriella was coming out of the bathroom. I expected an argument from her about the chair but got none as she sat and I rolled her outside and across the parking lot. Her dress had hiked up a bit and I could see her bare ankles. They were swollen larger than before. I stopped at the car and, while she was seated, checked her eyes. The whites appeared yellow. I put two fingers on her wrist and felt. Tachycardia—an abnormally fast pulse. Then I recognized tachypnea—her breathing was unusually rapid.

All were telltale signs of imminent organ failure.

ANDY

Clitter-click, step. *Clitter-click*, step.

The sound of my crutches became hypnotic. The rhythm stayed the same all the way along Clay Street, then when I turned the corner onto Rand Avenue. Thirty yards down the block was Keiser's Hardware Emporium, a bold name for a rinky-dink store. I took a hand off a crutch, flung open the door, hurried the hand back onto the crutch, and barely made it inside before the door swung closed and whacked me on the back. God forbid they invest in one of those self-opening doors.

The place was smaller than a basketball court, tiny for a modern hardware shop, and it made up for the lack of space with an abundance of ingenuity. Shovels, rakes, and hand tools hung from the ceiling. Aisles were packed tight and rose high, and at least one rolling ladder sat around waiting for customers to use if they needed to get an item from a top shelf. I found one tool that I needed. Of course, it was shelved four feet above my head. Even if I could get the rolling ladder, there was no way I could climb it.

"Hello?" I called out to the store, hoping to find someone rather than make my way to the front desk, then back again to the aisle. The less jostling of my leg, the better. "Hello?"

"I hear ya!" someone said from the next aisle. "Need help?"

"Yeah."

"Be right over."

The guy came around and smiled when he saw me. He was the guy who'd been at the plumber's van and had lent me the duct tape the day before.

"Hey! How's that duct tape holding up, my man? Remember me?"

"I couldn't forget you if I tried."

"Have you tried?"

"Yeah, it was easy."

"So who am I?"

"Alvin Einstein."

"Or was I Arthur?"

"One of those."

"So how you feeling?"

"Oh, just royal."

"No offense, but you look like my dog's ass."

"Do you often stare at your dog's ass?"

"If it was a choice between you and that mutt, I'd check out the dog."

"You're sorta lacking when it comes to customer service."

"Yeah, well, at least my leg ain't, like, held together with duct tape. So I got that going for me. Your face too. You got pretty beat up, huh?"

"Nothin' pretty about it."

"No, siree. So you come in for more duct tape?"

"Nah. There's what I need." I pointed up. "That handsaw. The battery-powered one."

"You sure? I hate those things. Get a corded saw."

"Can't do it. No electricity where I'm going."

"Out in the woods?"

"Huh?"

"Is that where you're working? In the woods? Where there's no power?"

"It's a complicated job."

"What kinda job? Tell me about it," he said eagerly.

"I'll fill you in later," I said, and immediately felt bad when a hurt expression spread across his face. "Sorry, I'm in a bit of a hurry."

He got the rolling ladder and climbed up to retrieve the saw. Then he came down and tried to hand it over.

"Do me a favor. Hold it. I want to read the specs."

"Just ask me. I can tell ya. I've used this one before. Right outta the box it's good. Batteries already charged. Thing is, this kind will only last you three months, then it dies. That's why I say get a corded one."

"Three months is fine," I said. I wouldn't need it for three hours, if everything went according to plan. "I'm only cuttin' some two-by-sixes."

"This'll work." He tried again to hand it over, realized my crutches, and said, "Guess you want me to carry it."

"If you could."

"That's what I'm here for."

"I thought you were a plumber."

"Nah. I help out Plumber Craig sometimes, then work here the other times."

"Just my luck."

"What else do you need?"

"Step stool."

Clitter-click, step. *Clitter-click*, step, as I followed him over two aisles.

"How high you going?"

"Two or three feet."

"How's this one?"

He took down an aluminum version, an unboxed step stool that weighed barely five pounds.

"Perfect."

"Holds three hundred pounds. Could put two of you on there and have weight left to spare."

"Good deal."

"What else you need?"

"One of those lamps you wear on your head. Like a miner."

"A lamp for your head?"

"Yeah. What's that called?"

"A headlamp."

"Who would have known?"

"Me."

"OK. Give me one of those."

It was in the same aisle, saving me a longer trip.

"What's next?" he asked.

"That's it for today."

"Let's ring you up."

He was behind me this time and saw the purple glittery back-pack.

"Going to school today?"

"Complicated story."

"You got a lot of those."

"I contain multitudes."

"Walter Whitman."

"Who's that? A friend of Alvin Einstein's?"

"I don't think they knew each other. Ol' Walter was the guy who first said that, about multitudes. Learned about him in high school. Never mind. So why you got that girly backpack?"

"It was the only one around the house."

"It yours?"

"My daughter's."

"Ain't she gonna miss it?"

I let that go without a reply. We put the three items on the counter.

"You got a loyalty card?" he asked.

"No thanks."

"It'll save you like twelve bucks on this stuff."

"I'm good."

He peeked toward the side office, then leaned over the counter to whisper.

"Can you get one? I gotta sign up ten customers a week if I wanna keep this job."

"Make you a deal: I'll sign up for the card if you take that saw out of the box. I don't need all the cardboard and stuff."

Ten minutes later the saw was unwrapped and in my backpack, along with the headlamp. The step stool wouldn't fit. I'd have to carry that.

I handed over the priest's money, glad to get it out of my hand.

"Well, you're all set, hoss." Then he searched the loyalty card form for my name. "Andy. Nice to meet you, Andy. I'm Ray."

"Thanks for your help, Ray."

"Need anything else?"

"Yeah. A ride. It's only eight blocks or so. Can you do it?"

"Sorry, man. I'd help you out in a second if I didn't have to work."

"I'll pay you twenty bucks."

"Carl!" Ray yelled toward the office.

Someone called back, "Huh?"

"I'm taking an early lunch, OK?"

. . .

I put the crutches in the back of Ray's weather-beaten, once-blue, now gray and rust-colored Camaro, then lowered my ass into the passenger seat ever so slowly to avoid bumping my tender leg. As he drove, I took the handsaw from the backpack. There was no use having it if it didn't work. I snapped in the battery pack and hit the trigger to test it. We both jumped at the sound, made louder in a small space.

"What are you gonna do? Cut my head off?" Ray said with undisguised concern.

"I wouldn't do that. Not while you're driving."

He gulped.

I revved it again, twice, felt satisfied, then returned it to the backpack.

"So where are we going?"

"Columbus Avenue," I said. That was next to Moore Street, where the abandoned house was. But I didn't want to clue him in on where I was ultimately headed.

"You ain't going to the woods, are you?"

"I never said I was. You assumed."

"Guess I was wrong."

"There's always a first time, Einstein."

"Do me a favor? Open that window."

"You've got the air-conditioning on."

"Yeah. I mean, don't take this the wrong way, but you smell a little ripe."

"How do you take that the right way?" I said while opening the window. He wasn't out of line, though. My leg was sweating under the jeans, made worse by the walk to the hardware store and the growing heat of the June day. Maybe I should have bought an air freshener back at the store, industrial sized.

He drove onto Columbus and I pointed to the corner, where it would be easier for me to walk around the block.

"Drop me here."

"Where you going?"

"A friend's house."

"Who's your friend? I know a lot of people on this street."

"He's a guy who doesn't ask a lot of questions."

Ray thought about that for a moment. His forehead crinkled. Then it smoothed. "Ohhh! You mean me! Sorry, hoss. Only curious, you know."

"All good. Thanks for the ride."

He pulled the Camaro over and, like a chauffeur, came around to open my door. I got out, put on the backpack, and took a single crutch.

"You forgot one of your crutches," Ray said.

"I only need one. I'll never be able to carry the step stool and use two crutches."

"I'll bring the crutch back to the store. You can pick it up later."

"Thanks, man. I appreciate it."

"No problem. You're a nice guy. I'd do anything for ya." He paused. "So where's my money?"

I took out a crumpled twenty and handed it over.

"Be safe," he said. "And get a doctor to check out that leg."

"Which one?"

"Which leg? The one that's cut up, ya nimrod!"

"I meant, which doctor? Who are you recommending?"

"Oh. I dunno. Go to the hospital. But be careful: I hear Locksburg General is so bad they might amputate your arm instead."

He drove away, and when he was out of sight I turned the corner and went to the abandoned house. It was dark and cool inside, reminding me of the feeling I'd had in the church. I rested by leaning against the wall in what had once been the living room. Then my phone rang.

"Yeah."

"You said you'd call me today," the priest said.

"It's still early. And I sorta had to put my leg back together after you fuckin' stepped on it."

"Where are the things?"

"I'm gettin' them. Hold your holy water."

"Where and when?"

"Give me about an hour. Maybe two. I'll call you."

"I'll be waiting."

"Yeah, you do that."

"You sound more cocky than you were last night, when you were whimpering on the floor. Easy to be brave when I'm not there, isn't it?"

"It's never easy to be brave," I said, and hung up on him.

NATHAN

I slept in my truck, parked in the lot at work. I'd driven there after Paula and I had our fight.

But is it a fight when only one person starts the battle, carries it on, inflicts the wounds, then leaves? More like an assault. Thoughts like that kept me awake before I finally fell into a rough sleep that ended in the morning when another worker pulled in fifteen minutes before our start time, his stereo blasting a country-rock tune.

You need to shut yourself off, I said to myself. *How does a surgeon cut into a living, breathing body? How do people do things that are repulsive, yet must be done? They close down their emotions. They worry about things later. That's what I've got to do. And in a few weeks, Paula and I will be on a beach somewhere, and I'll consider it all then, apologize to her, start our lives over.* This could be salvaged.

The eighteen-wheeler with LeeLee's cell phone taped to the undercarriage pulled away at 10:00 a.m., and within an hour the trash truck had come and emptied the dumpster. Those seemed to be good signs until a half hour later, when the warehouse door opened and the state police trooper, Detective Janson, entered. He dutifully spoke to Dennis, the floor manager, then went into the private room. Dennis walked over to me.

"Yeah, I know, it's fire-company business," I said before Dennis could speak.

Janson sat in the same seat as the last time we were in the room together. I took the one I'd taken before.

"Seems like old times," he said.

"Mmm-hmm."

"I was at the fire site yesterday." He waited for a reaction, got none, and said, "But you already knew that, didn't you?"

I only stared at him. Less than twenty-four hours ago I was disposing of a woman's body. I didn't trust myself to speak any more than the minimum.

"I saw you, riding by," he said.

"Right. I went fishing at Laurel Lake."

"Catch anything?"

"Nope."

"Then why do you go there? Why not the Susquehanna instead?"

"Maybe I'll try there next time."

"That was late to go fishing, huh?"

"I like it then. It's quiet."

"Didn't stay long. I saw you ride by, then ride back."

"Nothing biting."

"You're unlucky."

"Story of my life."

I got the feeling that he was casting around, like he was fishing too. He knew that something might be out there, though he couldn't be sure what or where it was. But something might bite, if he casted around enough. His problem was, I fished too, and I knew that a fish got caught only when it opened its mouth.

"I wanted to ask you a couple extra questions. Did you ever meet the victim before?"

"No."

"Until that day, of course."

"Right."

"When you were inside the house."

"Correct."

"And you're sure there was nothing else in there, that you saw?"

"Is there something you think I should have seen?"

"No. That's why I'm asking."

"I told you everything I know."

"And you were there, what, ten minutes before the ambulance showed up?"

"About that. From the time I arrived."

"So here's what I don't get. Everyone I talk to says you're a by-the-book kinda guy. You always follow orders. And Chief Naugle orders you to go to the hospital, and you say you will. But then you don't. You drive right back to your house."

"I felt better. I wanted to lie down."

"But your wife was at the hospital. It's not like you're scared of the place."

"I just didn't want to go."

"And now I'm asking you these questions, and you don't get defensive at all. It's like you've got the answers in your head, ready for me. It's weird. I trust you, I really do! But sometimes it doesn't add up, you know?"

He trusted me like I'd trust a rabid dog, and I was almost offended that he would lie so blatantly. Or maybe that's how he wanted me to feel.

"Here's another thing," he said. "I'm not from around here. But what I've noticed? When I speak with people? Everyone in Locksburg likes to talk. Ask 'em about the weather, and you get a twenty-minute sermon that goes from last summer's rain to next year's election. I went to get gas yesterday, and the guy behind the counter asked me my opinion on the new water-treatment plant. Couldn't shut him up. You, though, don't seem that way at all."

I stayed quiet for a moment, just to show him I felt no pressing need to speak, then threw out a question, if only to prove him wrong about my silence.

"Where are you from?"

"Huh?"

"You said you weren't from around here."

"Atlanta, originally. Then college in Philly. Now stationed in Harrisburg."

"City guy, huh?"

"Most of my life, yeah," he said. It was another quality to be wary of, as if I needed one. At the plant, I sometimes took product orders over the phone from customers around the country. Those who call in from big cities tend to repeat themselves to us, as if someone in a small town needed extra instruction. If you listen closely, you can sense the same tone in news reports or magazine stories about rural places written by those who live where the bright lights shine: there's an underlying self-importance that gives them license to tell us how we should feel and think, as if those who never stepped foot outside their own city's limits knew what was best for everyone else, everywhere. They seemed to believe that there was no better way to think than the way they did. Based on the people I know in this town, and the people I've talked to from cities, I think we're all, at various times, similarly smart or stupid. Yet one side has a sort of superiority complex that can come off as a kind of pity that only the other side can sense.

"But I'm not here to talk about me," the cop went on.

"Of course not."

"So when our man in the hospital wakes up, he'll back you on your story?"

"I can't speak for anyone else but me."

The cop tapped his pencil, eraser side down, on the table, thinking through his thoughts, or at least pretending to. He had nothing else. I'd bet he hoped that I'd tangle myself up, but I didn't, and I sat there quietly until he said:

"I'm leaving. If you got anything to say, you're going to need to say it now. Because after I walk out that door, every single bet is off."

With LeeLee dead, I'd gone too far. To admit what I'd done would make prison a certainty. To stay with the lies was at least to have some kind of chance.

I motioned to the door. He gave me a look that said I could go, and I left the room.

I went to my workstation and watched the private room door. It took him several minutes to leave. Maybe he waited that long to see if I'd return.

I'd considered it. But I knew I was all in from the moment I found the money.

There was no way out for me other than to keep going forward.

. . .

The first-aid box in the warehouse had a roll of gauze that I shoved into my pocket when no one was around. When I went back to the shop floor, Dennis mumbled, "How ya doin'?"

"Good. You?"

"Another day, another dollar. Or fifty-six cents, once the tax-man takes his share."

I laughed too loud.

"I told you that joke three times before, you never thought it was funny," he said.

"It's a sympathy laugh."

Dennis studied me up and down, then went back to his clip-board. I wondered if he noticed I was wearing the same clothes as the day before.

I said, "I'm feeling like heck. Must have had some bad bourbon last night. Can't wait to get out of here and go home to bed."

"You got the life, man. Drinking and fishing all the time, huh?"

"Fishing?"

"Saw you with the boat in your truck the other day. Heading up to the game lands."

"Oh yeah! Just, you know . . ."

"Get any?"

"Nah. That's why I've been drinking."

"Smart man."

I kept searching for something else to say—me, a guy who never liked small talk and ignored most opportunities to engage in it. Finally, I gave up, went back to work, and watched the clock so often that my eye muscles started to ache. I patted my pocket every few minutes to keep my mind on the gauze.

I found excuses to work through lunch: sweeping my work area, triple-checking things that I'd double-checked before, servicing a belt sander that was serviced days earlier and showed no signs of malfunction. At about one thirty, after everyone had come back, I announced loudly to Dennis:

"Aw, shit. I forgot to take lunch. I'll grab something now."

He nodded as if I needed his approval. While in the empty break room I ran the gauze around the inside of the trash can. There I found a discarded sandwich bag. I took a packet of sugar from the coffee station and sprinkled some inside the clear plastic bag.

When the bathroom was unoccupied, I went in and wiped the toilet seat with the gauze. Then lifted the seat and mopped up the drops of piss and whatever cringeworthy fluids were there, and sealed the gauze in the sandwich bag. The bag went into my pocket, where it would stay warm. At a little before five I went back in the bathroom and wiped the seat and rim again.

"Go get some sleep, man," Dennis said at quitting time.

"Gonna sleep until tomorrow morning," I lied. Then I got into my truck and went home.

Paula was at her late shift. I took a piece of raw chicken from the refrigerator, then put it outside in the sun, on top of the gauze.

The weather had been close to the nineties all day, and the humid June heat hadn't let up.

Within minutes, a dozen flies had landed on the meat and walked over the gauze. I couldn't stop watching their buzzing as they landed, fed, took off, returned. The vision would have disgusted me any other time. Now I welcomed it. I must have stood there for twenty minutes before going inside, wandering the house, then returning an hour later to find a swarm of flies. I tossed the chicken into the yard. Then I put the warm gauze back into the sandwich bag.

Now I would need to wait until night.

CALLIE

"Not good, huh?" Gabriella said, sounding winded, when we were both back inside the car.

"Not good," I said. "I need to get you to a hospital. I'm sorry, honey."

"Callie?" she said softly.

"Yeah?"

"Are you out of your fucking mind?"

"That's the first time I've heard you curse."

"It won't be the last . . . if we don't go to the beach."

"You don't understand."

"What? Are they going to save me? At some strange hospital? Is there a wonderful, magical cure around here?"

"Maybe they could make you more comfortable."

"I'm going to die. Don't let that happen in some hospital room. Especially not in New Jersey," she said in a pretty decent attempt at humor. She was breathing faster, though. She couldn't disguise that.

"At least let me give you a shot."

"C'mon. It's six more miles. Let's go. Then you can give me the shot. After."

I started to drive.

"Callie?"

"Yeah?"

"I'm sorry I cursed."

"It's OK."

"Callie?"

"Yeah?"

"Hurry," Gabriella said.

ANDY

I worked inside the abandoned house for two hours. It was a thirty-minute job, if I were uninjured and could get around without limping and without tripping over the debris and junk that were scattered throughout the place. But with my leg battered, most every move had to be plotted out. When I switched on the headlamp, stood on the step stool, and reached high above my head with the electric saw, I had to put the crutch aside, sometimes causing me to wobble and step off before falling. That forced me to start over and delayed the work, time and again.

I soldiered on. When I finished, I took a break and ignored the phone that was ringing for the third time that day. It was satisfying to know that the priest was on the other end of the unanswered calls, anxious and, hopefully, enraged.

Pain aside, the work had been comforting, as work has been to me since forgoing drugs. When I was a janitor or a maintenance man or a construction-site gofer, I found gratification in polishing a floor until it was shiny clean or fixing a leaky faucet until I knew it wouldn't drip again. I'd tried to channel that drive in recent years. When you're fixated on the job at hand, you aren't thinking about getting high. If that fixation lasts for only fifteen minutes, fine. Sometimes that's all you need to get through the roughest patch of a craving.

My daughter's smile, though. That worked best to keep me straight.

"Angie?" I said inside the house, quietly, as if in prayer. "I don't think you can hear me. I think you're sleeping, and I don't believe in heaven or any of that. But if you can hear, help me today on this, OK? I want to make sure this guy doesn't hurt anyone else. Then I'll see you soon, honey."

I wondered what she'd say, and for the third or fourth time that day, reconsidered the second part of my plan. Maybe I shouldn't kill myself afterward. When this was over with the priest, maybe I could go on to do something good, maybe live for Angie rather than die for her. If there was more to death than sleep, Kate was already with Angie, keeping her company. Maybe I could do things to help others, or at least stop those who hurt people. Assuming I survived today.

It was the kind of ridiculous moment that was typical for me— standing in a rat-filled abandoned house, holding a rechargeable saw, and wearing a headlamp while having a philosophical debate with myself.

When I'd finished the work, I started up the stairs. With great anguish I hoisted myself over the broken step that I'd fallen through the day before. In the bedroom, I flattened my body against the walls, like a man walking on a tall building's ledge, as I went to the closet to get the briefcase with the photo albums. Then I kept moving. At the corner farthest from the door, I collapsed and sat down, inhaling the dirty air that now carried a hint of sawdust. My cell phone rang again.

"No rest for the weary," I exhaled when I answered.

"What's that mean?" the priest asked.

"Or the wicked, apparently."

"Stop it with the games."

"Could you help an old altar boy, Father?"

"So why aren't you here?"

"Know why I'm not there? Because I came to this abandoned house to get your fucking photo albums, and now I'm sitting in the corner of a bedroom because I'm so tired and in pain."

"I have money."

"Then bring it to me," I said. "I'm on Moore Street."

"No. That's not the deal."

"Here's the new deal. The new deal is, you could have had anything you wanted. But then you broke into my house and stepped on my calf, and now I can hardly walk. So if you want me limping down the streets of Locksburg with all these dirty pictures under my arm, fine. I'll shuffle right over. And when the cops pick me up . . ."

"All right. I'll meet you in front of the house."

"I'm stuck up here, pal. I'm gonna need your help to get downstairs, the way I feel now."

"Give me the address again."

"Three twelve Moore Street. It's abandoned. But so's half the block. I'm in the top bedroom. Now listen: the steps are all fucked up. One of them is broken. It's where I fell the other day and hurt my leg. Walk over that step so you don't fall into it. Walk against the wall."

He hung up.

No matter where he was in Locksburg, he'd be over in ten minutes, tops. I used the time to worry if I'd gotten everything right. Then I worried that I was too worried. I was barely able to stand, let alone change the plan, so any late concerns were futile. Instead, I spoke again, this time to my wife.

"Kate? I already know what you'd think of this guy, because I feel the same way. So I'm taking care of it. And this may be the last thing I ever do, you know? Anyway, kiss Angie for me. And if you can, help me get this done without killing myself in the process. I've always been a bit of a fuckup, as you know."

I could almost hear her say, "I know." But in my mind I could also see how she looked at me like she sometimes did, with a hard-won love that I'd never gotten anywhere else before. I sat in the corner of that room, smiling at the memory of us.

Minutes later, a car drove slowly along the street outside.

I scuttled to the window and propped myself up. It was the priest's car. He coasted the block, then turned the corner. A minute later he came around again. He was circling, wary.

After another few minutes the priest waddled along the sidewalk. He'd parked somewhere away from the house. Downstairs, the door opened on rusty hinges.

"Watch those steps!" I called out. "There's a broken one!"

Wood creaked. Half a minute later the priest was in the bedroom doorway, across the room from me. I reached up to my forehead and switched on the headlamp.

"May the light of god shine upon you," I said, and aimed the beam at his eyes.

"Get that out of my face."

"Why? Too much light makes the baby go blind?"

"I'm not playing games with you."

He surveyed the room. I'd kept the closet door open, so he could see that no one was inside.

"Why are we in this place?" he said.

"I ducked in here right after I took the briefcase. I wasn't going to take that shit back to my house."

"What do you have for me?"

I nodded to the briefcase at my side, then shined the light down so he could see that it was his.

"Come get it," I said.

He appeared ready to move. But some innate sense stopped

him. He was a skittish animal, maybe some kind of reptile, one that was always wary of potential danger.

"Bring it to me."

"Where's my money?"

He pulled a round wad of bills from his pocket and held it up.

"That ain't ten grand," I said. He was experienced with junkies, that's for sure. Show them any amount of cash, and they'll do whatever you want or agree to whatever you say. I didn't care about the money but was miffed all the same—the prick was trying to shortchange me.

"It's all the money I have at the moment. Here." He held it out.

"Should I crawl over there like a crab for it?"

"Do you want this or not?"

"I do. Throw it over here."

"No."

"Then I guess we have a standoff."

A beam of late-day sun came through the window and lit the room a little better. I snapped off the headlamp.

"Does it get tiring, having to hide what you are?" I asked.

The priest examined me as if he were bored. I stretched my wounded leg out farther, tempting him to come over and step on it.

I said, "You have to know that your god's not gonna forgive you for fucking kids."

"I don't presume to know the mind of god, and neither should you."

"Well, I think it's safe to say that molesting children isn't on his list of things that you can get away with."

He cleared his throat involuntarily. Maybe I was getting to him. Best to keep going.

"Then again, it's not specifically in the Ten Commandments, is it? 'Thou shall not be a kiddie-screwing pervert.' You gotta—"

"I think you—" He got control of himself. Pulled against his anger. "I think we both know something about addiction, don't we? About things we can't control."

"Don't compare the two of us, pal."

"Haven't you hurt people, Andy? Didn't you do loathsome things for drugs? Do you have regrets? Any at all?"

I couldn't help thinking of Sophie that night in the Philly crack house. And thinking of the fragile old ladies who I knocked down while ripping their handbags from their arms, and the struggling corner stores I'd shoplifted from. I remembered the scams I'd pulled and—

"I can see you do," the priest said. "So you know how it is. But what you don't know is all the good I've done. All the times I've held off, wrestled with . . . desires."

"If you hurt one kid, that's too many. There's no way to offset any of that."

I know what he wanted: for me to charge at him, so this big man could swing one of his anvil fists into my jaw. I resisted the urge. I breathed deeply instead. Tried to calm myself. Then peered at him as evenly as I could.

"Know what I'm going to do, Father? I'm going to forgive you for the beating you gave me. How's that sound?"

"I'm uninterested in your forgiveness."

"Well, if you want it, here's your penance: leave those pictures here. Then go confess to the police."

"There's your money," he said, and tossed the wad of bills. It fell into my lap. "Now show me what's inside the briefcase."

I opened it. He saw the albums and nodded. I lifted the pairs of children's underwear. The guy had been restrained in his words, but he couldn't hide the craving in his eyes when he saw those. He was hypnotized by them, a disgusting and unmasked expression, a hundred times more sickening than anything I'd seen anywhere else, and I'd seen so much. The underwear was a remembrance of the things he'd done and a sign of his desire to do them again.

"Give those to me," he said, practically breathless. "Now."

I put everything in the briefcase, closed it, then pushed it forward. The briefcase slid on the dirty floor and stopped in the center of the room, halfway between us.

"Oops. I guess I'm not a good slider. But I'm also not a child molester. So at least I got that going for me."

We stared at the briefcase.

"Father," I said. "You can still walk away."

Maybe he considered it. Because he paused for half a moment.

Then the priest went to pick up the briefcase.

When he was three feet away from it, I panicked. Maybe the crossbeam that I'd cut out from underneath the floor wasn't enough to collapse it.

But then, a hideous crack.

The section of floor gave way.

The priest must have known, instantly, what was happening. He tried to move back. Too late. The thin, rotted floorboards, now unsupported by the two-by-sixes that I'd sawed off earlier in that space, snapped like twigs under the big man's weight.

The priest disappeared.

Poof.

One second he was in the room. The next, he was not.

An instant later, another *boom-crack!*

This one was clearer, louder, as he hit the ground floor. I'd gone into the cellar and cut those supporting beams out too. The priest's ten-foot fall turned into twenty as he smashed through the bedroom floor, then the living room floor, then landed in the basement.

Dust and dirt and everything from dried rat shit to old plaster kicked into the air, like the aftermath of an explosion. I had wanted to cheer at the priest's fall but went into a coughing fit instead.

I sat in the corner for minutes. The quiet was occasionally broken as parts of the floors gave way and dropped down. The dust cloud began to settle. I wanted to peer into the hole but wouldn't chance it. Instead, I crawled on my hands and knees, stuck close to the wall, and moved around the room then out of it. Then I got to my feet, and when I'd hobbled halfway down the staircase, looked up to see the hole in the ceiling, then looked down into the hole in the floor below. I switched on the headlamp and descended the basement steps.

The priest was on his back on the cellar floor, like some fat, struggling insect. He was trying to get up, but both of his legs had snapped. He apparently had landed first on his feet. From such a height, with all his weight coming down, one of his leg bones had thrust through his knee, pierced his skin, and now jutted out through his pants. The foot on his other leg had been turned around one hundred and eighty degrees. His arms were no better. One was twisted and bent behind his back. He raised his other hand, maybe to point, maybe to reach out in a futile motion for help. Blood squirted from two fingers that were bent to the side, barely held on by flaps of skin. He must have reached for something sharp on the way down and ripped his hand wide open.

To his right, the briefcase: it had opened in midair and the albums had released their photos. The pictures were still fluttering down, onto him, around him.

The priest tried to speak. No words came out. But in the beam of the headlamp, I could see his bloody lips moving, pleading for aid.

"Speak up!" I said. "Raise your voice to the lord!"

I shined the light in his eyes.

"Yeah, I wish I could help you, Father, but since you stepped on my leg and all, I'm afraid I'll never be able to get us both outta here."

He coughed up bubbles of blood. Tried again to speak, could only gurgle.

"I'm sure someone will come searching for you in a week or two. In the meantime, you can hang out with our rat friends. They're all god's creatures too, huh?"

It was tough to laugh, though I made the attempt, just to rub some salt in his wounds, so to speak. Before I went up the basement steps, I turned around.

"Yo, Father," I said. "I'm serious about this part: with all my sins, I'll probably be seein' you in hell. But I bet they'll give me a cooler seat than you."

Then I limped up the steps, turned off my headlamp, and left the priest down there in the pitch dark.

. . .

I hobbled out of the house and into the new night, wearing Angie's backpack and leaning on my crutch. Inside my pocket, the wad of money pressed against my leg. The pain in my calf was getting worse. I could smell the wound through my clothes, more pungent than before. If I didn't get the damage disinfected and stitched up, something would set in soon to kill me.

Or I could take the money and buy a big enough dose to end all my pain forever.

I limped along the street, trying to decide what to do. A block ahead, Brain Dead Brian turned a corner and, in his usual shuffle, began walking my way.

He could get me whatever I needed.

Or I could turn the corner before he saw me.

I wanted that hit so badly.

If I didn't get it, I'd be in nearly unbearable discomfort soon. Even if I went to the hospital, I'd be in agony tonight, tomorrow too, and for some time to come.

Go buy the biggest hit you can, a voice in my mind whispered. I imagined it grinning when it said, *It'll feel soooo fucking good. You*

won't have to worry about another day. You won't have to even worry about
tomorrow.

I considered it. Even licked my lips, imagining the dose.

Then another voice, quieter, whispered.

It was Angie.

She said,

Daddy:

The best part about

Tomorrow is that there will

Be more things to love.

NATHAN

Locksburg General Hospital has treated hundreds of burn victims over the years. In a county full of farms and machine shops, accidents and engine fires are an everyday occurrence. Just as common were return visits. Farmers would come in weeks later, in anguish over burns that had become infected when manure or some other germ-filled substance found its way into a wound. Too many times, the victims would end up hospitalized, their infections more life-threatening than the initial injury.

Paula often told me their stories. Similar tales were passed around the firehouse. Those wormed their way into my head whenever I thought about the burn victim. If he caught some kind of infection, he'd never make it out of the hospital alive.

It became a kind of game to envision what would happen if a fouled piece of gauze found its way under his bandages. Would anyone even discover it? A nurse changing his dressing would throw everything away, right? Then I considered how many people the guy killed with his drugs and his dealers and his money. If he died, wouldn't the world be a better place?

As everything started to close in on me, it was no longer a game played in my head. It was something that I began to actively plan, in case there was no other way to save myself, either from the police or from the pressures that threatened to drive me insane. I was now at that point.

When fighting with Paula, I kept telling myself that it was something in her or in the cop or in LeeLee or in someone else that was pushing me to do this.

But that was wrong.

It was something in me.

...

At ten o'clock at night I drove to the hospital and parked around back. I shut off the car and sat in darkness with the window open. Another car pulled in and parked twenty yards away. I slid down in the seat so the driver wouldn't see me.

It was Callie, the nurse. She went around to the front entrance, and a few minutes later opened the door to the MRI room from inside. She pushed a squeaking wheelchair that held a teenage girl, left her outside, then came around from the front of the building. When Callie was helping the girl into the car, I nearly went over to give them a hand. That's what I would have done any other time. Now, though, I stopped myself. I needed to act like someone else.

They drove away. I turned on the car radio. Tried to recall who won the last Phillies game. Anything to keep from dwelling on what needed to be done.

At ten thirty I knocked softly on the MRI room door. Waited. Knocked again.

I thought I could hear Paula standing on the other side breathing. I waited longer.

Then Paula opened it.

Her face fell. She couldn't stop staring, as if she'd never seen me until that moment.

Finally: "Why, Nathan?"

"I want to talk to him."

"No. You want to harm him. We both know it. And by opening this door, I'm now an accessory. A nurse, who took an oath to protect, will be an accessory to——"

"He's a drug dealer."

"I'll call the police. I'll call them right now. Let them take care of this. Do you want them to find you in that room?"

"You won't call them," I said. "I know you won't, so don't bluff me."

She blinked a few times, as if her vision would clear and I wouldn't be standing there.

"Let me by," I said.

"I . . . I honestly believed you wouldn't come here tonight. I'd have bet anything. I thought I knew you better than I knew myself."

"I told you I'd come."

"I thought, if he knocks on that door, I can't live with him anymore. And if I open the door, I can't live with myself."

"Paula . . ."

"But it didn't matter, because I never believed you would."

"Which room is he in?"

She kept staring at the ground. I moved past her and went inside.

"Which room, Paula?"

She looked at me with such bleak sadness that, any other time, I would have felt shame. There was no time for those feelings, though. Now I wanted to find the guy while I had worked myself into some kind of anger—anger at him, at Paula, at myself. That would spur me on.

"Everything I've ever known is wrong," Paula said, then turned and walked away.

I called after her in a hushed voice. Twice. She didn't stop. I decided, it doesn't matter, she'll forgive me no matter what I do. She always does. And she'll forgive herself for opening the door.

I walked down the hospital hallway, peeking into the small side windows of the rooms until I found the right one.

The guy lay on his chest, his eyes closed. His back was bandaged, and his face, turned toward the door, rested on a pillow. An oxygen line fed into his nose and hissed. Several machines surrounded him. They whirred and beeped.

I shouldn't have sat down to look at him. I should have surged forward, done what I had to do, then left. But I needed to think it through again, to stoke my hate. I took a seat opposite the bed.

To myself I said: All the drugs this guy had produced—who knows how many lives were ruined and brains were fried by his meth? Whose kids have died? I shouldn't have saved him. If I had done nothing, he would have fallen in that house and been burned to death in minutes. I had done the right thing and now could pay dearly for it. But I could take that back.

I put my hand into my pocket and took out the plastic bag with the gauze.

If he goes on to make any more drugs, I'll be responsible for it. But if I do this, Paula and I will be scot-free. I'm not even doing it for me. I'm doing it for her. We can still have a family. We can adopt a kid who will be good and who will go on to do something in life, not ruin people, like this guy.

There was a section of dressing on the guy's back where the tape could be pulled up, and where I could put the putrid gauze.

I think I got there—to the place where my hatred would let me do it. I stood.

The guy's eyes opened.

He looked at me standing above him. He blinked a few times. Tried to say something. Then shifted his face a little to make it easier to speak.

"Heyyy," he croaked.

I took a step back, surprised. I bumped the chair and sat back down.

"Hello," I said.

"Gotta drink? Water?"

A full pitcher sat on the table. I filled a cup, unwrapped a bendy straw, and moved it to his lips. He sucked up a sip. Stopped. Then drew another.

"Oh man. Thas good."

"Yeah."

"I'm in the hospital, right?"

"Locksburg General."

"You my doctor?"

"No. You don't know me." It started to come out as a question, but changed halfway and became a hope.

"Wait. Yeah, I know you. Fire guy, right?"

"Uh-huh. What do you remember?"

"I remember you helping me. Thanks, man."

I was still holding the infected gauze. I could tell him I was fixing his dressing, then slip it underneath. He wouldn't see. Wouldn't know.

"I saved your ass," I said.

"Uh-huh. Totally. I kept trying to get that fire out. Then all those chemicals went up, splashed on me."

"Well. Good."

He huffed. "Not really. This ain't good."

"The way I see it, better you than all the kids you'd have killed with that shit."

"What shit?"

"You make drugs. It's not only kids who get hurt by meth either. That stuff wrecks lives and families and whole towns. I don't know how you can do it. You're practically a murderer. Don't you feel any guilt at all?"

"You got the right room?" he said.

"I found you in that house."

"I know you did. I saw you with the bag too. So you know."

"'Course I know. All that drug money."

"Pal . . . we're talking about different shit here, I think," he said.

"What kind of shit?"

"You got the bag."

"Yeah. So?"

"So you know."

"That you were making drugs."

"I wasn't there making drugs. I hate drugs."

"Then what were you doing in that house?"

"Dude . . . we were counterfeiting," he said.

He looked at me, puzzled, and I returned the same kind of stare.

"What are you saying?"

"You got the bag. Didn't you check out the bills? All the serial numbers are the same. The paper is off a little too. That was the test batch."

"You were making meth."

"Naw. Me and Jerry. He's this genius college kid, smart as shit about stuff like that. He went into town for something. Left me there, told me not to smoke around the dyes and chemicals he was using on the paper. Fuckin' idiot, me. I lit a smoke and the chemicals exploded. Thank god you showed up."

"All those bills . . . ?"

"They ain't real. You didn't hold them up to the light?"

"I kept them hidden."

"Well, I know you ain't a cop, then. They been trying to catch Jerry for a while. Secret Service too—they're the ones who chase counterfeiters. They were getting help from the state police."

"All of the money is . . . ?"

"I'll give you some advice, and I'll be the one saving your ass this time: toss those bills in the trash, before you get in trouble. Jerry said it was only the first try, to get the printer and stuff primed. All his equipment probably burned, though."

We sat there in silence, him tired from talking, me trying to process what he'd said. After a long moment, I got up, went to the door.

"Thanks again," the guy said as I left the room. "You're the man."

I didn't know how to feel, so I felt nothing. I huffed once, almost a laugh at the absurdity. Shook my head.

Paula wasn't at the cheap desk that served as the nurses' station, and the reception area was unoccupied, as it usually was at night. I double-knocked on a door marked PRIVATE that the staff used as their lounge.

"Come in," a man said.

Old Dr. Willis was on the sofa reading a book, a mug of tea steaming on the table near him.

"Hello, Doctor."

"Good evening, Nathan," he said.

"Why are you here so late?"

Willis said: "I was called in. An injured patient arrived. The man had duct tape around his wounds! I've seen some strange things in Locksburg. So I'm usually not surprised. But he's lucky he won't lose his leg. He's asleep now in room—"

"Where's Paula?"

"I believe she went home."

"She was here like fifteen minutes ago."

"She said she wasn't feeling well. She asked if I could watch over things for a short while, until Nancy's shift starts. Nancy is late, as usual. I don't mind, though . . ."

"OK."

"Were you here to pick Paula up?"

"Yeah," I said, but I don't know if he heard it. I was already speed-walking toward the back door.

"You've got a good wife there," he called after me.

I drove off, wondering how to feel. Angry? Relieved? Confused? I tried them all, and each seemed to fit. I also felt disgust, that I was nearly a murderer, then denial, telling myself I never really would have done it. No. Not me. Paula was right. That's not who I was.

I felt great love for Paula then, mixed with great shame at what I'd put her through. That switched to joy when imagining how she was going to feel when we took the bag of bills from the attic and burned them in the yard, where I'd put my arm around her and beg her to forgive me for how I'd been, and tell her she was right, she was always right. And I'd stand there, pleading for her forgiveness, and tell her what I now knew: Who cares if we're in Locksburg or Fort Lauderdale? We will be together.

And that is what's good.

I drove across town and up the driveway to our house. Paula's car was parked outside.

I pushed the button, and the garage door began its rise.

The truck's headlights shined inside.

What came into view next I couldn't immediately comprehend—it was happening more quickly than my brain could process—but this is what I saw: As the garage door rose, it revealed the stepladder that was normally in the kitchen pantry. And at that moment—either because Paula was surprised by the opening of the garage door, or because she was already in the process of kicking it out from under her—the stepladder fell over.

Two feet, which were wearing white nurse's sneakers, jerked, then hung above the floor.

I was still perplexed. Then the garage door came all the way up to reveal Paula with a noose around her neck. The rope was tied to one of the rafters above her.

With no ladder underneath her, Paula was shuddering and swinging on the rope.

I bolted out of the truck and into the garage. I grabbed hold of Paula's waist. It was at the level of my shoulders. I lifted her body as high as I could to slacken the rope.

Paula made hideous choking sounds. She had tied the rope to itself, and there was no way to cut it down without leaving her to hang. I held her aloft to keep her from strangling. I thought it was working. I could hear her gasping. Some rough breaths were moving through her throat.

"Help!" I screamed out of the garage and into the night. "Help! Help! Please god, somebody help us!"

But no one would hear me. There were no houses within nearly two hundred yards of ours, and we were surrounded by trees that would stifle my screams, even this late at night. My cell phone was in the bedroom, where I'd left it so it couldn't be traced to show me at the hospital.

I held on to Paula, pushed her up as high as I could to keep the rope from tightening around her throat. Her breathing was raspy. But if I lowered her, I'd cut off her breathing, and the rope might snap her neck.

"My god, Paula! My god! I'm . . . I'm so sorry. This . . . you . . ."

I went quiet.

I didn't know what to say.

Then I told myself to keep going, talk to her, say anything. Talk to her as you never have before.

"Paula. I hurt you so bad. I'm so sorry for all I've done. I love you so much, and I know I hardly say that but it's true. From the first time I saw you in the hospital, remember? When I came in for stitches and you said I was brave? Of course you remember, you never forget anything. I love that about you. I love everything about you. Then the night we went to Dykeman Pond to take a walk, sorta like our first date, and we stopped there and you held my hand and then I swear there was no plan, I was nervous, true, but I had no real plan to kiss you and then all of a sudden we kissed and you said, 'I liked that a lot,' and me, like the idiot I was, said, 'Uh-huh,' and what I didn't tell you was you were only the second girl I ever kissed. I thought I had to be a big man and act like I'd been around the block with girls but I hadn't. They never liked me, but you did, Paula. You did."

Paula coughed. I pushed her up higher. My arms ached. The rope slackened but only a little. She was still breathing, harshly, and I didn't know what to do other than talk, keep talking to her.

"And all the years later, Paula, all the years later you made me so happy and now I'm going to make you happy. We're gonna burn that money, it's all fake, and I'm going to be happy now because I know. I know now that what I had, what we had, was good and real and is the only thing that matters, the only thing that really matters. I realize that now. I know it, Paula. I know it."

My arms were tiring. The muscles burned and hurt. I willed them to stay strong.

I said: "I know these things now.

"Please, Paula, forgive me.

"I know these things now.

"I don't want to leave. I don't want to go anywhere without you ever.

"I love you.

"I'm not letting you go. I'll hold you up forever if I have to.

"Stay with me.

"Stay."

CALLIE

We were three miles from the beach.

"Stare down at the floor," I told Gabriella as I drove.

"Why?"

"Neither of us has seen the ocean before. I don't want us to catch sight of it here and there, piece by piece. I want us to see it all at once. So don't look up, just in case. Stare at your shoes."

"What about you?"

"I'm only going to focus on the road."

I made that up on the fly, but it sounded like a good plan. We wouldn't really need it, though. At a traffic light I checked the GPS to find nothing but flatland until we met the water. I glanced over. Gabriella was staring at her shoes, a melancholy smile on her so-tired face. I was exhausted, but not in the way she was.

"I believe in God," Gabriella said. It came out of nowhere, yet didn't surprise me.

"That's good."

"I didn't want to say anything. 'Cause I don't think you do. Maybe you think it's stupid."

"I don't. It's not."

"I think He worked this out, so we could go to the beach together."

"He's an inept god, then, if I was the best that he could do for you."

"Please don't joke. Don't do that . . . You don't need to . . . Callie."

"I know. It's a defense thing, I guess."

"You're beautiful. And you're gonna . . . marry Paul one day, I bet."

I began to say, "Right, a one-armed man and a harelipped woman. What a lovely pair." But I didn't. I didn't want to think that way anymore.

"Talk to me about something. Anything," I said.

"Like what?"

"Tell me how it felt when you touched that guy's hand—Ben, was it? The guy in Bible study."

"I think . . . if I put it into words, I might lose it. If that makes sense."

"It does. Keep it, then. To yourself. Don't lose it. Hold it in you."

A sign ahead said: BEACH PARKING AREA. The sky was beginning to lighten. Our timing was perfect.

She was still staring at her feet.

Then all at once she was steeling herself against pain.

"Gabriella."

"Huh?"

"Are you sure . . . I can't give you a shot? Half a dose?"

She shook her head, then suddenly sucked in air, hard.

"I don't . . . want any of that . . . stuff," she said. She was laboring to get words out now. That was apparent with each breath.

"We're almost there," I told her, and in my head, for the first time since I was a child, I prayed to god—any god there could ever be. I asked for help. Then I looked over at Gabriella, who was holding in her anguish, and I didn't pray anymore. Instead, I demanded. Inside my head I said to that god: *You give her this. You give this girl just a little bit more time. You don't do this now. You don't.*

I pulled onto Ocean Drive and parked. A long, high dune blocked the view of the ocean. I got out, took the wheelchair from the back seat, and unfolded it as I raced around to Gabriella's side of the car and opened her door.

"Come on, honey," I said quietly. She tried to say something. And when she couldn't speak, I saw the realization in her eyes about what was happening to her, and what would follow very soon.

"Don't talk. I'll help you."

I leaned into the car.

"Put your arms around my neck."

She did, weakly. I pulled her up, blocked her knees with mine, then turned her and sat her in the chair.

"Good. Good. The sun. It's already up some. But remember, no peeking. Look down at the ground, OK? Look down."

I couldn't be sure if Gabriella was listening, but I was talking only to put sound in the air, to mask my own fears. I pushed the chair on the hard plastic walkway that led to the beach. The chair wheels squeaked and rumbled on the path, and I was caught between wanting to race forward and wanting to move slowly so as not to jolt Gabriella, who once let out a low moan when the chair jostled.

We went uphill until the path crested and opened toward the ocean.

"Almost there!" I said to her, fake cheer in my voice.

The walkway ended.

I could hear the surf. We were maybe fifty more yards from the water.

"I'm trying not to catch sight of the ocean. I don't want to see it until you do. We're going to do this together. Keep your eyes closed."

She said nothing.

"Can you hear me?"

She nodded once.

And that movement, that slight up and down of her head as she stared at the ground, is what broke me. I held it back in my throat until it hurt so bad.

I went around to the front of the wheelchair.

"Honey. Gabriella. Listen. The path ended. I can carry you, though. Put your arms around my neck. Just one more time. Can you do that?"

She moved them, giving me enough room to put an arm under her knees and one on her back to raise her into my arms. I'd known she was thin and light, but now there seemed to be so very little of her.

I could sense her quick pulse when I touched her. I could feel her rapid breathing on my neck.

Her body was now shutting down.

My throat hurt again, and a tear fell from my eye and onto her.

"We're almost there. Look at me. Can you do that? Look at me. It's OK if you can't but . . ."

Her eyes opened and stared into mine.

I began to walk with her in my arms. Our eyes on each other.

I stepped onto the sand.

"It's going to be beautiful," I said, still with that hopeful tone that I disliked. And I stopped that tone right there. Gritted my teeth. Fed off the pain in my throat.

"We're gonna get there," I said, and stared right at her with power or strength or whatever emotion I had in me then, one I wasn't about to analyze.

"I've been . . . so scared, Gabriella. I've been scared all my life. Everything scares me and I lie to everyone and I lie to myself and say I'm not lying but I am. And my face, I am so embarrassed by it. I am so, so embarrassed. They tell you not to be, but those are only words, it's impossible not to be. But I'm a little less scared now because of you. I really am. And I'm going to make sure that lasts and I am going to think of you and I'm . . . I can't lie. You know what's happening to you. And if there is a heaven, you are going there, I can guarantee that, and you and I will meet there one day. We'll see each other on a beach. And we'll hug and talk about this great night we had and we'll laugh and we'll smile when we see each other again."

I was looking at her as I walked. She was looking at me.

The surf rushed up and covered my feet. The breeze blew. And a mist of seawater touched our cheeks. Just like, sometimes, how a baby will brush your skin, so gentle.

"We're at the beach. The water's right there. We're both going to see the ocean for the first time. Are you ready?"

She smiled a bit.

"Close your eyes," I said. "Here we go."

I turned her so that she was facing the water.

"There," I whispered. "Look."

Gabriella opened her eyes. I watched her as she saw the ocean. Her expression was awe.

I closed my eyes and squeezed out the tears.

Then I turned my head toward the water.

I opened my eyes.

And all at once I saw the ocean.

Oh God, I saw it.

ACKNOWLEDGMENTS

When I learned that this novel was to be published, I celebrated first with my good-luck charms: Michele, Hope, and Troy Jaworowski. Hope, I'll remember that hug forever. Then I called four people who've supported me, drank with me, joked with me, and annoyed me for years. In other words, they're essential friends: Murielle Jacquemin-Harman, Jennifer Kitses (a terrific novelist herself), Lisa Reeves, and Rick Yost.

Speaking of essential, Doug Stewart, Tim Duggan, Anita Sheih, and Hannah Campbell define that word.

There are too many people with the last names Bier, DiPietro, Simons, and Wallace to mention individually, so thanks to all of you collectively. Joan and Gus Jaworowski too, of course.

I contacted some of my favorite authors, blindly, for blurbs and advice, and they came through, big-time: Ken Bruen, Dan Chaon, John Darnielle, Laura Dave, Jeffery Deaver, Fabian Nicieza, Jason Rekulak, Scott Smith, Willy Vlautin, and Chris Whitaker. I am in awe of these writers. Read them and you will be, too.

And to you, kind reader, so much thanks.

ABOUT THE AUTHOR

Ken Jaworowski is an editor at the *New York Times*. He graduated from Shippensburg University and the University of Pennsylvania. He grew up in Philadelphia, where he was an amateur boxer, and has had plays produced in New York and Europe. He lives in New Jersey with his family. *Small Town Sins* is his first novel.